"You are, without doubt, the most exasperating woman I have ever met."

And then Kit kissed her. It was a kiss of anger. Marina knew it was intended to show her that she could not stand against him.

She knew it. And yet she wanted to yield to him. The touch of his lips renewed the encounters of her dreams, when he had come to her in love and gentleness. Her body yearned for him. In spite of everything.

She was a fool!

"No!" she cried, pushing him away with all her strength as he raised his hand to her hair. "No! I will not be a pawn in your games, Mr. Stratton! Even a plain companion has a conscience, sir, and I intend to obey mine. Good day to you."

* * *

Rake's Reward
Harlequin Historical #697—March 2004

Harlequin Historicals is delighted
to present Mills & Boon author
JOANNA MAITLAND
and the sequel to her Regency
MARRYING THE MAJOR

Rake's Reward

Joanna Maitland

HARLEQUIN®

TORONTO • NEW YORK • LONDON
AMSTERDAM • PARIS • SYDNEY • HAMBURG
STOCKHOLM • ATHENS • TOKYO • MILAN • MADRID
PRAGUE • WARSAW • BUDAPEST • AUCKLAND

ISBN 0-373-29297-X

RAKE'S REWARD

First North American Publication 2004

Available from Harlequin Historicals and
JOANNA MAITLAND

Marrying the Major #689
Rake's Reward #697

Please address questions and book requests to:
Harlequin Reader Service
U.S.: 3010 Walden Ave., P.O. Box 1325, Buffalo, NY 14269
Canadian: P.O. Box 609, Fort Erie, Ont. L2A 5X3

Chapter One

'I have been waiting too many years for this, Hugo. Nothing you can say will make one whit of difference.' Kit Stratton spoke with quiet certainty, smiling calmly across at his elder brother as if they were discussing the turn of a cravat, or a new blend of snuff. He lounged back in his chair, with one immaculately booted leg thrown carelessly over the arm, and watched his brother. It might have been Kit, rather than Hugo, who was the owner of this comfortable, book-lined study.

Sir Hugo Stratton ceased his angry pacing and stood looking down at his brother in obvious exasperation. 'For God's sake, Kit, you must be out of your mind,' Hugo said bitterly. 'Stratton Magna has been in the family for generations, yet you would risk losing it to that old harridan on the turn of a card. You cannot intend to go on with this senseless charade. Besides, it all happened years ago. Cannot you let it lie?'

'No.' Kit shook his head decisively. 'You forget what she did to me…to us. She acted out of pure malice, Hugo, and I swore then that I would have my revenge on her one day. I mean to do it now.'

'And it matters nothing to you that you could lose the family estate in the process? By God, I wish—'

'You wish, now, that you hadn't persuaded John to leave it to me in the first place, don't you, Hugo?'

Hugo coloured a little. 'John will be turning in his grave,' he said. He sounded very near to losing his temper. 'And I…' He gave a snort of disgust. 'What a fool I was. I was the one who persuaded John to leave Stratton Magna to you, instead of to me. I was the one who said that you needed land of your own in England, so that you would stop playing the rake in Vienna. I was the one who thought you would—'

'Settle down and raise a brood of hopeful children?' finished Kit sardonically, rising to refill his glass. 'Never. Unlike you, I have no turn for the infantry, so I am more than content to leave the getting of Stratton heirs to you. You know very well that I have no intention of being caught in parson's mousetrap. Much too close for comfort with Emma. If she hadn't chosen you instead…' He allowed himself a wry smile. He had been the brother who compromised the heiress, but Hugo had been the brother who married her—for Hugo was the brother she loved. Hugo and Emma had been married for five years now, their happiness shadowed only by the deaths of Emma's father and of John, the eldest Stratton brother. Now Hugo was the head of the Stratton family, a baronet, and enormously wealthy. He had no need of the family estate at Stratton Magna.

Unlike Kit.

'Believe me, I do appreciate your generosity,' Kit continued, smiling still. He was determined to retain the upper hand in this encounter. 'I can guess what you were thinking, you and John, when you decided to leave Stratton Magna to me. But, as the oldest surviving brother,

you should have inherited the family estate, not I. If I
had known what you were planning to do, I might have
warned you of the risks you were running.'

'Might you?' said Hugo with biting sarcasm. 'If I'd
known what *you* were planning to do, I might have held
my tongue. As it is—'

'As it is, Stratton Magna is mine now and I can have
my revenge on Lady Luce without breaking my word to
you. I swore to you, then, that I would never gamble for
more than I could afford to lose. Until I inherited the
estate, I was in no position to come back to England and
face her. Now, I can,' Kit finished simply.

'You could have come back for good when John
died,' Hugo said pointedly.

Kit sank back into his chair. It was now well over a
year since John and his wife had died in that terrible
carriage accident. The family had expected Kit to remain
in England after the funeral, but he had not been prepared to oblige them. 'I had…other things on my mind,'
Kit said, staring down into his wine. 'Distractions, you
might say, one of whom is now in London.' He looked
up at his brother. He could see that Hugo's anger was
waning now. 'You may be sure that I learned my lesson
well over Emma. Resolved then to devote all my atten-
tions to ladies of…er…experience who would pose no
threat to my single state.'

'Provided their husbands did not catch you in their
beds,' put in Hugo sharply. 'You might not have come
off with a whole skin if they had challenged you.'

'As it happens,' Kit said with studied nonchalance, 'I
was caught out a couple of times. And I did come off
with a whole skin.'

'Good God!' Hugo was laughing in spite of himself.

He had always found it difficult to remain furious for long. 'And how many of the poor cuckolds did you kill?'

'None,' said Kit with a bland smile. 'That would have been ungentlemanly. I *was* guilty, after all. And the ladies in question were—'

Hugo shook his head decisively. 'Enough of your diversions, Kit. We are not here to discuss your successes in the petticoat line. Heaven knows, half of Europe seems to be aware of those. We are here to discuss this preposterous proposal of yours. You cannot be serious. You could lose everything to that woman. And after the last time, surely you—'

'After the last time, I have absolutely no intention of losing to her,' Kit said emphatically, rising to his feet. He put a hand on his brother's arm. 'Nothing you can say will change my mind, Hugo. You cannot imagine how demeaning it was for me to be forced to come to you, cap in hand, to beg for the money to pay those debts. I knew that you would have to take it from the dowry of the lady I had compromised. Can you imagine how that felt? I may have been only twenty-two at the time, but, believe me, Hugo, it rankled. And it rankles still. I was a hair's breadth away from utter disgrace.'

Hugo paused, gazing up at the huge portrait of Emma above the fireplace. He clearly had his temper well in hand now. 'I do understand, Kit,' he said at length. 'But it was all a very long time ago. Everyone has forgotten what happened. You will simply stir it all up again if you challenge the woman. Let it lie.'

'No. I cannot. I have spent five years waiting for this moment and I intend to relish it.' He raised a hand as his brother made to speak. 'Don't be so ready to assume that I will lose this time. Believe me, I have no intention of doing so.'

The corner of Hugo's mouth twitched slightly. The long scar on the side of his face was barely noticeable now, except where it twisted his smile. 'And precisely how do you plan to ensure that, brother? Are you become a Captain Sharp in your time on the continent?'

Kit smiled ruefully. 'No, though I have learned to recognise them pretty well. I have no need to cheat. All these years of play have improved my game immeasurably. You know well enough that I was always lucky with the cards and the bones. Nothing has changed there. I am just more practised than before. I have no doubt that I shall win…especially as I hear that Lady Luce seems to have lost her own knack for the cards. Did I not hear that she is called ''Lady Lose'' nowadays?'

Hugo nodded, somewhat unwillingly.

'Good. That improves the odds even more. Lady Luce tried to ruin me then. Would have done it, too, if you had not paid my debts. I owe you. And I owe her. With Stratton Magna at my back, I shall see her in the gutter. And I shall rejoice at her downfall.'

Hugo was shaking his head despairingly, as if he did not understand how Kit could harbour such hatred for another human being. And for so many years. But if Hugo had spent years exiled on the continent, he too might have just such a ruthless attitude to Society. Kit had long ago concluded that people were there to be used for his own advantage. It did not pay to become close to anyone. That way lay disaster.

The third Earl Luce was pacing his mother's opulent drawing room. 'Mama,' he said at last, 'you cannot continue like this.'

The Dowager Countess took a generous mouthful of

best madeira, savouring it as she swallowed. 'For God's sake, William, stop behaving like a caged elephant.'

The Earl stopped abruptly. He glanced at his reflection in the ornate, gilt-framed mirror—he was nothing like as large as an elephant. How dare she suggest anything so offensive?

She raised her lorgnette and peered at him. That piercing stare had unnerved him since he was five years old. Now, more than forty years later, it still did.

'Continue like *what,* precisely?' asked Lady Luce acidly.

Her son cleared his throat, ready to do battle on the one subject where he knew he had the whip hand. He was intending to enjoy this. 'You cannot continue to gamble with money you do not have, Mama,' he began. 'You—'

Lady Luce used the arms of her chair to push herself into a standing position. Even then, she was considerably shorter than her son, and looked more than twice as wide in her old-fashioned hooped skirts. 'And who, pray, is going to stop me?' she said in an awful voice.

'I am,' he said, as stoutly as he could, but avoiding her gimlet eye. 'I cannot afford to continue to pay your debts, Mama. You seem to forget that I have a family of my own to keep.'

His mother snorted. 'How could I forget? Never seen so many confounded brats. You're as bad as Clarence.'

'Mama! How can you say such a thing? It is highly improper for a lady to mention illegitimate children, even if their father is a royal duke. And you know very well that I have never been unfaithful to Charlotte.'

'No, because no other woman would look twice at you,' snapped his mother, 'even if you did have the money to dangle after them. It's quite your own fault that you have sired ten children. And I do not see why my style of living should be curtailed to pay for them, just because you cannot keep your—'

'*Mama!* Please!'

His mother looked hard at him and smiled nastily. She was clearly enjoying his embarrassment. One day, he would…

He turned his back on her and went to the window. If he did not have to look at her, it would be easier to tell her what she was to do. 'My children are not in question here,' he said, trying to keep his temper under control. 'My father provided you with a very generous jointure. You do not even have to pay for the upkeep of this house. You have the means to live in considerable comfort, but you choose to gamble instead, relying on the assumption that I will always stand behind your debts.'

'Balderdash,' said his mother roundly. 'You left me hanging in the wind when—'

Lord Luce spun round furiously. 'That was five years ago, Mama, and it only happened once. You knew that I could not raise such a huge sum just then.' He raised his hand to stop her from speaking. 'Besides,' he went on rapidly, 'you came about soon enough, when you won all that money from Kit Stratton, did you not? You had no need of my backing.'

'Did I not? I'll have you know, you miserable apology for a whelp, that—'

'No, Mama, you will not. You will listen to me. You will learn to live within your means. If you come to me just once more to pay your gambling debts, it will be the last time, I promise you. I shall let it be known that I will not pay in future. And who would accept your vowels then?'

'You would not dare,' she spat. 'Your name would—'

'Balderdash,' he said, enjoying the feel of the word on his lips. Let her have a taste of her own medicine. 'Society will agree that I have been too indulgent for too long. You may be an "original," Mama, but Society tires of such entertainments in the end. I am the head of the family and I mean what I say.'

His mother stamped over to him and poked him in the chest. 'Do you, William? Do you, indeed? Then understand this. I shall behave exactly as I please. If I choose to gamble, I shall do so, and nothing you can say shall prevent me. I shall stake my jointure and leave all my other bills unpaid. And I shall make a point of telling all of London that the Luce estate stands behind me, since otherwise I should end up in the Fleet. How would that please your sense of propriety, eh? The Dowager Countess Luce in debtors' prison because her son would not pay her debts. What would all your fine friends think to that? And your sons, too. I am sure it would make for splendid sport at Eton.'

The Earl's shoulders slumped. She had won again. She was not a woman, she was a witch.

'Well?' she said.

'Mama, you must understand that I cannot afford it,' he said, adopting a pleading voice. 'The income from the estate has been poor ever since the end of the war. If there are any more major calls on me, I shall have to start selling the unentailed properties. Surely you cannot wish me to do that? It is all I have to leave to the younger boys.'

Lady Luce grunted. 'I might think about it,' she said grudgingly.

His tactics had worked. That was as near to a concession as he had ever won from her. 'Perhaps if you

had another interest, something to divert your mind—'
he began.

'There's nothing wrong with my mind,' she snapped.

'No, of course not,' he said, trying to grapple with the
brilliant idea that had just struck him, 'but…a young
companion might be just the thing.'

She fixed him with a steely gaze.

He quailed a little but continued. He could not refuse
an opportunity to bridle the Dowager, however temporarily. 'Let me look about for someone suitable,' he said.
Then he added, as a clincher, 'I will undertake to pay
all the costs of her keep. Your jointure shall remain at
your sole disposal, as in the past.'

His mother gave him a very strange look. Then, to his
surprise, she nodded briefly. 'Yes, you are right. I could
do with a young thing about the place.'

Victory! The Earl bowed over his mother's hand. His
wife's bosom friend, Lady Blaine, would be bound to
know of a suitable candidate. He would enlist her aid
this very day. Now, he must make a speedy exit before
his mother changed her mind.

He had just reached the door when she said, airily,
'Just make sure she plays a good hand of piquet, William. At my age, I do not have time to start teaching
gels how to play cards.'

'Miss Beaumont?'

Marina spun round. She was being addressed by a
liveried footman who was taking no pains to conceal his
disdain at the sight of her shabby travelling costume and
worn bonnet. Marina raised her chin a fraction. She
might be poor and ill clad, but she was most certainly a
lady. She would not allow herself to be daunted by a
mere servant.

She narrowed her eyes as she looked at the young man. She was almost as tall as he was, she noted absently. 'I am Miss Beaumont,' she said in a frosty voice.

The footman could not hold her stern gaze. After a moment, he looked away. 'Will you come this way, miss?' he said, indicating the carriage that stood waiting to convey her across London to her employer's house.

It was only a small victory—but it mattered to Marina. If she was to live in Lady Luce's house, she must ensure that the Dowager's servants treated her with respect. 'Please see that my baggage is stowed safely,' she said, pointing to the two old valises that contained everything she owned. The footman did as he was bid, picking them up as though they weighed nothing at all. 'Thank you,' Marina said with a smile.

The footman seemed taken aback for a few seconds, as if he were suddenly seeing a completely different person. Then he remembered his place and helped Marina into the carriage where she sank back against the cushions with a sigh of relief. She had arrived in London, at last. And in a very short time, she would be making her curtsy to the Dowager Countess Luce, the old lady who wanted a gay young companion to brighten her declining years. Marina had decided during the journey from Yorkshire that she could fill the role pretty well. She had often acted as companion to her grandmother in her final years, reading to her, playing or singing for her, even playing cards with her. In those last years, Grandmama had become most exacting, almost as if she were still entitled to be treated as the sister of a viscount. Lady Luce could not be any worse. Reclusive elderly ladies were all much the same, weren't they?

Marina closed her eyes, trying vainly to shut out the noise and the overpowering smells. She had never imag-

ined that London could be so full of raucous sounds—
the cries of hawkers, each trying to outdo his neighbour,
the shouts of draymen anxious to make their way
through the bustle of traffic, the ring of horses' hooves
and carriage wheels, the underlying hum of a huge, pul-
sating city. At home, she had been used to the sounds
and smells of farmyard animals, the cries of wild birds,
and the howl of the wind across the moors. Nothing like
this. She resisted the temptation to hold her nose or put
her hands to her ears. If she was to live in London as
companion to Lady Luce, she would have to become
accustomed. She might as well start now.

Armed with this new resolution, Marina sat up and
looked out of the window. She had no idea where she
was, but the streets seemed to have become a little qui-
eter. They were certainly more genteel than before:
fewer hawkers, more gentlemen's carriages. The houses
had large windows and imposing entrances, some
flanked by columns like a Greek temple. This was much,
much grander than anything she had known in Yorkshire.

While Marina was studying the architecture on one
side of the street, the carriage drew up at a house on the
other. She had arrived! The footman, more deferential
now, had jumped down to open the door on the far side
and stood ready to help her out. As she stepped down,
the front door was opened by a stately old man in black
who was almost completely bald. What little hair he still
possessed was white as snow and sat round his pate like
a frill of cream round a pink pudding. He looked like
something out of a fairy tale, Marina decided, though he
should have been wearing a wizard's robe rather than a
butler's uniform.

'Welcome to London, Miss Beaumont,' the butler said

in an expressionless voice. 'Her ladyship is waiting for you upstairs in her drawing room. Will you come this way, please?' He turned and began to lead the way towards the imposing staircase.

Not now! Not yet! Marina looked down at her travel-stained clothing and her darned gloves. She needed time to make herself presentable before she was introduced to Lady Luce. The Dowager would take one look at her in this state and send her back to Mama by the first available coach.

Marina took a deep breath and paused just inside the door. 'I am sure her ladyship does not wish to meet me until I have rid myself of the dust of the journey,' she said in a voice that surprised her with its steadiness. 'Have the goodness to bring me to a room where I may wash and change my dress first. The footman may bring my valises.' Marina looked back to where the footman was extracting her luggage from the carriage.

The butler stopped short, then turned back and stared at her in apparent amazement for a few seconds. Finally, he coughed and resumed his earlier vacant expression. 'As you wish, miss. Will you come this way? Charles, bring Miss Beaumont's bags up to her room straight away.'

'Yes, Mr Tibbs,' replied the footman quickly, hoisting both bags with one arm so that he could close the front door noiselessly behind him.

Marina smiled to herself, a very little. She had just learned her second lesson. And so had Lady Luce's servants.

Chapter Two

Marina looked round her small, sparsely furnished bedchamber. She supposed she should be glad that she had not been banished to the attics, with the servants. As a lady's companion, she would be neither servant nor gentry, but something indeterminate in between. She must maintain her distance from the servants. Lady Luce and her guests would, in turn, maintain their distance from the companion. Marina would be alone.

The butler had informed her, in a somewhat fatherly manner, that she had been given a bedchamber on the same corridor as her ladyship's so that she would be within easy reach, should Lady Luce have need of her services at any time. Marina had deduced that she was to be at her ladyship's beck and call, twenty-four hours a day.

She shrugged her shoulders. What else had she expected? Her own grandmother had been equally exacting—and more than a little querulous towards the end of her life. Marina would just have to summon all her reserves of patience and understanding, and set about ministering to another old lady's whims.

I shall pretend she is my own grandmother, Marina

promised herself as she changed her gown. I learned forbearance then. I can surely do the same for another demanding old lady, especially as, on this occasion, I am being paid for my trouble.

She smiled at the thought of the money she would send to her mother the moment she received her first wages. Mama had said Marina would need to provide for her wardrobe, but surely she could manage with what she had brought from Yorkshire? A companion did not need many gowns to accompany her mistress when she took the air, or to wind her lady's knitting wool. Marina had long ago decided to confine herself to what she already had. Her first duty was to her own family.

She considered her image in the glass that had been thoughtfully provided. It would do. Her grey gown, though creased from its time in her valise, was clean and neat, and set off with a fresh white collar. She looked like a lady, not a servant, she decided, with a small smile of satisfaction. Her dark brown hair had been neatly rebraided and pinned to the back of her head. Her newly washed complexion glowed with health. Her head was bare—she might be almost at her last prayers but, at twenty-three, she was not yet condemned to the spinster's cap—and she wore no jewellery except the mourning ring that had been on her finger almost since the day she had learned of her father's death. She nodded at her reflection in the mirror. Lady Luce would see, in her, the model of a demure, biddable lady's companion, well worth the wage she was to be paid. The Dowager would have no reason to send Marina back to her family. That must be avoided at all costs, for Mama desperately needed every penny Marina could spare.

And now she must go down to meet the lady who

would have the ordering of her life for months, perhaps years to come.

Marina took a deep breath, straightened her shoulders and made her way out into the corridor. Tibbs, the butler, was hovering not far away, waiting for her.

'This leads to her ladyship's chambers,' he said, indicating a door near the head of the staircase. 'No one else sleeps on this floor, except when her ladyship has guests. Though now there is yourself, miss,' he added, apparently as an afterthought.

'Does not the Earl stay here when he is in London?' Marina asked.

'No, miss. Her ladyship and her son…' He coughed. 'His lordship has his own house in town. He always stays there.'

'I see,' said Marina. It was understandable that a grown-up son would not wish to live under the eye of his mother, even for a day or two. The butler seemed to have been about to say something about the pair, something that had sounded for all the world like the beginning of backstairs gossip. Marina, not being a servant, should deliberately shut her ears to it. And yet she found herself wondering about the Earl and his relationship with his mother. Was she too demanding for his comfort? Elderly ladies often were. And a gentleman's patience could be quickly exhausted.

The butler led Marina down to the floor below and to a room at the front of the house. With a grand gesture, he threw open the door and announced, in stentorian tones, 'Miss Beaumont, your ladyship.'

Marina passed through the door that Tibbs was holding and heard it close quietly at her back. This sumptuous straw-coloured drawing room seemed to be empty.

She could see no one at all. But surely…? The butler had seemed in no doubt…

Marina hesitated by the door.

'Don't just stand there, girl. Come into the light where I may see you.' The sharp voice came from the depths of a chair by a large window overlooking the street.

Marina moved forward to find the source of that peremptory command. Only when she had reached the far side of the room could she see that the voice had issued from a tiny figure who was dwarfed by the chair she sat in. Lady Luce was richly dressed in plum-coloured silk, but in the style of more than forty years earlier, with wide skirts and an abundance of fine lace at her throat and wrists, and a powdered wig on her head. Although her skin was dry and wrinkled, the delicate lines of her bones showed that she had once been very beautiful. Now she resembled nothing so much as a miniature exotic fruit, so shrivelled and fragile that it might shatter if it was touched.

'Good gad, they've sent me a beanpole,' Lady Luce exclaimed.

Marina could feel herself blushing. It had been a matter of regret throughout her adult life that she had inherited her father's height and build. Her slight figure made her seem even taller than she actually was. Compared with Lady Luce, she must seem a veritable giantess. Marina curtsied. 'How do you do, ma'am?' she said calmly, trying to manage a smile for the tiny—and extremely rude—Dowager Countess who was to be her employer.

The Dowager did not immediately reply to Marina's polite greeting. She was looking her up and down, her sharp old eyes missing nothing of her new companion's dowdy appearance. 'Thought one of the Blaines would be better turned out,' she said. 'Wouldn't give a gown like that to a scullery maid.'

This was not a good start to their relationship. The Dowager must be instantly disabused of the idea that Marina was 'one of the Blaines,' or that she could afford to be better dressed. Marina knew she must set matters straight between them, even if Lady Luce sent her packing as a result. She had no choice.

'I think you must be labouring under a misapprehension, ma'am,' Marina began. 'My name is Beaumont, not Blaine. I am only distantly related to the Viscount's family, through my grandmother, but she was not acknowledged by them, not after her marriage.'

'Hmph,' snorted the Dowager. 'Nothing "distant" about it. Your mother and the new Viscount are first cousins, are they not?'

'Yes, but not—'

'You're a Blaine,' said the Dowager flatly. 'The old Viscount's father was a tyrant and a blackguard, but that don't change the bloodline, not in my book. Your grandmother was daughter to one Viscount, and sister to the next. You're a Blaine, all right.'

It was clearly going to be difficult to argue with Lady Luce, perhaps even to get a word in, Marina decided. But, on this delicate subject, she must try.

'Forgive me, ma'am,' she began again, 'but you must understand that the Beaumonts have never been acknowledged by the Viscount's family, not even when my grandmother's brother succeeded to the title.'

'That's because he was just like his father,' interrupted the Dowager, with a grimace, 'which was only to be expected, since all the Blaine men—' She broke off to scrutinise Marina's face for a moment and then said, 'I see you know nothing about your noble relations, young lady. Well, I may choose to enlighten you—perhaps—one day. But there are other, more pressing matters. For a start, we must do something about that frightful monstrosity you are wearing.'

Worse and worse, thought Marina, but before she had a chance to say a word in defence of her wardrobe, the Dowager was laying down the law on dress, just as she had on the subject of blood.

'It is fit only for the fire,' pronounced Lady Luce. 'Or the poorhouse. Though, even there, I dare say the women would turn their noses up at it. Have you nothing fit to be seen, girl?'

'I do have one evening gown, ma'am. Apart from that, I have very few gowns, all similar to this one. What spare money we have must be spent on my brother's education. Harry is at Oxford,' she added, with sisterly pride, 'and he is destined for the Church.'

'Don't approve of spending every last farthing on boys,' said Lady Luce quickly. 'You educate them, and where does it get you? Eh? Take your every penny and fritter it away. If it's not land drainage, or enclosures, or something equally unnecessary, it's fast living and loose women.'

'Harry does not—'

Marina's protest was cut short by another disapproving snort. 'Not *your* brother. Don't know the first thing about *him*. He may be a pattern-card of rectitude, for all I know. But the sons of noble families…' Lady Luce shook her head. Her message was clear. The sons of noble families were not to be trusted with money. Presumably that also applied to her own son?

'A lady has to be independent enough to lead her own life, in just the way she wants,' said Lady Luce, warming to her subject. 'Especially once she is widowed,' she added meaningfully.

At last, Marina understood. Lady Luce's unusual views on female independence were clearly to be applied to her own case, and probably to that case only. It was unlikely she would care about the plight of Mama, or any other gently bred widow who had fallen on hard times.

'You give 'em an heir and your duty is done,' said Lady Luce. 'Least a husband can do in return is to provide for a comfortable widowhood. But husbands seem to think that the heir should have charge of everything, even his mother!' She stopped, looking up at Marina once again. 'And just what do you think you are laughing at, young madam?'

Marina had not realised she had begun to smile at the old lady's spirited defence of her own interests. 'I beg your pardon, ma'am,' she lied quickly, 'I was thinking only that you reminded me of my own dear grandmother. I miss her greatly.'

'Balderdash,' said Lady Luce roundly. 'You were thinking that I was talking dangerous nonsense, but that I could be forgiven my revolutionary views because of my great age. Well? Were you not?'

Taking a deep breath, Marina said, with sudden resolution, 'Yes, ma'am, I was. I admit it. But I see now that your arguments should not be dismissed on such spurious grounds. You are obviously a redoubtable opponent, for woman or for man, and your great age has nothing to do with the case.'

Lady Luce gasped. For a second, Marina held her breath, thinking how foolhardy she had been to speak so. The Dowager would ring a peal over her head and then despatch her post-haste back to Yorkshire. But nothing of the sort happened. Her ladyship stared sharply into Marina's face, now mercifully straight, and then said, with a crack of laughter, 'Yes, you'll do. Once we have done something about your wardrobe, of course. I shall see to that tomorrow. You are not fit to be seen as you are. Turn round.'

Obediently, Marina turned her back.

'Again,' said the Dowager.

Marina turned to face her once more.

'Sit down, girl,' said Lady Luce, nodding towards a low stool at the side of her chair. 'It's giving me a stiff neck trying to look up all that way.'

Marina allowed herself a small smile as she obeyed. The Dowager's bark was extremely frightening, but Marina now fancied that her ladyship's bite was a little lacking in teeth, like a pampered old lapdog, yelping and snapping uselessly at every visitor.

'Now, Miss Beaumont. Tell me about yourself,' began her ladyship. She was obviously pleased to see that Marina, once seated on the stool, was shorter than she was. 'What do they call you?'

'Marina, ma'am,' replied Marina, puzzled. How could Lady Luce have agreed to employ a companion when she did not even know her given name?

'Marina. Hmm. Unusual name, is it not?'

'I am not sure, ma'am. I was named for my father's mother, I believe.'

'Foreign, was she?' Lady Luce's voice betrayed her distaste.

'I understand so. I never knew her. My father's family had served in the army for generations. All the women followed the drum.'

'Your mother, too?' Lady Luce's voice had a clear undertone of disapproval now. She probably felt that such behaviour was not appropriate for a niece of the Viscount Blaine.

'Yes, ma'am. But after the Peace of Amiens, my father decided that his wife would be better in England, since my brother and I were so small. We settled in Yorkshire.'

'And your father? What was he?'

'He was a captain in the 95th Rifles, ma'am. He died nine years ago, at the battle of Ciudad Rodrigo, along with my uncle.'

Lady Luce nodded in understanding. Marina wondered whether she, too, had lost loved ones in the wars. Many titled families had.

'But your mother was provided for?' Lady Luce clearly had no qualms about enquiring into the most intimate detail of her companion's circumstances. And she would doubtless persist until she received her answer.

'No, ma'am. At least, not well.' That was true, though it was not the whole truth. 'My mother supplemented our income by taking pupils.' Seeing her ladyship's look of surprise, Marina added, 'My mother is very well educated, ma'am. Her father was a great scholar. He educated his daughter exactly as he educated his son.' She smiled fondly. 'Unlike my mother, my uncle had no inclination for scholarship. He was army mad, almost from his cradle. A great disappointment to my grandfather.'

'Hmph,' said Lady Luce. It was not clear whether she approved or not. 'And who was he, this scholar grandfather of yours?'

Marina was beginning to dislike her ladyship's sustained questioning very much, but she did not think she could refuse to answer. 'He met my grandmother when he was the Viscount Blaine's private secretary, I believe, ma'am.'

Her ladyship smiled suddenly. 'And he was remarkably handsome, too, was he not? Tall, with fine features and dark hair, and a beautifully modulated speaking voice?'

'Why, yes. Grandmama did describe him in much that way,' Marina replied. 'Did you know him, ma'am?'

Her ladyship continued to smile, a rather secretive smile, and a faraway look came into her eye. 'Aye, I knew James Langley. All the girls were mad for him, I remember. Handsomest man we had ever seen…but quite unsuitable…quite.' She looked sharply at Marina as if looking for some resemblance. 'Your grandmother kicked over the traces for his handsome face, did she, eh?'

Marina blushed and nodded dumbly. Her ladyship's salty turn of phrase was not what she was used to in Yorkshire with her very proper mama.

'And her father cast her off as a result?'

Marina nodded again.

'Just what I'd expect from that family. Don't hold with such cavalier treatment. Don't hold with it at all.' Lady Luce shook her head so vigorously that a little cloud of powder rose from her wig. 'If I had had a daughter—'

The door opened to admit the butler. Bowing stiffly, he announced, 'His lordship is below, your ladyship, and begs the favour of a few minutes' conversation with Miss Beaumont.'

'Does he, indeed?' said Lady Luce, frowning.

Marina was astonished. What on earth could Lady Luce's son want with the companion?

'I suppose I must humour him, in the circumstances,' her ladyship said, grudgingly. 'Conduct Miss Beaumont below, Tibbs.'

Wonderingly, Marina followed the butler out of the room and down the staircase to the bookroom on the ground floor. Perhaps the Earl wished to look over his mother's companion, to decide whether he thought her suitable? But what if he did not? Marina doubted that her son's objections would make any difference to Lady Luce, not once she had made up her mind.

The Earl was standing by the window, looking out into the street. He was several inches shorter than Marina, and noticeably corpulent. Unlike his mother, he wore the newest fashions, even though tight pantaloons did not flatter his figure at all.

He waited until the door had closed before turning. He made no move towards Marina. And he did not attempt to shake hands.

Marina understood. To the Earl, she was only a servant. She curtsied, waiting for him to speak.

Like his mother, he surveyed her keenly. Marina caught his lofty expression and responded automatically by lifting her chin. Had not Lady Luce just insisted she was a Blaine?

'Miss Beaumont,' he said, in an affected drawl, 'you have arrived at last. We had looked to see you somewhat sooner than this.'

Marina did not attempt to make excuses for the timing of her arrival. His lordship might travel post, but she could not afford such luxury. She looked calmly across at him, waiting.

'However, it is of no moment now. We have more important matters to discuss.'

Marina's surprise must have been evident in her face, for he said, 'I take it Lady Blaine did not tell you about my requirements?'

'No, sir. Lady Blaine said nothing at all about the nature of the post. She wrote only—'

The Earl clearly had no interest in what Marina wished to say, and no compunction about interrupting a lady who was no better than a servant. 'What her ladyship wrote is of no interest to me, Miss Beaumont. What matters here are the instructions that I shall give you. Your role in this household is to prevent my mother from indulging in extravagant foolishness. No doubt you have heard that she has a predilection for gambling?'

Marina shook her head. 'I know nothing at all about her ladyship's manner of living, sir.'

The Earl snorted. He sounded worse than his mother. 'I see,' he said. 'Very well. The facts are these. My mother is overfond of gambling. On occasion, she has been known to risk considerably more than she can afford. Your role, Miss Beaumont, is to ensure that she does not.'

Marina gulped. How was she supposed to ensure such a thing? Surely Lady Luce would never have agreed to have her son's agent foisted on her? 'I do not understand, sir,' Marina said.

'It is quite simple,' snapped the Earl. 'Even a woman should be able to grasp it. I am employing you to stop my mother's gambling. The means I leave to you.'

Ignoring his rudeness, Marina tried to grapple with his astonishing statement. 'I had understood that I was employed by the Dowager Countess,' she began, but she was permitted to go no further.

'Ostensibly, but all the costs of your position fall to me. *I* am employing you. And your role will be as I have described.'

Marina swallowed hard. The task was impossible, surely? And the Earl was obnoxious. 'Is the Dowager

Countess content with this arrangement?' she asked quietly. It would sound presumptuous for a mere companion to speak so, but the question had to be asked.

The Earl was beginning to look angry. 'I require you to say nothing to her on the subject. If you do, you will be discharged instantly.'

Marina paled.

Lord Luce smiled nastily as he continued, 'Remember, Miss Beaumont, that it is I, not my mother, who pay you. And that it is to me you will answer, if you fail in your appointed task. That is all I wish to say to you. You may go.'

There was nothing more to be said. Marina automatically dipped a brief curtsy and left the room. Her heart was pounding madly. She understood at last why Lady Blaine had written that short, cold letter to Mama. At the time, Marina had wondered why her haughty relation should suddenly offer to recommend her to a comfortable position, after decades of estrangement. But since pride was a luxury that the Beaumonts could not afford, Marina had had to accept the crumbs from the rich man's table. Now, too late, she could see that the crumbs were laced with poison.

She was trapped. And she was alone in London. She could turn to no one for advice. If she was loyal to Lady Luce, the Earl would dismiss her. If she acted as the Earl's instrument, Lady Luce would soon suspect and send her packing. After all the money that had been spent on her passage to London, it seemed she would soon become a burden to Mama all over again. She would have squandered her only chance to help her family.

She shook her head defiantly. No. She must do her duty. Somehow, she must find a way to satisfy both the

Earl and his mother, and to earn the money to send home to Yorkshire to keep Mama from penury.

She must.

She would.

Chapter Three

'Good gad! I thought you said you had an evening gown. Is that the best you can do?'

Face flaming, Marina stood rigid as the Dowager's sharp little eyes travelled over every detail of her drab appearance. She was wearing the best of her meagre Yorkshire wardrobe, a dove-grey gown made high to the neck, but relieved with a tiny ruff of precious lace. It was plain, and not in the least fashionable, but it was clean and neat. And, unlike most of Marina's other gowns, it bore no visible evidence of mending.

Lady Luce's distaste was manifest in the narrowing of her eyes and the slight thinning of her lips. She rose from her chair, shaking out her wide silken skirts. The fall of fine lace at her bosom quivered indignantly. 'I suppose that *is* your evening gown?' she said in withering tones.

'You are correct, ma'am,' replied Marina, refusing to drop her gaze. She would not be made to feel ashamed of her appearance. Her dress was perfectly adequate for a near-servant. 'This is quite my *best* gown,' she added daringly, remembering the lesson she had learnt when she first arrived. The Dowager relished a sharp opponent.

Lady Luce gave a snort which might have been suppressed laughter. With a tiny shake of her powdered head, she said, 'We shall see to your wardrobe tomorrow, as I promised. Don't suppose it will matter much tonight. Shouldn't be taking you to Méchante's in the first place, of course, not a gel like you.' She turned for the door, talking all the while. 'Too prim and proper by half. Just what I'd expect from William.'

'Excuse me, ma'am,' began Marina, daring at last to interrupt her ladyship's meanderings, 'but who is Méchante and why—?'

'Why should you not go there?' Lady Luce spun round to face Marina. She seemed remarkably nimble for her years. Her eyes were full of wicked laughter. 'My dear, Méchante—Lady Marchant—is not a proper person for a lady to know. She is the daughter of a Cit, and her history is…ah…more than a little colourful, besides. Most of the company at her card party tonight will be male. As to the *ladies* you may meet there…' She chuckled. 'Suffice it to say that you would do best to pretend never to have set eyes on them. You would be wise to make yourself as unobtrusive as possible. Try to blend into the background.' She looked Marina up and down once more. 'In that gown, it should not be difficult.'

Marina stared, but Lady Luce was already making for the door which opened, as if by magic, just as she reached it. The butler stood in the hall, waiting. No doubt he had been listening to every single word. Before morning, Marina's plight would be the talk of the servants' hall. She could feel herself flushing yet again as she followed Lady Luce to the door, head held high and eyes fixed on the Dowager's ramrod-straight back. The servants might mock in private, but they would never detect the slightest sign of weakness in Marina's outward behaviour.

Throughout the short journey through the still-bustling streets, Marina worried at the information about the dubious Lady Marchant and her card party. Méchante—Marina knew it meant naughty, or wicked, in French. If the lady's past was as colourful as the Dowager had hinted, she probably deserved her nickname.

Marina quailed inwardly at the thought of this first test. Why did it have to come quite so soon? She began to rack her brains for ideas to stop the Dowager's gambling but came up with nothing practicable. If she claimed she was ill, the Dowager would simply send her home. If she tried to intervene in the game itself, the Dowager might well dismiss her on the spot. And if she betrayed the Earl's instructions, the Dowager would probably stake every penny she had, and more, just to spite him, for she had made no secret of the fact that she despised him. Marina chewed at her bottom lip. It did not help.

'Pull yourself together, child,' said the Dowager sharply. 'Méchante won't eat you, you know. You might even enjoy yourself…get rid of that Friday face. You *do* play cards, I take it?'

'Yes, ma'am,' replied Marina quickly. As a companion, she might be lacking in many ways, but she could certainly hold her own at the card table. Her father had delighted in teaching her how to play cards, and she had been an apt pupil, but she had never yet had an opportunity to discover whether she had inherited his appalling luck. Nor did she wish to. Captain Beaumont's gambling losses had been the major cause of his family's poverty. 'However, I never gamble. I believe that—'

'What you believe is of no importance. You will soon

discover that everyone gambles, whether they can afford it or not.' She stared hard at Marina for a second. 'I collect that you have no money?'

'I believe that gambling is wrong, whether one has money or not,' said Marina stoutly. 'It ruins too many lives.'

The Dowager continued to stare, narrowing her eyes assessingly, but she said nothing until they had reached their destination and were preparing to alight. 'Do not share your puritanical opinions with the guests tonight, Marina,' she said. 'It would do no good. And it could do you a great deal of harm.'

Marina nodded dumbly and followed Lady Luce into the brightly lit entrance hall of Lady Marchant's extravagant London house.

'Why, Lady Luce, is it not? Good evening, ma'am.'

The Dowager stopped so suddenly that Marina almost collided with her. As it was, she stepped on the hem of her ladyship's train and had to extricate herself carefully from the fine material. By the time Marina looked up once more, Lady Luce was staring coldly in the direction of the handsomest man Marina had ever seen. He had stationed himself between Lady Luce and the staircase and his presence seemed to fill the marble hallway. He was extremely tall and dark, with beautiful features that would not have looked out of place on a statue in a Greek temple. His exquisitely cut clothes seemed to have been moulded to his form, yet he wore them with an air of nonchalance.

'Such a pleasure to meet you again, ma'am.' The gentleman's drawl had an unpleasant edge to it, Marina noticed, and his finely shaped mouth curled in disdain as he looked down at the tiny lady whose path he was blocking. 'It must be…what?…all of five years? I look forward to making your acquaintance again. You *do* still play, I take it?'

'Oh, I play, Mr Stratton, you may be sure of that.' Lady Luce's voice was acid. 'I had not thought Méchante was quite so short of guests, however, as to need to invite just *anyone* to make up her numbers. I see that I shall have to take more care in deciding which invitations a lady should accept.' With that, she marched forward, forcing her tormentor to make way for her. He did so with easy grace, Marina noticed, and he continued to watch with narrowed eyes as the Dowager mounted the elegant branching staircase to the reception rooms above. He spared not one glance for the grey companion.

By the time the Dowager reached her hostess's drawing room, she was white with anger. Her thin lips were pressed tightly together as if to prevent her from speaking words that she might regret.

'Ma'am—'

'Have nothing to do with Kit Stratton, child,' said Lady Luce sharply before Marina had time to begin her question. 'He is dangerous. More dangerous than you could ever imagine.'

'But—'

'Good evening, Méchante.' Lady Luce was holding out her claw-like hand to a voluptuous blonde dressed in a gown of diaphanous pink silk. It was doubtful whether Lady Marchant wore much by way of petticoats beneath her gown. It seemed to cling to her almost like a second skin.

Marina had never seen anything so brazen. She caught herself staring and forced herself to look away. Their hostess's nickname was well deserved. She seemed to relish it, too. At Lady Luce's impudent greeting, Lady Marchant smiled contentedly, accentuating her slanting

green eyes. There was something remarkably feline
about that look, Marina decided. She was probably devious, as well as wicked.

Marina longed to ask questions, but could not. Who
was the haughty man in the hallway? His name seemed
vaguely familiar, but she could not place it. What was
between him and Lady Luce? Enmity, for sure, but why?
Marina had no opportunity to say a word, far less ask a
question, for Lady Luce and her hostess were already
mingling with the throng of guests. There was no sign
of the incredibly handsome Mr Kit Stratton.

Marina forced her thoughts back to practical matters.
She must not stand alone in the doorway as if she were
an outcast. She must heed the Dowager's warning and
blend into the background. The huge draped velvet cur-
tains would provide just what she needed. They were far
enough away from the candelabra to cast quite a deep
shadow. In her grey gown, Marina would appear to be
almost a shadow herself.

Safe in her dark corner, Marina surveyed the company. Almost all the guests were men. There were soldiers in scarlet coats, some of them quite senior, some
of them so young that they still had the downy cheeks
of a girl. Marina was forcibly reminded of her younger
brother, Harry, and how very proud he had been on the
first application of his cut-throat razors.

Of the non-military gentlemen, a few were dressed in
expensive and well-cut coats, but most reminded her of
Lord Luce. They looked well fed and well-upholstered
and, in more than one case, well on the way to an early
grave.

The ladies—no, that was too flattering a term—the
women were few. Apart from Lady Marchant and Lady
Luce, there were only three, none of them in the first

blush of youth. They wore fine but slightly grubby gowns, all very low cut indeed. Two of the women had painted their faces. Lady Luce was right. Méchante's house was one that no virtuous young lady should ever enter. Why then had she been so insistent that Marina should accompany her tonight?

The noise in the room was almost deafening. It seemed that all of the gentlemen were well into their cups and each was almost shouting to make himself heard above his fellows. Marina found herself shrinking somewhat into the velvet shadow and wishing that she had been able to avoid coming to this place.

Where was Lady Luce? She and her hostess seemed to have disappeared. Marina supposed they must have gone into an adjoining room. Should she follow her employer? Or should she stay here where, for the moment at least, she seemed to be relatively safe? She hesitated, but only for a moment. It was her duty to protect the Dowager, somehow, from her gambling folly. What if she were gambling in the very next room?

Marina straightened her shoulders. She must follow her employer and do her duty.

'Well,' said a male voice at her elbow.

Marina smelt the nauseating mix of stale alcohol and sweat even before she turned. Where had this man come from? She was being accosted—there was no other word for it—by a middle-aged man in a rusty-black evening coat. He was quite as raddled as the worst of those in the room. His skin was almost as grey as her gown; he had the eyes of a man who had not slept for days on end.

She gave him the look that had cowed many an upstart in Yorkshire and made to pass on. It was not to be. The man's hand grabbed her arm and forcibly brought her to a halt.

'Not so fast, missy,' he said, in a drawl that sounded half drunk, half affected. 'And who might you be?'

Marina tried to shake him off, but failed. 'My name is of no moment, sir,' she said in icy tones. 'I will thank you to let go of my arm.'

'Indeed?' His red-lidded eyes narrowed nastily. He looked her up and down. 'This one has her nose in the air,' he said at last. 'Don't see why.' His contempt was obvious from the set of his lips. 'With looks like yours, you should be glad that any man deigns to take notice of you. Don't reckon you're worth a guinea of any man's blunt.'

Marina gasped. She knew just what he thought her to be.

With a final, rather undignified wrench, she pulled her arm free and ran through the doorway, praying that her employer would be in the room beyond. She was disappointed. The adjoining room held only card tables where little groups of gentlemen were deeply engrossed in piquet and whist. At the table nearest the door, one of the gentlemen, clearly disturbed by her hurried entrance, indicated irritably that she should be silent.

Marina felt herself flushing. She halted her headlong dash. The man who had accosted her might not think her a lady, but she would try to behave as she had been taught. Even in a house such as this.

Head held high, she walked slowly and calmly through the room to the doorway on the other side.

It was another room for gambling, but considerably less decorous than the previous one. A noisy dice table stood near the door; on the far side, there was a roulette wheel, with a number of players clustered eagerly round it, including two more painted ladies.

Marina suppressed a shudder. There must be a way out of this nightmare. Where on earth could Lady Luce have disappeared to?

Kit watched with narrowed eyes as Lady Luce mounted the stairs to the galleried landing. Five years seemed to have changed her very little. She was as rude as ever, but he had expected nothing less. Did she suspect his intentions? Possibly. She was bound to know of the change in his circumstances. Society tabbies such as the Dowager made it a point of honour to know everyone's business.

He took out his gold snuff box and tapped it with a manicured fingernail. Mechanically, he opened it and took a minuscule pinch. His eyes were still on the landing above.

Where was she? Would she dare to play when she knew he was here, watching, waiting his chance?

Of course she would. Lady Luce was a soulless harridan but she was no coward. She might avoid Kit if she decently could but, faced with a direct challenge, she would never retreat. All he had to do was wait for the right opportunity. One day, it would come. Perhaps even tonight?

With a little nod of satisfaction, Kit mounted the staircase. Unlike Lady Luce, he did not take the branch leading to the reception rooms. He had long ago made it his business to spy out the layout of Méchante's labyrinth of a house. He knew precisely where the high-stakes games would be played. And, like a skilled hunter, he knew that the best tactic was to conceal himself and lie in wait for his prey.

* * *

Marina was bewildered. She had made her way through room after room encountering only drunken gamblers with too ready hands. It seemed to have taken hours to come this far. Now she was back on the landing, but still there was no sign of Lady Luce.

At the far side of the landing, a door opened. A slurring voice said, 'So this is where you are. Don't think you fool me by pretending to run away. I learnt the tricks of your trade before you were born. And I know exactly what you have in mind. Exactly.'

Marina whirled round, took one look at the man weaving his way round the gallery towards her and instinctively backed away. Feeling a doorknob against her side, she quickly entered the room, leaning back against the door with a sigh of relief.

Here was yet another gambling room. This one was much smaller than the others and was generously hung with deep blue damask. A pointed archway in the wall led through to the adjoining room, also blue. In each, there was a large oval table where a group of gamblers was playing in complete silence. Marina looked in horror at the piles of coin, notes and vowels heaped on the green baize. The guests here were playing for very high stakes.

From her position by the door, Marina could not see any sign of Lady Luce. Perhaps she was not gambling, after all?

At the table in front of Marina, Lady Marchant was acting as banker. Marina took half a step forward, but stopped when Lady Marchant gave her a slight shake of the head. Obviously, Marina's presence was unwelcome here.

What was she to do?

Behind her, someone tried vainly to open the door. A

second later, it was pushed sharply into Marina's back. Surprised, she stumbled forward.

Lady Marchant frowned and shook her head angrily at the interruption, motioning to Marina to leave the room immediately. Unjust though it was, Marina knew better than to protest. She turned to do as she was bid. What choice did she have?

She stopped abruptly. There in the doorway, propping himself up against the jamb, was her drunken pursuer, the man she had been trying so hard to avoid. He was leering at her, waiting.

He thinks he has me now, Marina thought. But I will not allow myself to be used like a common street-walker.

She pulled herself up to her full height—which was a little taller than the drunk—and stared haughtily down at him. Her flashing eyes dared him to approach her. But in his befuddled state, would he heed her warning?

Through the archway, there came a cry of triumph. It was Lady Luce's voice. She was in the very next room!

Marina spun on her heel and cried out as she collided with a man directly behind her. He must have risen from Lady Marchant's table just as Marina turned.

For a split second, Marina felt herself falling, but then strong arms gripped her and held her upright. She found she was staring at a gold cravat pin in the shape of a swooping bird of prey, its cruel head set off by a blood-red ruby eye. She could not move. She was standing transfixed in a man's arms while the warmth of him invaded her limbs. Her mind was refusing to function. She could think of nothing but the obvious fact that he was even taller than her father.

Then she glanced up into his face.

It was Kit Stratton. And he had the hardest eyes she had ever seen.

Chapter Four

Kit set the grey lady back on her feet. It crossed his mind that she had no business to be in a house like Méchante's where all the females were either members of the muslin company or hardened gamesters like Lady Luce.

The grey lady seemed remarkably tongue-tied. Perhaps she was simple? That would certainly help to account for her presence here.

Kit looked over the grey lady's head to the swaying figure in the open doorway. Even in his cups, the man had a predatory look. Kit glanced down at the grey lady, wondering what the man could have seen in her. She was hardly worth pursuing, unless to puncture that strange air of 'touch-me-not' surrounding her. Yes, that must be it. It might be amusing to watch how she dealt with her would-be lover.

The drunk took a step towards them. 'I'll thank you to unhand my woman,' he said, enunciating each word with exaggerated care. 'I saw her first,' he added, as if to clinch the matter.

Kit stiffened at the man's brazen challenge. Not even drink could excuse it. He stepped smartly round the grey

lady and confronted her pursuer, bending down so that
their heads were almost touching. He forced himself to
ignore the stink. 'You are out of your depth here, my
friend,' he said in a low, menacing voice, 'and I find
your presence offensive. Go and put your head under the
pump.'

The man goggled up at him.

It seemed that hard words were not enough for this
man. Kit seized him, spun him round and quickly twisted
one arm up his back. Then he propelled his squealing
victim out on to the gallery and threw him to the floor.
Kit smiled grimly at the sound of bone crunching against
wooden balusters. Stone would have been preferable, he
thought, closing the door on the sprawling figure.

The grey lady had turned to watch. She was looking
at Kit through narrowed eyes. Clearly, he had been
wrong about her. There was nothing in the least simple
about this female.

'Good manners require me to thank you, sir, for saving me from a fall,' she said in a voice of cold, educated
politeness. She did not meet his eyes. 'As to the other—'
she glanced briefly towards the closed door '—I shall
try to pretend that I was not witness to such a vulgar
display.' With a moue of disgust, she turned and moved
serenely through the archway.

She holds herself like a duchess, Kit noted absently.
How very strange.

He felt a sudden desire to laugh. For once, he had
rescued a damsel in distress instead of ravishing her.
And his reward? She had simply looked down her nose
at him. He should have known better. Women were all
the same. Next time—why should there be a next time
with such a woman?—if there was a next time, he would
make her sorry she had ever tangled with Kit Stratton.

* * *

Marina was glad to be able to seek out her protector on the far side of the arch. Kit Stratton was Lady Luce's enemy. Everything about him shrieked danger. Beneath that fine, polished veneer, the man was a flint-hearted savage. It had taken every ounce of her self-control to conquer her body's weakness and give him the set-down he so richly deserved. She was proud of her actions. She had shown she was a lady still.

At the table, they were playing Faro. Lady Luce had clearly been there all the time, hidden by the dividing wall.

Marina's heart sank when she realised her employer was acting as Faro banker. This was no mere flutter. This was serious gambling. Heavens, why did this have to happen? And why Faro? Faro was the game that she hated above all others, the game that had ruined her father. It could be a game of infernally high stakes and incredible losses. Men played and played, always hoping to recoup their losses on the next card, until eventually they had nothing left to stake. Faro had led many a man to blow his brains out. Her father might eventually have done the same, if he had lived through the war.

No one had taken the least notice of her entrance. She leaned back against the wall alongside the arch, trying to steady her rapid, anxious breathing. She forced herself to think logically and sensibly. She must not panic. Surely Lady Luce would not play for higher stakes than she could afford? And besides, as banker, she would certainly have the odds in her favour. There must be a good chance that she would leave the table a winner. At that thought, Marina began to feel less uneasy and craned her neck a little in order to watch the play without disturbing those at the table.

There were five players besides Lady Luce. All were

men. All had their backs to Marina. Lady Luce was gathering up a pile of coin and notes. Her crow of triumph had been justified, to judge by the amount she was pulling towards her. So far, she looked to be on top. With expert fingers, she broke a new pack and began to shuffle the cards. The discarded pack had been swept to the floor.

The only noise to be heard was the slap of the cards. The players seemed to be frozen in their seats. Then a deep voice broke the silence from beyond the archway. 'You seem to have remarkable luck, ma'am,' it said. 'Do you dare to raise the stakes for this next deal? Shall we say a minimum of twenty guineas? Or would you prefer to pass the bank?'

Marina did not need to look round in order to recognise the speaker. It was Mr Kit Stratton. His tone was light, but mocking. It was as near an insult as it was possible to be.

Marina saw the spark of indignation in Lady Luce's eyes and the sudden frown as she looked across at her rival. 'By no means, Mr Stratton,' she said in remarkably even tones. 'I have no intention of surrendering the bank just yet. But I certainly agree that the stakes have been too low. Did you suggest twenty? Why, I would not dream of proposing such a paltry sum. What say you to fifty?'

The gentleman sitting opposite the Dowager rose immediately. 'Too steep for me,' he said and left the room.

Mr Stratton strode forward and very deliberately put his hand on the back of the vacant chair. He and Lady Luce stared each other out. Marina knew, even from behind, that he was daring her employer to continue. She also knew that Lady Luce would never back down against this man.

What was Marina to do? She racked her brains, but for some reason she seemed unable to think straight. In her very first day in her new post, she was failing to prevent her charge from gambling for enormous stakes. What on earth was happening to her?

At length, Mr Stratton's voice replied, 'Fifty? Certainly. Unless you wish to go higher?'

Marina prayed silently that Lady Luce would not accept this further challenge. Surely it was bad enough with the stakes they had already agreed?

Lady Luce smiled slowly, first at Mr Stratton, and then at the other players. 'Gentlemen,' she said, 'as banker, I will accept any stakes that Mr Stratton cares to name.' She looked across at him once more. The gleam in her eyes suggested she was sure of her victory now.

For what seemed a long time, Mr Stratton said nothing at all. Then, in a very quiet, calm voice, he said, 'Madam, you do me too great an honour, but it would be ungentlemanly to disappoint you. A lady's whims must always be humoured. Shall we say…two hundred pounds?'

This time the gasp echoed round the room. Two more of the gentlemen made to rise, muttering excuses. Such stakes were almost unheard of.

Mr Stratton did not move an inch as the players left the table to congregate by the archway. He laughed, though Marina could detect no mirth at all in the sound. 'It shall be a snug little party, then, my lady,' he said, pulling out his chair.

Marina was beginning to feel quite light-headed. She put a hand against the wall for support. This could not be happening. Two hundred pounds was a fortune—and it was to be staked on the turn of a single card. She moved a couple of steps nearer, in hopes of drawing the Dowager's attention to herself. Perhaps she could signal to Lady Luce, distract her, somehow make her stop?

The movement caught Lady Luce's eye. 'So there you are,' she said caustically. She pointed to an empty chair at the far end of the table. 'Sit down, and do nothing. This is too important to allow of any distraction.'

Marina moved across the room and sank into the chair. The Dowager's sharp glance indicated very clearly that she must neither speak nor move.

She closed her eyes and rested her chin on her hand. If only she could *do* something. Her only hope was that Lady Luce would win. Her overpowering fear was that Mr Stratton—bold, ruthless Kit Stratton—would ruin her mistress.

And herself into the bargain.

Kit watched the tiny hands deftly shuffling the cards. Keeping his eyes fixed on the cards helped his concentration. It also helped him to spot any sign of cheating though, in this case, he expected none. Lady Luce was much too proud to stoop so low, even if she knew how, which he doubted. No. This would be a straightforward test of skill and nerve. Kit's well-trained memory for cards would probably cancel out some of the banker's inbuilt advantage.

After that, it was all down to luck.

Lady Luce gathered her cards together and pushed the pack towards Kit. 'Do you care to shuffle them yourself, sir? Perhaps one of the other gentlemen would cut?'

Kit stretched out a hand. 'I am sure the cards are well enough mixed already,' he drawled carelessly, not bothering even to glance at his opponent. 'I will gladly cut, however. Then, perhaps, we may get to the business of

the evening?' He cut the cards to her with a decided
snap.

Marina saw how the Dowager's lips thinned under the
lash of his scorn. Mr Stratton seemed to be seeking to
force a quarrel on her, in addition to everything else.
How could two people have come to detest each other
so? It was quite beyond Marina's understanding.

'Stakes, gentlemen, please,' said the Dowager in a
hard voice.

Without hesitation, Mr Stratton extracted a fat pocket-
book and, peeling off two banknotes, laid them on the
nine in the livret of cards on the players' side of the
table. Lady Luce watched impassively, waiting for the
other two gentlemen to decide on their wagers. The bald
man nearest Marina scribbled a vowel but then sat undecided, his hand hovering between the five and the six
in the livret. The very young man at the far end was
much more decisive, quickly pushing a heap of notes
and coin on to the queen.

As the bald man's hand continued to hover, Lady
Luce cleared her throat ominously, staring across at him.
He coloured slightly and dropped the scrap of paper on
to the six.

Marina held her breath, waiting for the first card to be
faced. Her father had always said that it was an omen
for the whole game. Normal Faro deals consisted of two
cards—the banker won on the first, and the players on
the second—but the first and last deals were banker's
cards only. Papa had been convinced that if the banker
won on that first card, the players would lose heavily
throughout the game. Marina had never really believed
it—it had not prevented her father from losing his
shirt—and yet she found herself offering up a little
prayer that the Dowager's card would win. It needed to

be a six, or a nine, or a queen. Best of all if it matched Mr Stratton's nine. She wanted to see him lose.

Lady Luce took her time. Indeed, she smiled round at the three men before she even touched the deck. She seemed remarkably confident.

She faced her first card and laid it to the left of the deck. Nine!

Lady Luce gave a little nod of satisfaction and collected the stake from Mr Stratton's losing card.

He did not even blink. Marina decided he now looked even more like a marble statue—beautiful, cold and stony-hearted. Greek gods had been said to amuse themselves by treating human beings as pawns in their Olympian chess games. Kit Stratton looked as if he felt exactly the same about his opponents.

He threw two more bills on to the nine in the livret, never once raising his eyes to look at the banker or at any of the other players. He seemed to be focused totally on the cards.

Marina recognised that stare. She had seen it on her father. Mr Stratton was almost certainly a practised player with the ability to remember every card played. She had been taught to do the same herself. The knowledge helped improve the odds, especially towards the end of the game when few cards remained to be dealt. Kit Stratton was very definitely playing to win.

The Dowager faced the cards for the next deal. A king for the banker, followed by a two. No winners. With so few players, there could be several such barren deals. If the banker moved quickly through them, it would be more difficult than normal to memorise the cards. Marina set herself to doing so, too. The task would help her to remain calm, especially if Mr Stratton were to win.

Three more barren deals followed in quick succession.

Marina knew exactly which cards had been played. Did Kit Stratton? It was impossible to tell from his face.

Lady Luce faced a six on to the banker's pile to the left of the deck. The bald man groaned and muttered an oath as his stake joined the heap in front of the banker. He started to scribble his next vowel even before the players' card had been dealt. The man at the far end drew an audible breath. Another nine! Lady Luce placed it carefully on the heap of players' cards. Then she picked up the two bills that Mr Stratton had lost earlier and, holding them between finger and thumb as if they were contaminated, dropped them on to the nine in the livret.

Mr Stratton smiled down at the money for just a second before returning to blank-faced impassivity. He laid his hand flat on the bills, fingers spread in possession. He had well-kept hands, Marina noticed, momentarily distracted from the cards. Strong, too. Marina doubted they were gentle hands. He would like nothing better than to put those long fingers round the Dowager's throat and squeeze the life out of her.

What on earth had made her think that? Marina was suddenly horrified by the picture his lean fingers had conjured up. He was only a gambler. Ruthless, yes, but a gentleman, surely?

Without raising his hand, Mr Stratton slid all four bills from the nine to the ten. The moment he lifted his hand from the table, Lady Luce dealt another banker's card. Another nine!

The bald man gave a crack of laughter. He made to comment on such amazing luck, but the Dowager frowned him down. It was not surprising that she wanted no distractions in this duel. She dealt the *carte anglaise* with careful deliberation. This time, the players' card was a queen. The young man won. With a quick side-ways glance, he pocketed his winnings and moved his original stake to join Mr Stratton's on the ten.

He, too, senses that this is a battle to the death, Marina thought. And he has chosen to side with the men, and with youth, against one solitary old woman.

Marina forced her thoughts back to the cards. Thirteen had been played. She could remember every one. Kit Stratton had staked four hundred pounds on the ten. There were still thirty-nine cards to be faced. And among them were four tens.

Marina was having difficulty remembering the cards. It had never happened to her before. She had prided herself on that ability, yet now, when it really mattered, it seemed to be deserting her. It was something to do with those strong, lean hands. She could not take her eyes from them. What was it about them? Mostly, they lay relaxed and utterly still on the baize table while Kit Stratton watched the deal of every card. He was like a hawk—a detached, ruthless hunter, ready to launch itself on any quarry that became even slightly vulnerable.

There were only nineteen cards left. And still not a single ten had appeared.

Beyond the archway, a knot of onlookers was gazing across at Lady Luce and her cards. Clearly, Lady Marchant's table had broken up in order to watch the excitement of the duel between Mr Stratton and the Dowager. Lady Luce frowned across at her unwelcome audience, and then returned her attention to the players. The bald man was leaning back in his chair, trying to appear nonchalant. The youngster was all excitement. He did not speak, but his eyes kept flicking back and forth from the money lying on the ten to the banker's set face.

There were beads of sweat on his furrowed brow. His fate was bound up with Kit Stratton's…and the elusive ten.

Lady Luce faced another pair of cards. The bald man's card won. Impassive, the Dowager pushed his winnings across the table and waited while he decided on his next wager. The pile of paper and coin in front of her was now pitifully small. She desperately needed a winning card.

Marina could see the increasing tension in the Dowager's fixed smile. Her lips were becoming thinner and thinner. Her hands were absolutely steady, however, as she turned up the next card. A nine to the banker. Useless.

And then the players' card. A ten.

There was a tiny gasp, quickly muffled, from one of the watchers by the archway. The young man at the table was grinning from ear to ear, but Mr Stratton had not moved a muscle. He was still gazing at the cards.

The Dowager pushed her last two bills across to the young man. With what seemed to be an apologetic glance at Mr Stratton, he pocketed his winnings and moved his stake from the ten to the queen. Lady Luce had no more bills. Rather than count out two hundred pounds in coin, she reached for pen and ink to scribble a vowel for Mr Stratton's winnings.

His raised hand stayed her.

Marina held her breath, knowing instinctively what was to come.

With a long finger, Kit Stratton indicated that his winnings remained on the table.

This time, Marina herself could not stifle a groan. Kit Stratton was riding his luck. If he won again, the Dowager would have to pay him seven times his stake. That was nearly three thousand pounds!

Lady Luce reached towards the cards. Marina closed her eyes, not daring to look. There were still three tens in the pack under the Dowager's hand.

A groan from the bald man made her open her eyes once more. The bald man had lost. And Kit Stratton had won with another ten.

This time, Marina knew exactly what he would do. That long finger moved again. All his winnings—against a prize of fifteen times his stake!

Three more deals, and no more tens appeared. The young man lost on his queen. The bald man won on a king.

Kit Stratton sat as if turned to stone.

There were only seven cards left.

Marina forced her whirling mind to concentrate on the cards. What were they? She ought to know.

She frowned into the silence, pushing every other thought out of her mind. Her brain cleared quite suddenly, as if a curtain had been drawn back from a chalkboard on which the cards had been written. Two aces, a two, a three, a knave…and two tens.

The bald man had two hundred pounds on the ace. The young man had put his stake on the six. Clearly he had no ability to remember cards.

Mr Stratton's hand lay carelessly on the green baize, his index finger extended towards one corner of the ten.

It seemed that no one dared to breathe while they waited for Lady Luce to face the next pair of cards. An ace for the banker. And a three for the players.

Lady Luce reached out to remove her winnings from the ace. Marina offered up a silent prayer of thanks. Now, let the same happen with the ten. Please.

The bald man was not prepared to retreat. He looked a little shiftily at the other players and then placed a stake on the ten. It seemed he had decided that Kit Stratton's luck was in.

With calm deliberation, the Dowager faced her next card. It was a useless two. She paused a moment, then quickly turned over the *carte anglaise*.

Ten!

The bald man gave a little crow of triumph. It was followed by a pregnant silence as everyone in the room watched to see what Kit Stratton would do. He could take his money now—six thousand pounds—or he could let it ride, in hopes of redoubling his winnings to thirty times his original stake.

For several seconds he sat as still as a statue. What was he thinking? There were only three cards left. Such an experienced gambler must know that the banker now had two chances of winning while the players had only one. The bald man had quickly pocketed his money. He was wise to do so, Marina judged. Surely Kit Stratton could not win again? Only the most hardened gamester would play on.

It seemed that Kit Stratton was a gambler to the core. With total nonchalance he tapped his pile of winnings into place. He never once raised his eyes from the cards.

But, for the briefest moment, an ironic smile pulled at one corner of his mouth.

Marina's heart was racing. That twitch of the lips had told her everything. Kit Stratton was well aware that the odds were against him, but he was prepared to run with his luck in order to defeat a woman he detested. And if he did not succeed now, he would make sure there were other occasions. He was the Dowager's enemy.

Marina looked towards Lady Luce. Under her old-fashioned face-paint, her skin was grey. Yet her eyes sparkled angrily. She had accepted Mr Stratton's latest challenge. Better to risk an unlikely loss of twelve thousand than to pay out on a certain loss of six.

Surreptitiously, Marina crossed the fingers of her right hand. She was not superstitious—she prided herself on being too well educated for such things—but she could not resist the impulse. She must not cross the fingers on her left hand, for that, she remembered a little guiltily, would bring bad luck. She forced herself to watch. Like the Dowager, she would show she was no coward.

Three cards remained—an ace, a knave, and a ten.

Lady Luce's tiny wrinkled hand hovered over the pack. Then, like a cat pouncing on a mouse, she faced the first of them with a snap. The ace.

Marina dug her crossed fingers into the palm of her left hand. Two cards only. The chances were equal now.

Lady Luce smiled calmly across at the players, but Mr Stratton continued to stare at the table. He could not see the banker's defiance as she turned the card that could be her ruin.

Ten.

Kit Stratton had won twelve thousand pounds.

With a gesture of disgust, Lady Luce faced the final, useless card. It was over. She had taken on the challenge and she had lost. She visibly straightened her back and waited for her adversary to speak.

He did not. He sat, as still as ever, staring at his winning card. Then, very slowly, his eyes narrowed and his mouth stretched into a taut, venomous smile. It made the hair on the back of Marina's neck stand on end. There was something almost devilish in Kit Stratton's expression.

He raised his head a fraction and stared at the Dowager, with that nasty smile tugging at the corner of his mouth. Marina was reminded of a cobra, its head rising before its victim as it prepared to strike. How could she ever have thought him handsome? Hatred and the lust for vengeance had put hideous lines into that remarkable face. She wanted to look away, but she could not. Opposite Mr Stratton, the Dowager was ashen. She seemed to have shrunk. She looked suddenly very old, and very frail.

Mr Stratton seemed to be waiting for Lady Luce to speak, to concede defeat. Yes, he would enjoy that. He wanted to humiliate her to the uttermost.

Lady Luce did not manage a smile, but she nodded casually towards her opponent as if nothing out of the way had occurred. Then she began to gather up the cards with deft, steady hands.

Marina's own hands were nothing like as steady. She kept them hidden in her lap. She must *do* something.

Slowly, languidly, Kit Stratton rose from his seat. He was enjoying this. From his great height, he looked down on Lady Luce, still smiling nastily. After a moment more, he spoke in a soft, sibilant voice. The cobra again. 'Success is mine on this occasion, I see,' he said.

Lady Luce scribbled a vowel and pushed it across the table. She said nothing. Her self-control was unbelievable.

'But I am in no hurry to collect what is due to me.' Mr Stratton narrowed his eyes balefully and lowered his voice even more. 'I shall look for settlement of this in, shall we say, seven days?' He bowed from the neck, never taking his eyes off the Dowager. 'I shall now bid you good evening, ma'am.'

Lady Luce said nothing. There was no need. The expression of loathing on her face was eloquent. Marina thought she could also detect a hint of fear.

Kit Stratton put the sheet of paper in his pocket and turned to leave. He had triumphed. Marina had fallen at the very first hurdle. The Earl would dismiss her forthwith. Her only chance of employment would be ruined, at a stroke, by this handsome, hateful man. Someone must stop him.

Almost without knowing it, Marina rose from her place and moved to put herself between Mr Stratton and the archway into the adjoining room. 'Sir...' she began, putting a hand on his arm to stay him. He turned sharply to look down at her. She had never seen eyes so cold, so hard. He was ruthless, implacable, and full of hate. Nothing would move such a man. 'Sir,' she began again, hardly knowing what she was going to ask of him, 'will you not—?'

She was not permitted to finish her sentence. With a sneering curl of that beautiful mouth, Kit Stratton lifted her fingers and removed them from his coat, dropping them instantly as if they were diseased. 'No, *madame*,' he said hoarsely. 'Whatever it is you would ask of me—' he looked her slowly up and down '—the answer is no.' He had a fine cambric handkerchief in his left hand—it seemed to have been conjured out of the very air—and, quite deliberately, he flicked it across his immaculate sleeve where Marina's touch had sullied it.

Marina was outraged. How dare he?

One eyebrow quirked upwards by the tiniest fraction. He was pleased at her reaction. What a villain he was! Marina could not think of words harsh enough to describe such a man. He was—

He was gone.

And with him went all Marina's hopes.

Chapter Five

Kit passed out through the silent onlookers who fell back to make way for him. There was awe on some of their faces. Probably none of them would have dared to take such risks.

Out on the landing, the drunk was long gone. The entrance hall below seemed to be deserted.

Kit walked slowly down the elegant staircase, his mind a blank. He could barely remember what he had done, except that he had had his revenge at last. He ought to feel elated, exhilarated, triumphant—but he did not. He felt nothing. Absolutely nothing.

He turned to watch Méchante's luscious figure descend the stairs, swaying seductively. The silk of her gown was almost transparent, leaving little to the imagination. In recent years, Kit had come to prefer his women a little more restrained. Unlike Méchante, Kit's current mistress did not peddle her wares to every man in sight. The Baroness Katharina von Thalberg offered herself only to him—and to her husband, of course. Kit could hardly object to that.

He waited for Méchante to join him, mentally comparing her with his delectable Katharina and finding his hostess a little wanting. Yes, he would go to Katharina. Losing himself in her body would give him back a measure of sanity after this night's madness.

'Must you go, Kit?' Lady Marchant purred. 'May we not drink a glass of champagne to your victory? And to old times? I have a fine vintage on ice in my private apartments.' She gazed at him with wide green eyes and stretched up to whisper in his ear, pressing her body sensuously against his. 'My guests can do without me for an hour or so.'

Kit's body did not react at all to her blatant invitation. Bedding a beautiful woman was a pleasure as normal—and as fleeting—as winning a hand of cards. But Méchante left him cold. She had been his mistress once, five years ago, and she had betrayed him.

He lifted her hand to his lips so that she could not read the expression in his eyes. 'No, my dear,' he said silkily, 'I never go back. And I never share.'

'Be careful, my friend.' Lady Marchant was not purring any longer. There was an edge of malice in her voice and her feline eyes had narrowed to slits. 'Your Katharina takes too many risks. Her husband may not be quite so forgiving, now that you are no longer in Vienna. There, he was just another minor aristocrat. Here, he is a diplomatic representative of the Hapsburg Empire. A scandal would ruin him.' She dropped a tiny, impudent curtsy. 'And it could happen so very easily, do you not think?'

Clever. And still dangerous. She was well named. Kit looked her full in the face. Yes, they understood each other. 'I thank you for your invitation, Méchante. And for your wise words.' He bowed again and turned to take his hat and cane from the servant. 'Now, I must bid you goodnight. A most interesting evening. I am indebted to you.'

Her brittle laugh followed him down the steps and into the crisp night air.

It was very late. Katharina would have tired of waiting for him. She would have gone back to her husband. She would have been mad to stay till now.

Kit closed the door quietly behind him and made his way up the stairs of the snug Chelsea house he had rented for their assignations. He would sleep here for a few hours. Tomorrow—later today, rather—he would find Katharina and apologise. She would forgive him... probably. And if she chose to exact a penance, well... that would be enjoyable, too.

He smelt her perfume even before he opened the door to their bedchamber. He breathed it in deeply, trying to conjure up memories of her body under his. Such a pity that she had gone.

'Kätchen!'

The Baroness Katharina von Thalberg lay sprawled across the huge bed, idly leafing through a magazine. She turned in surprise at the sound of her pet name and, for a second, a tiny frown creased her brow. '*Du kommst spät,*' she began, rolling over on to her back to look up at him with huge dark eyes full of hurt and accusation.

'*Auf Englisch*, Kätchen,' he said wearily. She had every right to complain of his lateness, but he was in no mood for one of her scenes. She need not have waited, after all. He returned to the charge. 'You are in London now. Here, you must speak English.'

The Baroness made a face. 'So you say,' she replied. 'I do not see why so. We are alone, are we not? We may speak in any language we choose. *Français, peut-être?*'

Kit pressed his lips together to suppress a sharp retort. She could be remarkably provocative, his little Austrian. And this was the wrong time. 'No, *madame*. English,' he said firmly, beginning to strip off his coat. He stretched his long body on the bed beside her, propping himself up on one elbow. 'But words are dangerous. They can betray us…in any language.'

He ran a lazy finger down the inside of her deep décolletage until it came to rest in the shadow between her perfect breasts. He began to stroke her skin as gently as if he were wafting a feather fan across a rose petal. Katharina closed her eyes in ecstasy.

'And what need have we of words?' Kit whispered. His lips were so close to her cheek that each word was a caress on her skin. She sighed out a long, shuddering breath.

Kit gazed down at the ravishing picture she made. His body was beginning to heat. At last.

'You have it exactly, my dear,' he said softly.

Lady Luce's hand was shaking as she raised the brandy balloon to her lips and tossed off the contents. 'I should have left that house the moment I saw him,' she said bitterly, collapsing into her favourite chair by the window. 'He is the very devil. With the devil's own luck.'

Marina nodded her understanding. There was no need to ask who was meant. It was strange to see the Dowager so…deflated.

Lady Luce groaned. 'And as for William…' She shook her head angrily at the thought of her son. 'He will positively relish raking me down. Not that he will be given the chance,' she added, straightening her shoulders a little. 'Thought he could fool me. Foisting a gel like you on his mother to keep her in order. Who is the fool now, I say?'

So the Dowager had known all along. Marina was not at all surprised. The old lady was very sharp. And her son was...not his mother's equal. Not that it made any difference, as far as the companion was concerned. The Earl might be somewhat lacking in brains, but he had the ability to send Marina packing.

The Dowager held out her balloon to be refilled. Obediently, Marina fetched the decanter and splashed some of the amber liquid into it. Lady Luce snorted. 'That's not even a mouthful.' She shook the glass impatiently until Marina added considerably more. 'Better,' she said. 'And you should have some, too.'

'Oh, no, ma'am. I never drink spirits. I—'

'Fetch another glass. You will need it. You have a difficult day ahead of you. William will see to that. Just the sort of thing he enjoys.'

The Dowager was right. In the next twenty-four hours, Marina was like to be dismissed. Her stomach turned over at the thought of the coming interview with Lady Luce's dreadful son. She sipped tentatively at her brandy and gasped as it burned its way down. 'Good grief,' she choked out at last. 'Do people really drink this for pleasure?'

Lady Luce laughed. She reached out her scrawny hand and placed it over Marina's smoother one. 'You have courage, Marina. I'll give you that. And I'll not let that arrogant son of mine bully you, or send you packing.'

Marina looked up in surprise.

'Why did you think I took you to Méchante's tonight? Did you think it was chance?' She shook her head at

Marina's obvious incomprehension. 'I have no intention of permitting William to order my life. Not in any way. I took you to that gambling den to show him—and you—that I shall play whenever, and wherever, I wish. He cannot stop me. And setting up a chit of a governess to watch over me will not stop me either.'

Marina felt herself blushing. 'I...I did not...'

'No, you did not. I'd have discharged you myself if I had thought for a moment that you were William's tool. As it is, he promised me a companion, all expenses paid. I shall hold him to our bargain.'

Marina gulped. Life was like to become extremely unpleasant if the old lady and her son used her as a pawn in their endless trials of strength. And with a loss of twelve thousand pounds to sharpen the contest...

Lady Luce held out her glass for another refill. Then she sat for a long time, cradling her brandy and staring vacantly towards the wall.

She must be thinking about the money, Marina decided. She cannot possibly find such a huge sum. Especially not in one week.

'He was determined on his revenge,' said the Dowager, musingly. 'I suppose I cannot blame him. He was word-perfect, too. I should have known he would be.'

'I beg your pardon, ma'am? I'm afraid I do not quite follow...'

'No reason why you should. And I wasn't talking to you, in any event.' At Marina's sharp intake of breath, she softened the merest fraction. 'Oh, you will come to learn it all in the end, I suppose. Best that I tell you myself. Can't have you hearing gossip from the servants. Wouldn't get the facts right, I dare say.' Lady Luce chuckled a little at her own wit. 'There is not much to tell. Several years ago, when Kit Stratton was barely out of leading strings, he lost five thousand pounds to me. I was in pretty deep myself at the time and could not afford to give him time to pay…or even an opportunity to recoup his losses. I demanded payment in seven days. I used those very words. He has been waiting his chance for revenge ever since.'

The story did not sound in the least plausible to Marina. Gentlemen lost thousands of pounds at play all the time. Why should Kit Stratton be bent on vengeance? Against a woman, too?

Her doubts must have been obvious, for Lady Luce looked somewhat shamefaced. 'He paid,' she said hoarsely, 'on the nail. I found out later that his brother Hugo had given him the money—out of his wife's dowry. They had been married less than a week. Kit was sent abroad soon after.'

'Oh,' breathed Marina. No wonder Kit Stratton had felt humiliated. And what of the brother? What had Hugo Stratton thought of it all? Had Hugo Stratton really sent his brother into exile? He— Hugo Stratton? *Now* she knew why the name had seemed familiar!

The Dowager was beginning to ramble. It must be the effects of too much brandy. 'Can't say I blame the boy. My own fault. Let him think I was doing it out of malice when it was really William's fault. Insisted he couldn't afford to tow me out of River Tick. I couldn't admit *that* to young Stratton, could I? But to use the very same words…' She raised her glass yet again.

'Do you know Hugo Stratton, ma'am? The brother?'

'What? Yes. No. Well…we are barely acquainted, but everyone knows about him. He's as rich as Croesus since his brother died, never mind the money from his wife. Doesn't come up to London much. Got out of the habit after the war, they say, because he hated being stared at.'

'Stared at?'

'He was badly wounded. Waterloo, I think.' The Dowager frowned. 'Why all this sudden interest in Sir Hugo Stratton? What is he to you, miss?'

Marina swallowed. 'I think he may have served with my father, ma'am,' she said quietly, gazing down at her skirts. 'In Spain. I think he fought in the battle where my father and my uncle died.'

Lady Luce said nothing. She simply reached for the brandy decanter and tipped a generous measure into Marina's glass.

Marina tried in vain to find a comfortable position in her bed. It must be nearly dawn. Her head was pounding, but she could not possibly sleep. What on earth had possessed the Dowager to give her brandy? Her brain was refusing to function.

She tried again.

Kit Stratton was Sir Hugo Stratton's younger brother. And a Captain Hugo Stratton had been her uncle's closest friend. They had served together for years. According to Uncle George, Hugo Stratton was the best friend, and the staunchest comrade, that a man could wish for. It was partly due to Captain Stratton's influence that Marina's father had joined the 95th. It was not Captain Stratton's fault that the brothers had died so soon after.

Kit Stratton could not be as bad as he was painted. It was not possible. Not if he was Hugo Stratton's brother. And he must be. It was an unusual name. Perhaps Kit had had other reasons for his hatred of the Dowager. Perhaps his insult to Marina herself was simply an unconscious continuation of his harshness at the card table. Perhaps...

There was no way of knowing, unless she found out for herself.

Yes, that was the answer. She would seek out Kit Stratton and ask him to forgive the Dowager's debt. If necessary, she would ask him to do it in memory of her uncle and her father—and for his brother Hugo's sake. No gentleman could possibly deny such a request.

The thought of such an interview made her stomach churn. She would have to abandon the last shreds of her pride to make her appeal, and if he treated her with the same degree of contempt as before... She shivered. She was not sure she could bear that.

Was he a gentleman at all?

It was true that the Dowager had rambled on for what seemed like hours about Kit Stratton's way of life, his mistresses, his fine clothes, his carriages, his horses... He had all the outward attributes of a very wealthy gentleman. But did he have a sense of honour to go with his high-couraged horses?

Marina smiled weakly. The horses had provided her solution. She rather wished they had not. Kit Stratton exercised his horses in the park every morning, come rain, come shine, no matter how great his indulgence the night before. According to the Dowager, it was one of his few saving graces.

He would be in the park tomorrow morning. No—in just a few hours. She had only to go there and confront him. As a gentleman, he could not fail to listen to a lady's pleas.

That was not true.

He could spurn her without a moment's hesitation. He had done so once already, knowing perfectly well that she was a lady. He could do so again, unless she could find some way of breaking through his armoured exterior.

Her own pride did not matter. It was her duty to protect her family—and to do so, she must retain her position with Lady Luce. To save the Dowager, she must challenge Kit Stratton.

Why did he have to ride such a huge animal? Kit Stratton's bay stallion must be seventeen hands or more. Marina felt completely dwarfed by horse and rider. Would he even condescend to rein in to greet her? He could not mistake the fact that she wished to speak to him.

Kit touched his crop carelessly to his hat, using his other hand to bring his horse to a stand with practised ease. There was a sardonic gleam in his eye as he looked down at her. 'You are about betimes, ma'am,' he said. His gaze wandered lazily around the park before coming back to rest on Marina's shabby figure. 'And you appear to have…mislaid your maid.'

'A companion does not have a maid,' snapped Marina, 'as you know very well, Mr Stratton.'

His eyebrows shot up. Then he nodded slowly, once. 'No. She has the tongue of a shrew instead, it would seem.'

Marina was suddenly sure she was blushing. Confound the man! This was not at all what she had intended for this interview. She swallowed hard. She must start again. 'Mr Stratton,' she said, as evenly as she could, 'I should be most grateful if we might have a private word. About…about last night. I—'

He frowned. 'You are come as Lady Luce's envoy? Believe me, ma'am—'

'No! No! She knows nothing of this, I promise you. I have my own reasons for wishing to…to consult you. You see…'

His expression was changing even as she spoke. He was almost smiling, but there was nothing in the least pleasant in it. Marina felt a sudden urge to flee. She swallowed again. He was doing everything he could to make her position impossible. He had not even dismounted, as any true gentleman would have done. That thought gave rise to a spark of anger. Heedless of risk, she fanned it. He was trying—deliberately—to overset her. He despised her, a poor plain companion, for daring to approach rich, handsome Kit Stratton.

'You mistake me, sir,' she said crisply. 'I am not come at Lady Luce's bidding but at my own, to ask a…a favour of you.' There. It was out. And Kit Stratton's face was dark with anger. 'Not for her ladyship's sake—I know that is impossible—but for—'

'A favour?' Kit snarled. 'A favour for whom? For you, ma'am? Believe me, I do not do favours for ladies. Not unless they have earned them.' He glanced quickly over her thin person, his eyes narrowing.

Marina stood stock still. She could neither move nor speak. This could not be happening. Was he really saying that—?

'I see that you take my meaning, ma'am. Good.'

He leant down towards her. The fresh, clean scent of his cologne assailed her. It seemed completely at variance with the black-hearted man who wore it. She forced herself to stand her ground.

'If you wish to…discuss the matter of last evening's events, ma'am, I will be pleased to give you a hearing. I shall be free at…eleven o'clock this morning. You may present your petition then. In private.' He gave her an address in Chelsea. To Marina, a stranger in London, it meant nothing.

He sat back into his saddle and took up the slack in the reins. 'I shall expect you at eleven. Do not be late.'

Chapter Six

Kit looked up from his newspaper as the long-case clock in the hall began to strike the hour. He had done her the courtesy of being here, because she was a lady. But he had known she would not come.

He turned back to his newspaper. He would just finish the report he had been reading, and then he would leave for his club. No doubt the story of his winnings would have done the rounds by now. He was like to hear about nothing else for a se'enight.

He leaned back into his leather wing chair, relishing the peace of the cramped Chelsea sitting room.

Five minutes later, a quiet knock on the door was followed by the entrance of the tiny woman who looked after the house. 'There is a…a person to see you, sir,' she said, bobbing a polite curtsy. 'She will not give a name. She—'

'The lady is come by appointment, to discuss a matter of business,' Kit said firmly, to quell the speculation in the housekeeper's eye. He rose to his feet. 'Show her in, Mrs Budge.'

The grey lady was liberally spattered with mud. Kit looked quickly towards the window. He had been so absorbed, he had not noticed the rain. Had she walked all the way? Had she no sense at all? She was already unattractive enough, even without the addition of brown mud to her grey appearance.

And still she thought to sway him?

He shook his head wonderingly. She seemed ill prepared for the mammoth task she had undertaken.

He raised his brows enquiringly. 'Good morning, ma'am,' he said politely. She had stiffened noticeably. Surely she did not feel insulted by his treatment of her? A woman—a lady—who had come to a private meeting in a gentleman's house?

He waited for her to speak. He would not help her.

'Good morning, sir,' she said at last. The poke of her drab bonnet dipped a fraction.

Was that a token bow? It seemed he would receive nothing more. Kit returned it in kind, from his much greater height. She dropped her eyes. She was nervous, clearly. He waited once more.

'It was good of you to see me,' she said, as if their meeting was the most normal thing in the world, rather than an outrage against the rules of Society. 'You said I might... The truth is, I wanted...I wished to ask you to forgive Lady Luce's debt. Oh, I know it is a fortune, but you are a very rich man, whereas she is old and—'

'And poor?' finished Kit sardonically. 'If your mistress is poor, ma'am, it is because she has gambled away her substance. She has no one to blame but herself. Do you not agree?'

She looked guilty but said nothing. Her silence was beginning to annoy Kit. He realised, in that moment, that he did not know her name.

'Do you not agree, ma'am?' he said again. 'Pardon me, but I have not had the honour of an introduction.'

He bowed politely. 'You are Miss Smith, I suppose?' he found himself adding sarcastically. There was something about this lady that vexed him intensely.

She lifted her chin and looked shrewdly up at him. 'No, Mr Stratton, I am Miss Beaumont,' she said calmly, holding up her muddy skirts so that she might drop him a disdainful curtsy.

She had the pride of a duchess—in the garb of a scullery maid. If he was not careful, she could best him in this encounter. And that he would never permit. Not from any woman.

'Well, Miss Beaumont,' Kit began quickly, motioning her to the second wing chair, 'just what have you to offer me that is worth twelve thousand pounds?'

She stopped short in the act of sitting down. The colour had drained from her face in an instant. She had become almost as grey as her gown.

'I *beg* your pardon?' she said in a voice raw with hostility.

Kit allowed himself to smile down at her. She recoiled gratifyingly, but she did not look away. She had a degree of courage, this grey lady.

'Many a man has allowed himself to be leg-shackled for a mere fraction of twelve thousand pounds, Miss Beaumont. It is, as you said, a fortune. And yet you would have me forgo it.' He took a step towards her. They were so close now that the muddy hem of her dress was trailing on his boots. 'You place a very high value on what you have to offer, Miss Beaumont,' he said, making his voice almost a caress.

Her head came up sharply and colour flooded back into her cheeks. She made to slap his face.

'No, Miss Beaumont,' Kit said, catching her wrist with his left hand and twisting it behind her back. 'I am afraid I do not permit ladies to strike me.' He looked down into her face. She had hazel eyes, flecked with gold. They were wide with fear. Was she so naïve that she did not know what she risked, visiting him like this?

He pulled her hard against him, unintentionally twisting her wrist a little in the process. Her lips parted on a tiny cry of pain.

He immediately relaxed his grip, but his gaze was caught by those invitingly parted lips. She needed to learn her lesson, once and for all. He brought his right hand up to cradle her head and lowered his mouth to hers.

She was not willing.

Her free hand clawed at him, her nails mercifully sheathed in her cheap gloves. Without raising his mouth from hers, he quickly imprisoned both her wrists in one lean hand.

Now she was truly caught.

Gently, unthreateningly, he began to pull at the strings of her bonnet. Her lips parted a little more as if to bid him welcome. She was yielding to him at last. He had expected no less. Women always yielded…sooner or later. He started his assault in earnest…

Without warning, a heavy boot kicked him hard on the ankle.

Kit drew in a sharp, painful breath. Automatically, he pulled away, but he knew better than to let go of his attacker.

What a picture she made! Her bonnet was askew and her dress was filthy, but her slim bosom was heaving and her eyes were ablaze with fury. She had a perfect complexion, he noted absently, especially when she was aroused. What a pity that anger, rather than desire, was the cause.

'I will thank you to let me go,' she said hoarsely. She sounded hard put to it to retain even a vestige of politeness.

Kit slid his hands up her arms until she was firmly gripped once more and held her at arm's length. She was unlikely to attempt another kick from that position. 'My dear Miss Beaumont, do you take me for a complete fool? I will let you go when I have your word to behave like a lady, and not before.'

Anger changed to embarrassment. She was actually blushing!

'You have it, sir,' she said stiffly. 'Do I have yours that you will behave like a gentleman?'

Kit was surprised into a shout of laughter at her temerity. What an astonishing woman!

He shook his head somewhat ruefully, but did not slacken his hold. 'Whoever told you I was a gentleman, Miss Beaumont? I fear you have been misinformed.'

She stared up at him. Her eyes were still blazing, but it did not seem to be anger now—or not wholly. 'I do not believe you, sir,' she said staunchly. Then she simply turned her head to stare down at the hand that was grasping her left arm. 'If you please, Mr Stratton…' She stood absolutely still, waiting.

Kit shrugged his shoulders and let his hands fall. What did it matter? He did not care to kiss a woman who was more than half wildcat. And who would fight him every step of the way. This interview needed to be brought to a speedy, and final, conclusion.

He crossed to the bell-rope and pulled vigorously. The door opened almost immediately. 'Send the boy out for a hackney, Mrs Budge,' he ordered. 'My visitor is leaving.'

The moment the door closed again, Miss Beaumont

began to protest. 'Mr Stratton, I have no desire for a cab. I shall leave on foot, as I came. Besides, we have not finished our business—'

'Miss Beaumont, there is nothing more for you to say,' said Kit firmly, advancing on her until she backed away. A low chair prevented her further retreat. 'I suggest you sit down. Good. Now, in the matter of the hackney, there is nothing to discuss. It is not my habit to permit ladies to walk the streets of London alone. In that, at least, I am a gentleman. The boy will pay the jarvey to take you wherever you want to go.'

She made to protest again but he stopped her with a raised hand.

'As to our *business*... You want me to forgive Lady Luce's debt. Twelve thousand pounds, payable in seven days. Very well, Miss Beaumont, I will do so.'

Her eyes widened in surprise, but she said nothing. Perhaps words were beyond her. That would certainly be the case in a moment or two, he'd stake his honour on that.

'There is a price, of course,' he continued, 'but you knew that when you accepted my invitation to visit me here, did you not?' He paused, waiting for a reaction. There was none. 'The price, Miss Beaumont, is you. In my bed. Willingly.'

That had done it. She was truly terrified now. She had learned her lesson at last. She would not trouble him again.

Not after this.

'You—' Her voice cracked. She cleared her throat and tried again. 'You are very direct,' she said hoarsely. 'May I ask how this...arrangement is to be achieved?'

Her response was much braver than he had expected. It was hardly surprising that she would not look straight

at him now. Still, he must play this little charade to the
end.

'Nothing easier, Miss Beaumont,' he said on the ghost
of a laugh. 'You will write to me here, naming the day
for our…meeting. It will, of course, take place *before*
the debt falls due,' he added, watching her face for signs
of duplicity. 'On the agreed day, you will be walking
early in the park, just as you were today. A plain, closed
carriage will draw up beside you. It will have a white
silk scarf tied to the handle of the door. You will step
into it.'

'And how, pray, is my absence to be explained to
Lady Luce?' Miss Beaumont asked witheringly. 'She
will wish to know where I have spent the day…and the
night. And then she will dismiss me on the spot.'

Kit delivered his *coup de grâce*. 'Oh, do not fear that
I shall detain you long, Miss Beaumont. Our…business
can be quickly dealt with. Darkness is not required, you
know. You will be home long before you have been
missed.'

Her head came up then. She was terrified still, but her
fear was overlaid with loathing. There was a hint of
something more, too—

The door opened. The interruption could not have
been worse timed. 'The cab is at the door, sir. The driver
has been paid.'

'Thank you, Mrs Budge. Tell him to wait. The lady
will be out in a moment.'

As the door closed, the grey lady rose from her chair
and stared proudly across at Kit. 'I will go now, Mr
Stratton,' she said quietly, 'but I shall take the liberty of
telling you that you are not worthy to be called Hugo
Stratton's brother. For he is a man of honour. While
you…'

She turned on her heel. In the space of a heartbeat, she had whipped open the door and disappeared down the hallway.

By the time Kit reached the front door, the hackney had almost turned the corner, its wheels throwing up great splashes of muddy water as it raced away.

Marina leaned back against the creaking leather. She would *not* faint. Not now. She had kept her self-control throughout that appalling interview. There was no point in giving way, not now that it was over.

Kit Stratton was a fiend. He was the very devil.

Had not Lady Luce used those exact words? But she, Marina Beaumont, thinking she knew better, had not heeded the warning. She had broken all the rules to visit him in his lodgings— No, that was wrong. No man of means would live *there*. Even a stranger to London could tell that. Her erstwhile host probably used that modest little house to entertain his mistresses. If Marina accepted his bargain, he would probably bring her there to...to... Oh, she had been well served for her arrogance. Kit Stratton had offered to forgive the Dowager's debt in return for Marina's honour.

He must have known she would not—could not— agree. He must have known.

Why then had he made her such an offer? It made no sense. He neither liked nor admired her.

What a stupid fool she had been, driven by her desperation to find some way of retaining her post. She had seen his arrogance, but she had thought she could find a way to move him, by appealing to his better nature.

Madness! Kit Stratton had no better nature. He had no feelings at all.

She closed her eyes, willing the memories to leave her. They returned, stronger than ever.

She had been in his arms. She had fought him…but not enough.

In all her life, she had never been kissed with any degree of passion. She had not known how it would feel. She had not imagined that she would respond, against everything she had been taught. Kit Stratton had been forcing himself upon her. She should have repulsed him but, for one incredible second, she had felt herself softening under his assault and welcoming the touch of his lips.

He had been right to treat her like a street-walker. She had behaved no better!

His final offer had proved it. He would take her innocence without thought for the consequences, as if her virtue was worth no more than the turn of a card on the Faro table. She would spend an hour—perhaps less—in his bed. And then he would send her back to Lady Luce, a little used, to be sure, but the bearer of a gift of twelve thousand pounds.

Would Lady Luce be grateful? Marina doubted it. If she ever found out, the lady would probably laugh.

No. Nothing would ever make Marina accept Kit Stratton's humiliating offer. Not even—

The hackney drew up outside Lady Luce's house. The front door opened just as Marina was stepping down on to the flagway.

The Earl's corpulent figure seemed to fill the doorway. 'So there you are at last, Miss Beaumont,' he said ominously. 'I shall not ask where you have been. We have much more important matters to discuss.' He looked her up and down, taking note of her dishevelled state. 'There is no need for you to change for this interview,' he said with a sneer. 'Our business will take but a very few minutes. How you dress thereafter will be your own affair.'

Kit poured himself a second glass of madeira and downed it in a single swallow, as he had the first. He looked across at the window and shook his head at the drab grey skies. He had gone too far. She had been foolish and naïve in her quest, but still…he had gone too far. She was, after all, a lady, but he had treated her like the veriest doxy. That final remark about how long… Had he really said something so unforgivably crude?

He must be losing his mind. He was definitely losing his self-control and he *never* did that with women. Never.

Not for more than five years.

Since that mad moment when he had compromised Emma Fitzwilliam, he had never allowed himself to utter a word or move so much as a finger without carefully calculating how the lady in question would react to his advances. He had thought he knew how to read them all.

But Miss Beaumont was not predictable. She had not succumbed to his practised lovemaking. She had thrown his words back in his face. And she had even compared him unfavourably to—

Hugo! How did Lady Luce's grey companion come to know of Hugo Stratton? They could never have met, could they? She would have been little more than a child when Hugo returned from the wars. And then he had married Emma Fitzwilliam.

If the grey lady had had dealings with Hugo, they must have taken place since his marriage to Emma. Well, well. That did not sound in the least like his upright brother. But no…it made no sense. What could Hugo want with such a woman when he had Emma?

Emma was blonde, beautiful, vivacious, loving—a perfect wife. Miss Beaumont was grey and rather gaunt. She did not seem to know how to laugh. And she prickled with pride. What could Hugo ever see in her?

The unexpected.

She was not like any of the women Kit had bedded. She fought him. And she spoke of honour, and of the worth of a gentleman.

She could not be Hugo's mistress. There must be something else between them. It was a puzzle. And it would plague him until he had resolved it.

Kit rose and made his way to the door. No point in staying here. Katharina was long gone and could not be with him again for several days. Sometimes, unfortunately, a husband had to take precedence. Kit might as well go to his club and face the inevitable gossip.

The cold brass handle served to remind him that the weather outside was foul and that he had no carriage in Chelsea. He opened the door to order another hackney, this time for himself.

Had she gone straight back to Lady Luce? Would she ever dare to venture out alone again? She would not be found walking early in the park again, that was certain. She had fled from him like a frightened doe.

He thought back through their tense encounter and found he was no longer quite so sure. He had never discovered precisely why she was so intent on begging him to forgive the Dowager's debt. To be honest, he had given her no chance to explain anything. He had simply pounced on her.

It would be madness for her to meet him again, knowing, as she did, what would happen between them. But how could he be sure—certain sure—that she would not accept his challenge?

His answer was clear enough. He must leave orders that any letter was to be brought round to his lodgings immediately.

And he must be prepared to hire himself a plain, closed carriage.

Chapter Seven

Marina only just succeeded in reaching her bedchamber. She did not even have the strength to reach the bed before her legs crumpled under her. She sank to the floor and dropped her head into her hands.

She was dismissed!

So much for the Dowager's promise of protection. That had gained her nothing. Lord Luce was insisting she leave his mother's house before the day was out. Mr Kit Stratton would wait in vain for her letter—Marina would be long gone.

How would she ever explain to Mama? Was there even enough money in her purse to pay her fare back home?

Damn Kit Stratton! It was all his fault!

'Twelve thousand! Are you saying that stupid chit stood by and watched while you lost twelve thousand pounds?'

'She did not stand and watch,' Lady Luce snapped. 'She was seated throughout.'

He ground his teeth.

'You need not play the martyr, William. The debt is mine, not yours.'

'Indeed? And you have twelve thousand immediately to hand, do you, Mama?'

For once she said nothing, pressing her lips together in a tight, angry line.

'No. Nor do I. I shall have to go to the moneylenders until I can sell the unentailed land. And there will have to be strict economies. For both of us.' He looked down at her, frowning darkly. 'Your useless companion leaves today, of course, and this house—'

'What? You have absolutely no right to dismiss her. How dare—?'

'I pay her, Mama. She is become an expense I can no longer afford.'

And his mother had long been another such, he thought grimly. It would be so very satisfying to tell her so. If only he could—

'Petty revenge, William. You seek to humiliate your own mother. I had not thought even you could stoop so low.' She looked at him with scorn.

Lord Luce was shocked into silence for a moment. He would almost have said she hated him. 'Mama, I…' he began. He cleared his throat and tried again. 'Mama, I truly cannot afford to pay Miss Beaumont. But, by all means, let her remain for a few days more. I admit it would be unkind to pack her off in this appalling weather.'

His mother looked at him in sudden surprise. Then she nodded.

'Perhaps you will tell her, Mama? If I am to arrange the money in time, I must set about matters immediately.'

He made to leave, then stopped, hesitating. 'Mama,'

he began in a softer voice, 'please stop doing this. I grant that you have a right to choose how you order your own life. If I have seemed to interfere, I…I apologise. But if you continue to gamble, you will ruin us all. Truly. I beg of you to stop. For the sake of your grandchildren. Please.'

He looked pleadingly across at his mother's tiny figure. There was no sign of softening in her features. This time, his tactic had failed.

'I see. No doubt we shall meet again in church tomorrow,' he said with freezing formality. 'I bid you good day.' He bowed and left her.

Lady Luce walked over to her favourite chair and slowly took her seat. For several minutes, she stared vacantly at the window and the street beyond. The driving rain was pouring down the panes so that it was difficult to see out.

The Dowager's bony hand reached for the bell on the table beside her. Almost before the sound had died away, the butler appeared.

'Have you seen Miss Beaumont this morning, Tibbs?'

'Why, yes, m'lady. She was with his lordship earlier, and then—'

'Never mind that,' snapped the Dowager. 'What was she doing before that? I sent my woman to her room and she was not there.'

'She…er…she went out early, m'lady. Walking, I supposed.'

Lady Luce snorted. 'When did she return?'

'Er…just after his lordship arrived, m'lady. He interviewed her in the bookroom.'

'I see. What are you waiting for, man? Go and fetch her! What is the point of having a companion who provides no company? Go and fetch her at once!'

* * *

Marina paused at the foot of the stairs to straighten her skirts. At least she was no longer mud-spattered, as she had been during that degrading interview with Lord Luce. She would have looked even worse, if Kit Stratton had not sent her home in a cab. Should she be grateful? It had kept her dry. And she had not got lost, as she had done on the way to Chelsea. Then again, if she had been forced to walk, Lord Luce might have been long gone by the time she arrived back. A curse on Kit Stratton! Everything was his fault.

Tibbs had already announced her. She had no option but to face her second accuser.

'So there you are at last, miss!' snapped Lady Luce, the moment the door closed behind Marina. 'Perhaps you would be good enough to explain where you were this morning?'

Oh, dear. Marina had been *almost* sure that her ladyship would not wake before noon, that her absence would not be noticed. Yes, she had been a fool, on that count also.

'I assumed that you would sleep late, ma'am,' she said, 'and so I went out for a walk. I—'

'A walk? In the pouring rain?' Lady Luce's tone was scathing.

Marina lifted her chin. 'I am well used to the rain, ma'am,' she said with quiet dignity. 'In Yorkshire, it rains a great deal. If one ventured out only when the weather was fine, one would take no exercise at all.' Marina looked directly at the old woman, marvelling at her own ability to fence with half-truths. Kit Stratton's devilry was rubbing off on her, it seemed.

Lady Luce snorted in disbelief. 'Very well,' she said sharply, 'but in future I expect you to be here when I send for you.'

'In f…future?' Marina hid her hands in the folds of her drab gown to conceal their sudden trembling.

'Sit down, girl. You are as white as a sheet…and if there is one thing I cannot abide, it is missish young females who swoon at the slightest reverse.'

'I shall not faint, ma'am,' said Marina, trying to sound as if she was fully in control of herself. 'It…it is just that his lordship said I must leave at once. I—'

'His lordship was incensed by your behaviour. Not unnaturally,' she added, in a voice that tried, but failed, to convey a degree of sympathy with her son's feelings. 'But he does not dispute that it is for me to decide whether you shall go or stay.' Lady Luce gave a tight little smile that made Marina's heart sink. 'For the moment, I wish you to stay. Is that understood?'

'Yes, ma'am,' said Marina meekly. What on earth was going on? The Dowager had won the battle with her son—that was clear—but why had she bothered to fight?

'Now,' said the Dowager briskly, 'there are a number of matters that I must attend to this afternoon.' She looked disdainfully at Marina's shabby gown, wrinkling her nose in distaste. 'The first of them shall be to find you a suitable gown.'

'Ma'am—'

'You are to be ready to accompany me in ten minutes. Do not be late. That is all.'

There was nothing further to be said. Marina rose quickly, dropped a curtsy to the Dowager's back, and hurried away to find her bonnet and pelisse.

'Well? Do you, or do you not?'

Marina came suddenly back to earth. What had the Dowager just said to her? 'I beg pardon, ma'am. I fear I was wool-gathering. You asked…?'

'I asked, miss, whether you were satisfied with this gown, or whether we must seek another,' said Lady Luce testily. 'Well?'

Marina looked at herself in the glass. It was a very simple muslin gown, totally plain, but in a most becoming shade of pale green. She could not remember when she had ever worn anything but browns and greys, serviceable colours for a young woman who walked, and worked, in all weathers. This was sadly impractical...but she loved it. 'It is delightful, ma'am, but—' Marina tore her eyes from her reflection '—I fear I cannot afford to buy any gowns at all until I have my first quarter's wages. And since Lord Luce said I was to leave, I do not think I should—'

'Balderdash!' her ladyship declared. 'You will leave when—and if—I say. And I refuse to have a scullery maid for a companion. What would your cousin, Lady Blaine, say if she saw you?'

'But Lady Blaine has never laid eyes on me, ma'am, and—'

'For heaven's sake, child, will you never learn when to stop protesting? I say you shall have it. And the evening gown also. They are a gift. You will not be required to pay for them.'

'Oh.' Marina let out a long sigh. How wonderful. And now she would not have to meet Kit Stratton in her dowdy grey dress. He would not—

What was she thinking of? She was not going to meet that handsome devil at all. Never again. She had made up her mind to that, the moment she left his squalid little love-nest. She would not forfeit her honour, even to save her position with Lady Luce...even to save Mama from penury. It was impossible. Mama would be repelled by the very thought of such a sacrifice.

But Mama need never know.

Marina tried to close her mind against the siren voices trying to lure her to her doom. Mama might never know, but Marina herself would be only too aware of her transgressions. She did not think she would be able to live with herself, no matter how worthy the cause. She—

'Marina! I am waiting!' The Dowager was becoming angrier by the minute. This time she was clearly waiting for Marina to change back into her old gown, so that they could leave the modest dressmaker's that the Dowager had thought appropriate for a penniless cousin of the Viscountess Blaine.

'I beg your pardon, ma'am. Excuse me. I shall be ready in a very few moments.'

And this time, she was, having ruthlessly suppressed every urge to lapse yet again into wondering about the maybes and might-have-beens of her life.

It was much more difficult during the rest of the afternoon, however, for her ladyship rambled on and on about the places they visited, the people they saw, and the problems of life in London. Marina tried to play her companion's role. She smiled, she nodded, she murmured agreement at, she hoped, the right moments, but she was not seeing what Lady Luce saw, nor sharing her ladyship's thoughts. A terrifyingly handsome male face kept intruding into her mind. The skin of her arms and shoulders tingled as though his hands still held her. And her lips felt soft and yielding, waiting for the next brush of—

She groaned.

'Are you ill, child? You cannot feel faint, surely? Not on account of a short carriage ride and two new gowns.'

Marina forced a smile.

'I warn you,' said Lady Luce sternly. 'If you take to collapsing on me, I shall send you back to Yorkshire, no matter what your noble relations may think.'

This time Marina did not rise to the Dowager's bait. She remained calm and matter of fact. 'I have never fainted in my life, ma'am, and I do not intend to start now.'

Marina sank, fully clothed, on to her pillows. Peace at last! The blessed silence wrapped around her like the softest goose-down coverlet. Now she could try to resolve her future, without the Dowager's never-ceasing commentary on Society life and living.

That was not really fair...and Marina knew it. In more settled circumstances, Lady Luce's sharp-tongued comments would have been most entertaining but, today, too many of them had been directed at Marina herself. And she had deserved them all. She had never been one for allowing her thoughts to wander into might-have-beens. Indeed, her mother had often said that Marina was too commonsensical for her own good. Here, in London, she was supposed to be a paid companion, anxious for her lady's comfort, not a day-dreaming fool who had constantly to be recalled to her duty.

It was all Kit Stratton's fault!

He had disrupted her peace by his scandalous proposals and his even more scandalous behaviour. She had tried all day to banish his image, his voice, his touch...

She had failed. If she closed her eyes now, she could see him still, his beautiful features made sinister by the hard, calculating gaze he was bestowing on her.

She forced her eyes open. The image retreated. She dare not allow herself to sleep lest it come again. She was afraid of what she might do if she permitted Kit

Stratton to invade her dreams. Here, waking, she had some shreds of morality to cling to. There, if he took her in his arms again, she might be tempted to forget them all. For just one more taste of those lips...

She jerked upright. Heavens, she was starting to doze. She must not. Not until she had reached her decision.

She sprang up from her bed and began to pace about the room. That was better. Sleep was banished now. She must think, and weigh, and decide.

She could not yield her person to Kit Stratton. It was wicked, and immoral, and against everything she had been taught. A woman should remain pure until she married. She should give herself to her husband alone, in order to bear his children. Marina had seen quite enough of the treatment meted out to fallen women, even in rural Yorkshire. It was a terrible fate.

And it could be hers if she gave herself to Kit Stratton.

He would use her and discard her. He would not suffer—it was the way of the world that men walked free while women bore the burden of both their sins—and he would probably condemn her for yielding to his threats.

And yet the yielding might be so sweet...

She touched her fingers to her lips, remembering the feel of his mouth on hers, the way the heat of him had seemed to light an answering fire in her limbs—

No! She must not! Kit Stratton was a practised seducer, an out-and-out rake. He had known exactly what he was doing to Marina. No doubt he had intended to make her melt in his arms, to welcome his advances. She must not imagine that he had *felt* anything for her. She was just one more poor gentlewoman to be conquered...and forgotten.

Marina's pacing was becoming more and more frenzied. She forced herself to stop, holding on to a simple wooden chair for support. She must not permit him to rule her like this. She must find a way of giving him his own again. She must outwit him.

There must be a way. And it must be done soon, before the Dowager's debt fell due.

She would find a way to best him if she had to spend all night devising it. He had thought to trick her into his bed, had he? Well, she had a trick or two up her sleeve also, and she could play as dishonourable a hand as any man alive.

She had found her solution.

Her father had taught her to cheat at cards. While she had never used her skills for real, she had become most adept. Her father and her uncle had laughed aloud when she trounced them, time and time again, so perfectly that neither of them could ever catch her out. Oh, how carefree they had all been then. She could still see her father's smiling face and long, lean body, so well suited to the dark green of the rifle brigade. On their last leave, the two men had made much of her, a gawky fourteen-year-old with no pretence to beauty. For those few weeks, she had felt so very special. And then, in the depths of a Yorkshire winter, the terrible news had come. The laughter had disappeared for good from her mother's eyes. In a single day, Mama had lost her only brother and the husband she loved, but Marina never saw her weep, even when they discovered that Papa's gambling had left them almost penniless. Mama simply became silent and serious, devoting all her energies to finding a way of supporting her two young children. By calling on all her scholarly abilities, she had succeeded, though it had been hard for them all.

Marina twisted the mourning ring on her finger. It was all she had of her beloved father…apart from his lean

looks, and an ability to fuzz the cards. She would use
her skills against Kit Stratton, in a way that would have
made even her father marvel!

She carried her candle to the little table by the window
and sat down, pulling a sheet of paper towards her. She
dipped her pen in the standish and wrote the salutation
with a firm hand. *To Mr Christopher Stratton. Sir…*

She stopped, pen poised. What was she to say? He
was expecting a letter naming the day for an assignation,
not an invitation to a game of cards. And where was it
to take place? It would be madness to go alone to his
Chelsea house—if she wished to leave there with her
virtue intact. Perhaps she could challenge him at Méchante's? She would need to persuade the Dowager to
take her there again—and soon—and not to betray that
fact that Marina would be writing vowels with no money
to back them. Perhaps—

Marina laid down her pen in disgust. Her common
sense seemed to have deserted her completely. Was she
going out of her mind? There was no way, no way at
all, in which she could cheat Kit Stratton out of twelve
thousand pounds in the next five days. Not unless she
went alone to his house. There, she could—

No. There must be another solution.

She picked up the pen once more and rolled it round
in her fingers. They were long, and clever, and—with a
little practice to regain their old skills—they could produce a card as from nowhere, but in this case they would
not provide the answer. She had been prepared to consider a thoroughly dishonourable course of conduct, in
order to avoid even worse dishonour, but—

But there *was* another way. Less sure, perhaps, but
still…

She dipped her pen once more and began to write,

pausing now and then over her choice of words. The letter must appear totally innocuous, to anyone other than Kit Stratton. That was vital.

She wrote until, at last, she was sure she had achieved her aim. She sat back in her chair to read her completed letter.

Sir, it began, *With reference to our recent discussions, you will appreciate that the property I have to offer is too valuable to be traded, except against payment in advance. I would therefore ask you to forward to me the paper in your possession at your earliest convenience. I will undertake to make all necessary arrangements for the conclusion of our business as soon as I am in receipt of the document in question.*

She nodded in satisfaction and added her signature to the sheet. He would not mistake her meaning. Of that, she was sure. He would send the Dowager's vowel for twelve thousand pounds, expecting Marina—as a woman of her word—to surrender her virtue to him. But she would not.

She could not!

Somehow, once she had the vowel in her possession, she would find a way of depriving Kit Stratton of his prize. The reward for his infamy should not be Marina's virtue.

Even if she had to behave in a thoroughly dishonourable fashion to achieve it, she would make sure his wicked plans were thwarted. She would begin practising at once to regain her skills with the cards…just in case they were needed.

And she would laugh in his face when she triumphed.

Chapter Eight

Kit looked up, annoyed, as the study door opened. He had given specific orders that he was not to be disturbed.

'Hugo!' he cried, his frown clearing immediately. 'What are you doing back in town? How long do you stay?' He strode across the room to shake his brother's hand.

'A short time only, perhaps a week or two.' Sir Hugo Stratton smiled enigmatically. 'Business, Kit,' he said.

Kit raised an eyebrow. He knew his older brother well enough to recognise that smile. 'You mean that you have heard about my…er…exploits and wish to satisfy yourself that nothing untoward is afoot. You really ought to stop concerning yourself about me, you know, Hugo. I am well able to look after myself now.'

Hugo laughed. 'That is what worries me. You do look after yourself. But someone has to look to the family's reputation, and by all accounts, *you* are not…' He stopped suddenly and put a friendly hand on Kit's shoulder. 'Why don't you tell me what has been happening since last I saw you?'

Kit nodded. In this mood, his brother would not be thwarted. It was easier just to give in gracefully. 'I will.

Just give me a moment to finish this letter.' He sat down at his desk again and set about folding and sealing the papers he had been working on when Hugo arrived. 'Pull the bell, will you, Hugo? I must send this off.'

The door opened just as Kit rose with the thick letter in his hand. 'See that this is delivered this afternoon,' he said, handing it to the butler. 'And make sure that the messenger remains anonymous.' The butler bowed impassively and withdrew.

'Can't afford to let the good Baron know the source of his wife's correspondence, can you?' commented Hugo wryly. 'I should do the same in your shoes, I suppose.'

Kit grinned. 'I might have known you would have heard about Katharina. How do you do it? You are supposed to be buried in the country.'

Hugo laid a finger along his nose and tapped twice. 'Family secret,' he said, failing to keep the amusement out of his voice. 'As head of the family, I have to have some advantages, you know.'

Kit shook his head resignedly and moved to pick up the heavy crystal decanter. 'I collect that Emma's formidable aunt has been gossiping again. Might I ask what tales she has told you this time?'

'You are too sharp for your own good sometimes, Kit,' replied Hugo, taking a glass of madeira and settling himself in the armchair opposite Kit's mahogany desk. 'You are right, of course. Emma's Aunt Warenne has been keeping us up to date. She says that your Baroness is a diamond of the first water. And that she has a remarkably possessive husband.' Hugo looked questioningly at his brother.

'There is no need to worry, Hugo. He is possessive, I grant you, but he is a very poor shot.'

Hugo choked over his madeira.

'Do take care, brother,' said Kit impudently. 'I really have no desire to take over your role as head of the family, even temporarily.'

'By all accounts, you are unlikely to live long enough to do so,' replied Hugo. 'Even your possessive Baron could have a lucky shot, you know. I can understand that you wished to make her your mistress in Vienna, but it is bound to be much more dangerous to continue the liaison here in London. As a diplomat, the Baron has a very great deal to lose.'

'True,' said Kit. Hugo was clearly waiting for him to say something more, but Kit kept all his attention on his glass.

With a sigh, Hugo continued, 'The *on dit* is that, since it took you almost a twelvemonth to seduce her from the path of virtue, you were unwilling to give up the spoils when her husband was called to London.'

Kit said nothing. He continued to savour his madeira.

'I take it that the Baroness was the reason you would not return to England after John's death?'

Kit swirled the wine in his glass. 'She seemed to be…unaccountably attached to her virtue for a considerable time after I returned from the funeral,' he said at last. 'I am glad to say that she has tired of it now.'

'Does it never occur to you, Kit, that seducing virtuous matrons is…is wicked?'

Kit tried to stifle a chortle.

'Yes, very well, perhaps that was a rather melodramatic way to put it, but… Let me tell you, Kit, that if any man tried to seduce Emma, I should put a bullet in him without a moment's thought.'

Kit looked up. One corner of his mouth tugged into a slightly mocking smile. 'But I'd wager your Emma would never be seduced. That's the difference, you see, Hugo. Katharina's seduction was long and drawn out because she *enjoyed* the chase. Make no mistake, she had decided almost at the outset that she would succumb…eventually. Fortunately, I was the only one to see that. Most of the Embassy fellows were sure she was virtue incarnate. Wagered I'd never succeed with her. She won me a tidy sum, I'm delighted to say.'

'How very calculating that sounds,' said Hugo, with obvious distaste. 'But if she means nothing to you, why did you follow her to London?'

'Because it suited my other plans. If Society was convinced I was deep in love with the beautiful Baroness, the tabbies were unlikely to dwell on what else I might have in mind. I prefer my…er…victims to be taken unawares.'

Hugo laughed shortly. 'And she was, I collect. To the tune of twelve thousand pounds. Was that not a bit steep, Kit? She won only five from you, after all.'

'True,' said Kit evenly, 'but five years of exile adds a great deal to the debt, in my opinion. I think twelve thousand would be a fair settlement.'

'Would be?' queried Hugo. 'You don't say Lady Luce will not pay?'

'Cannot? Will not? What does it matter? I am sure that she *cannot* pay without calling on her son for help. And he is far from willing to support her gambling. All London knows that. On the other hand, how would it look if he—?'

'If he left her hanging in the wind?' finished Hugo. 'We all know the answer to *that*. No one would receive either of them. Luce can't allow that to happen, not with his top-lofty shrew of a wife. She would make his life

a misery, without a doubt. Never met a woman so devilish high in the instep. Or one with so little cause.'

'One of the dangers of parson's mousetrap, Hugo,'
said Kit.

Hugo shook his head despairingly at his brother. 'Not
if you marry a woman who loves you, Kit. Don't you
think you—?'

Kit rose quickly from his seat and headed for the door
before the conversation could take an even more unwelcome turn. He should never have mentioned marriage in the first place. 'I've arranged to meet some
friends at the club,' he said lightly. 'I take it you will
accompany me? If we don't leave now, we shall be late.'

Hugo cast his eyes up to the ceiling, but he did not
try to pursue the topic any further. Kit was relieved. He
had the greatest of respect for his brother, and he certainly did not wish to be at outs with him. On the other
hand, if Hugo continued to drop these heavy hints about
marriage…and love…

Women! They created nothing but problems!

Struck by a sudden thought, Kit wrenched open the
door and called impatiently for his butler. 'That letter I
gave you,' he said sharply, before the man had time to
catch his breath. 'Have you despatched it yet?'

The butler flushed guiltily. 'I was just about to summon a messenger, sir, and—'

'Don't bother me with your lame excuses, man. Hand
it over.'

The butler produced the letter and retreated with rather
more haste than normal.

Kit strode across the room and threw the letter down
on his desk. 'It is your fault, you know, Hugo,' he said
with a wry grin. 'You reminded me—unwittingly, I admit—that it does not do to respond just when, or how,

a lady expects. I think that, on this occasion, the lady shall be made to wait a little longer. You never know, it may do her good.'

He turned to where Hugo stood, intrigued, and clapped his brother on the shoulder. 'And now,' Kit said smoothly, 'if you are ready, shall we go?'

'Beware, Kit,' said Hugo. 'One day it may be you on the receiving end of such cavalier treatment.'

Kit looked hard at his brother and shook his head. 'Not I,' he said firmly. 'Not from any woman alive.'

Approaching the receiving line, Marina followed dutifully two steps behind Lady Luce. It was a very grand affair indeed. Marina's simple amber silk gown, which she had thought so splendid when she first tried it on, was very dull by comparison with the finery of the other guests. She would be able to merge into the background, yet again.

Introductions completed, the Dowager led the way into the ballroom and stood for a moment surveying the scene. She called Marina close with a beckoning finger. 'Do you see those two ladies over by the window?' she whispered, indicating with her fan a pair of richly dressed matrons. 'The one wearing that appalling puce gown is William's wife, Charlotte. Never did have an ounce of taste! Never a beauty, either.'

The Dowager's daughter-in-law was both plump and plain, but she had a decided air of consequence, even from a distance.

'She was passable when she was younger, I'll admit. Lost her figure—and her looks—through too much child-bearing. Much too much. Ten children, indeed! An heir and a spare should be enough for any man.'

Marina was hard put to stop herself from laughing

aloud. But the Dowager's next words banished any hint of mirth.

'So—what do you think of your exalted cousin?' Seeing Marina's obvious surprise, the Dowager said, 'The lady standing beside Charlotte is the present Viscountess Blaine.'

Marina saw a thin woman with an overlong nose and a modish but very unflattering hairstyle. She was wearing too many jewels. 'She looks…' Marina could not find any words. Even to the Dowager, she could hardly say that Lady Blaine looked like a horse.

'Quite,' said Lady Luce with a tight smile. 'Come. Let me make the introductions.' She strode across the room much faster than seemed possible for such a tiny person, forcing the other guests to make way for her. Marina followed in her wake, more than a little reluctant to face one of the relations who had treated her family with such contempt.

'Good evening, Charlotte. Good evening, Lady Blaine.'

The two younger women returned Lady Luce's greeting without any sign of pleasure. Both ignored Marina completely.

'I should like to present my new companion, Miss Beaumont,' said Lady Luce neutrally.

Both ladies turned to glance at the companion for a second. They were clearly far from satisfied with what they saw. Neither offered a hand.

The Dowager eyed Lady Blaine with disfavour. 'Surprising that you have not met before, is it not?' she said. 'Considering Miss Beaumont's mother is full cousin to your husband. But then, he has been out of the country for some months, has he not?'

The younger Lady Luce had started in surprise and

now lifted her lorgnette to inspect Marina more closely. Marina felt as if she were being examined for flaws like an insect impaled on a pin. She lifted her chin, turning all her attention to the Dowager and Lady Blaine.

'So this is the gel I recommended to you,' said Lady Blaine at last.

She had the kind of voice that reminded Marina of fingernails scraping across a chalkboard. How could anyone bear to be in the same room with her?

'I hope she is giving satisfaction,' continued Lady Blaine, for all the world as if Marina were not present. 'You must understand, ma'am, that I recommended her only because of the urgency of your son's request. I could think of no one else who could be procured at such short notice. If I had had a little more time, I am sure I could have found someone to suit you admirably.'

The Dowager's eyes narrowed dangerously. 'You have made yourself quite useful enough, my dear,' she said. 'I suggest you take your satisfaction from that. Leave the good deeds to those more accustomed to them. Come, Marina.' The Dowager moved Marina away before Lady Blaine's affronted gasp could be turned into words.

'Ignore her,' continued the Dowager. 'She has no breeding. Blaine married her for her money, of course. The men of that family always marry money and spend it on their mistresses.'

What an outrageous old woman she was! To be able to say such things! As a poor relation, Marina must always mind her tongue, but living with the Dowager would certainly never be dull.

The Dowager immediately began to point out other notable guests and to regale Marina with salty stories of their exploits. It was most entertaining. 'That beanpole of a gel over there,' she continued, pointing most impolitely with her fan, 'is Lady Blaine's eldest. Milly, or Tilly, or some such. Her face has too much of the dead horse for perfect beauty.'

Marina's eyes widened. How could she?

'Gel like that will never take. Especially since her mother persists in dressing her in white. Makes her look positively ill with that sallow complexion. The woman has even less taste than Charlotte.'

Marina tried not to nod. Her brother would be ashamed to learn that his sister could do anything quite so uncharitable, however satisfying it might have been to learn that her cousin was even less attractive than herself. In Miss Blaine's case, a handsome dowry might provide some slight compensation.

'Oh,' breathed Marina, catching sight of a couple dancing the waltz, 'who is that beautiful fair-haired lady?'

'What? Oh, that one,' said the Dowager, suddenly less animated than before. 'That, child, is Lady Stratton, who was Emma Fitzwilliam before her marriage. She is waltzing with her husband, Sir Hugo Stratton. Don't hold with it myself. Living in each other's pockets like that.' She shook her head.

The dancing couple turned at that moment so that Marina could see Sir Hugo's face. Even though this man was much older, and his face was visibly scarred, the likeness to Kit Stratton was very strong.

'Oh,' breathed Marina, 'is he—?'

'Yes, he is Kit Stratton's brother,' said the Dowager grimly, 'and as plump in the pocket as any man in London. Emma Fitzwilliam was the catch of the Season when he married her. No doubt her money helped to compensate for the scandal.'

'Scandal? I...I don't understand, ma'am.'

'No. Why should you? You're too young to know. It is just one more reason to beware of Kit Stratton, that is all. He ruined Emma Fitzwilliam, but he refused to marry her. Left that task to his elder brother. That's why he has spent the last five years abroad.'

Marina looked back at the couple on the floor. Sir Hugo Stratton and his wife were smiling at each other in a way that made Marina's heart turn over. Whatever might have been the reasons for the marriage, there was no doubt in Marina's mind that it was a love match now.

'Good gad!' exclaimed the Dowager a moment later. 'There's no avoiding the man, even here. Keeps turning up like a bad penny.'

Kit Stratton had just entered the room and was threading his way through the crowd of guests. Marina's stomach lurched at the sight of him. Her palms had become damp inside her borrowed evening gloves. Why did he have to be here? Why now? Would he recognise her?

He stopped some distance from them and sketched an elegant bow to a haughty dame in a feathered turban. Their exchange was very brief. Then, with a barely suppressed grimace, he left her for the dance floor, where he tapped his brother on the shoulder and impudently stole his partner. Sir Hugo simply smiled on the departing couple and strolled off, stopping here and there for an animated conversation with some of the other guests. He did not glance back even once towards his brother. Instead, he looked lazily round the ballroom, as if to assess how many of the guests he knew. His glance flickered over Marina and the Dowager, hesitated barely a moment, and then moved casually on.

'There seems to be no bad blood there,' Marina said, unwisely voicing her thoughts.

'Hmph,' snorted Lady Luce in disgust. 'It's all for show, I don't doubt. Come, Marina,' she added, turning for the door. 'I have no intention of remaining here a moment longer. I had not expected the air at this ball to be quite so polluted.'

With a final lingering glance towards the colourful throng of swirling dancers, and Kit Stratton's tall, elegant figure, Marina followed her mistress to the exit, totally unaware that she was not the only lady taking an interest in that arrestingly handsome gentleman. Miss Tilly Blaine, half-hidden by a pillar, was gazing on Kit Stratton with wide, glowing eyes, as if she had never beheld anything so beautiful.

Marina spent a disturbed night and then an uncomfortable day, trying vainly to give all her attention to Lady Luce's At Home. At least neither the younger Lady Luce nor her bosom bow, Lady Blaine, had put in an appearance.

As soon as the drawing-room door closed behind the last of her callers, the Dowager sank back into her favourite chair and straightened her powdered wig. 'Thank heavens for that,' she said. 'I was beginning to think that pair of harpies would never leave.'

Marina smiled but said nothing. The Dowager had obviously enjoyed the afternoon's verbal sparring with her visitors. The problem with the last two was their failure to fight back when lashed by the Dowager's acid tongue.

'And what, pray, are you smiling at, miss?' asked the Dowager.

Marina considered for a second or two, and then said, 'I was musing on the definition of a harpy, ma'am. I was always taught that they were fearsome mythical beasts, with murderous claws. But it seemed to me that there was nothing in the least mythical about Mrs Varity and her daughter—'

Lady Luce choked on a laugh. Mrs Varity was a remarkably large woman and totally unsuited to figuring in any myth, except in the guise of a well-padded cushion.

'And their claws seemed to have been drawn long before they even entered the house,' finished Marina, undaunted. 'I cannot think why that should be so. After all, it is not as though your guests are received with anything other than the utmost kindness.'

Lady Luce struck Marina on the wrist with her fan. It was quite a gentle blow, however, and the lady's eyes were sparkling with appreciative amusement. 'That is quite enough from you, young lady,' she said. 'I fear I am nurturing a viper in my bosom, keeping you here.'

'I fear so, ma'am,' agreed Marina, nodding gravely.

'Hmph! And I will not have you defending that Varity woman, either. She only came in hopes of finding out exactly what happened at Méchante's t'other evening. Wanted to crow over my losses, that was all. Like a cock on a dunghill!' She opened her fan and waved it aimlessly to and fro for a moment. 'I fancy I showed her the dangers of that!'

'Indeed, ma'am,' said Marina, non-committally. In fact, Mrs Varity had quit the field in full retreat, and Lady Luce was clearly relishing her victory. Now might be the time to tackle her on the touchy subject of Kit Stratton. 'Are you expecting Mr Stratton in the next few days, ma'am?' she asked quietly.

'What business is that of yours?' snapped Lady Luce, her geniality gone in an instant. 'Fallen for his pretty face, have you, eh?'

'No, no!' Marina felt sure she was blushing. 'It was just… I was wondering whether, as a gentleman and so very much your junior, he might not decide that it was…unseemly to collect on the debt.'

'Not he!' cried her ladyship, with an explosion of harsh laughter. 'Kit Stratton does not have a gentlemanly bone in his body. He would sooner cut his own throat than—' She looked up as the door opened. 'What is it *now*, Tibbs?'

The butler bowed stiffly, indicating the salver he carried. 'A letter has been delivered, m'lady. By hand. The messenger did not wait for a reply.'

Lady Luce stretched out her hand towards the salver.

'It is for Miss Beaumont, m'lady,' said the butler, offering the tray to Marina.

It had come! At last!

Lady Luce sat back in her chair with a grunt of disapproval. Marina could feel those sharp little eyes boring into her as she took the letter and calmly nodded her thanks to the butler. In a moment, the Dowager was going to question her about it. What could she say? Penniless companions, newly arrived in London, did not receive letters by special messenger—especially if they had no acquaintance in the city. She should have been prepared for this.

Marina weighed the letter in her hand. It was heavy enough to contain an enclosure. And it must be from Kit Stratton. The handwriting was bold and firm. Definitely not a lady's hand. Feeling the Dowager's increasing curiosity on her, Marina stuffed the letter hurriedly into the pocket of her gown.

'You may open your letter if you wish, child,' said her ladyship airily. 'You must be wishing to know who has written to you.'

Marina shook her head quickly. Too quickly. 'Oh, I know that already, ma'am,' she said. 'There is only one possibility, since I have no friends in London. There is a…a London clergyman who may become a patron to my brother, Harry,' she said, trying to make the hasty lie sound convincing. 'You may recall that he is to enter the Church when he leaves Oxford. The reverend gentleman promised that his wife would seek me out when I came to London. It is most kind of them both, I think, since they know nothing of Harry's sister. The letter can only be from her.' Marina tried to smile confidently at the Dowager. Would she be believed? It seemed a remarkably unlikely story. What if the Dowager asked Marina to produce this clergyman?

Lady Luce looked assessingly at Marina for a moment. Then she said sharply, 'You are here as companion to me, my girl, not to be running off to some do-gooding parson. Bad enough to have to listen to them on Sundays, without other days of the week as well.'

Marina tightened her lips to hide her smile. Lady Luce made no secret of her trenchant views on the clergy. If she disliked a sermon, she made sure that the whole congregation knew it. She had done so on the previous Sunday, smiling in satisfaction while her son squirmed with embarrassment. Marina had felt it, too, but in truth the Dowager's outrageous behaviour had been the least of her worries. She had spent Sunday, and most of Monday, wondering whether Kit Stratton would reply. At least she had her answer now.

'You may visit this parson in your own time,' Lady Luce continued. 'Not in mine. Is that understood?'

'Yes, ma'am,' said Marina meekly.

'Oh, get along with you now. Go and read your letter,

since it is burning a hole in your pocket. I shall not need you until dinner.'

Marina could scarce believe her luck. It seemed the Dowager believed her story. And as for the degree of indulgence she was showing…

'Thank you, ma'am. You are very kind,' she said, rising from her chair to drop a curtsy. 'I—'

The Dowager waved an impatient hand. 'I suggest you go before I change my mind,' she said tartly.

Marina retreated, as quickly as dignity permitted. The butler was hovering in the hallway, so she mounted the stairs at a measured pace until he was out of sight. Then she scampered up the remaining flight and along the hallway to the safety of her room, trying not to slam the door in her haste.

The letter was sealed with a wafer that did not wish to be removed! She cursed softly, trying to tear it apart. At last, the thick paper was undone. Yes, there was an enclosure. Kit Stratton must have taken the bait!

In her haste, Marina dropped the outer letter on the floor. No matter. She would read it in a moment. First, she must be sure that she had the Dowager's vowel in her hand.

She spread the folded sheet on the little table and smoothed her hand quickly across it. Disappointment hit her like a blow. It was the same black handwriting as the address. Why had Mr Stratton written her two letters?

The answer came in a moment. The inner letter was addressed not to Marina, but to the Dowager herself. And Marina was clearly intended to read it. That was the only reason why he would have left it unsealed.

Marina glanced quickly down the sheet, hardly daring to breathe. Then she let out a tiny cry of triumph. It was

as good as forgiveness of the debt. He wrote that he
would return the Dowager's vowel when he called upon
her at the end of the week—and that he would not demand the money.

Marina closed her eyes and clasped the letter to her
bosom. It seemed almost too good to be true. She had
set a trap—and her quarry had walked straight into it.
Her future must now be secure.

For almost a minute she sat immobile, while pictures
rose in her mind of Mama, comfortably circumstanced
at last, and beaming gratefully at her daughter. In just a
few short weeks, Marina would be able to send home
her very first contribution to that small, spartan household. How wonderful that would be.

Provided Kit Stratton could be tricked out of the second part of the bargain!

Marina opened her eyes with a start. She still had to
deal with Kit Stratton's designs on her virtue. But at
least she had secured the Dowager's debt. That was the
first, vital step.

She bent down to retrieve Mr Stratton's outer letter.
What would he have to say to her?

The letter was very short indeed. It contained barely
two lines. There was neither salutation, nor signature.

*White scarf. Tomorrow. The letter is post-dated and
can be publicly revoked.*

It made no sense. What on earth…? Marina scrabbled
around on the table for the inner letter and forced herself
to read it carefully, one sentence at a time.

Then she understood.

The letter was dated two days hence and addressed to
the Dowager Countess Luce. Its tone was curt and for-
mal. *Madam*, it said, *Your intermediary has prevailed
upon me not to collect on your recent debt. I shall call*

*upon you tomorrow, as agreed. Your vowel shall be re-
turned to you then. Christopher Stratton.*

In her haste, she had overlooked that one significant
word—tomorrow. And the date. The letter was worth
nothing, nothing at all, until that day. She had been
duped.

How arrogant, how stupid she had been to think for
one moment that she could outwit a practised deceiver
like Kit Stratton. He had taken her stratagem and turned
it back on her. She had demanded payment in advance
and he had provided it, but so cleverly that she could
not make use of it until after she had delivered on her
side of the bargain. Nor could she now retreat, as all her
senses were urging her to do. If she did not meet him
on the morrow, he would no doubt make their bargain
public immediately, using Marina's letter as proof of his
allegations against her. It would cost him nothing. He
had no reputation to lose. But Marina would be cried a
liar, a cheat and a wanton, to boot. Lady Luce would
discharge her on the spot—she would have no choice.
Marina would be forced to return to Yorkshire with not
a penny to her name—a name that would be dragged
through the mud in London and, eventually, in Yorkshire, too.

Marina would be an outcast. Mama would be shamed,
dreadfully shamed. There would be no more pupils—no
father would permit his child to enter such a household.
They would have to rely on Harry for their very bread.

Harry! What of Harry? He would probably suffer, too.
He might even be asked to leave Oxford, for who would
give a living to a man with such a sister?

A tear squeezed its way out and down Marina's cheek.
Angrily, she brushed it away. What was the point of
tears? She had brought all this on herself, by her own

stupidity in sending that incriminating letter. And signing it, too! If her family suffered, she alone was to blame. Oh, why had she ever set eyes on Kit Stratton?

He had won. It mattered not how many curses she called down on his head. He had won.

He expected her to be in his carriage on the morrow. And, heaven help her, she now had no choice but to comply.

Chapter Nine

Marina had not slept.

As soon as she heard the first stirrings of the household below, she rose and began to make ready for her fateful meeting with Kit Stratton. She felt like the condemned preparing for the scaffold.

She stripped off her nightdress and washed every inch of her skin with the freezing water left from the night before. The cold should have brought her body to life, but it did not. She barely shivered.

Then she hunted through her meagre supply of underthings to find those with the least evidence of mending. She shivered then, to be sure. He would see them…all of them, but her pride would not permit him to discover the full extent of her poverty. He must be made to remember that she was a lady and—in that at least—his equal.

She shuddered again at the sight of the pretty green gown hanging from the rail. Had she really considered wearing such a thing for this meeting? She had truly been mad.

Hastily she donned the most severe of her drab Yorkshire gowns, plain, long-sleeved and high to the neck.

Only then did she pause to look at herself in the glass. Her face was almost as grey as her gown. The mass of chestnut hair curling around her shoulders contrasted starkly with her pale skin, like a wig on a corpse. With shaky fingers, she braided her hair and pinned it back into her usual neat knot. That was better. No…it would not do. She unpinned it and did it over again, much tighter. Her hair would be barely visible now, especially under her bonnet.

But he was bound to insist that she remove it. And then every other stitch of clothing she was wearing…

Swallowing her fears, Marina forced herself to look around the gloomy interior. The carriage was far from elegant. And it had a vague, musty smell to it, as if it had lain long unused in some damp coach house. Involuntarily, she wrinkled her nose.

'I apologise for the carriage, Miss Beaumont.' Mr Stratton was leaning carelessly back in his seat to let his frank gaze wander over her body. 'It is not mine, you understand. Mindful of your reputation—' He quirked a sardonic eyebrow at Marina's start of surprise. 'Oh, yes, ma'am. Mindful of your *reputation*,' he said again, with emphasis, 'I have hired this anonymous vehicle, rather than use my own. It is not quite what I should like…but then you will not be in it for long, will you?' He leant forward and slid one lean hand out behind the closed window blind. After a moment, he sat back once more, carefully folding the white silk scarf that had been attached to the door handle. 'I would not, for the world, draw attention to your presence here,' he said in a soft, almost menacing voice.

Marina stared dumbly at the floor. It was none too clean.

'Remove your hat and gloves, if you please.'

Marina looked up with a start and then complied, struggling a little with the strings of her bonnet. She had made the bargain. He would make sure she kept it.

'Now, give me your hand.' His long fingers enfolded hers in a strong grip. With a single movement, he pulled her from her seat and on to his lap, lowering his mouth to hers.

Without thinking, Marina tried to push him away.

He raised his head and looked down into her eyes. His expression was unreadable. 'Willingly, Miss Beaumont,' he said softly. 'That was what was agreed. Have you so soon forgotten?'

'Willingly in your *bed*, Mr Stratton,' snapped Marina, 'not in a dirty, smelly carriage.'

Kit gave a great shout of laughter. '*Touché,* Miss Beaumont,' he said, grinning. 'Perhaps you would like to resume your seat?'

Without giving Marina a chance to respond, he grasped her round the waist and placed her back on her seat as though she weighed nothing at all. Then, still grinning broadly, he lounged back in his own place once more.

It was the first time Marina had ever seen genuine humour in his face. For once, his eyes had softened. His whole expression was alive with amusement. He seemed years younger…and devastatingly handsome. If this was the face he showed to his conquests, it was no wonder they all succumbed. Marina, too, could feel the pull of his attraction. She wished—

She turned away before her resolution failed her and busied herself with replacing her bonnet on her tightly braided hair. Even without her gloves, it seemed that her fingers wanted to tie themselves in knots.

Kit leaned towards her, smiling mischievously. 'Shall I help you, ma'am?' he said, stretching out a hand. 'I am accounted…adequate in dealing with ladies' clothing.'

Appalled, Marina batted his hand away and turned even further from him. He was doing it quite deliberately. He was determined to ensure she was thoroughly unsettled. As if his mere presence was not enough to do that.

At last her bonnet was tied and her gloves restored to her hands. She clasped them together in her lap and sat round in her seat. She would not let him see how much he affected her. 'May I ask where we are going, sir?' she said quietly.

He nodded approvingly. Confound the man! It was as if he could read her mind and was awarding her marks for self-control.

'I am taking you to my house in Chelsea, ma'am. It is far enough away from the fashionable streets and perfectly suited for the…business we have to conduct. I take it you do not object?'

'I was not aware that I had any choice in the matter,' Marina replied acidly.

'No, but it does no harm to observe the niceties of polite conversation, do you not think? It serves to make a tedious journey pass the more quickly.'

He was laughing at her! For just a second, she saw it in his eyes, before his expression became a bland mask, as usual. With difficulty, she suppressed an urge to slap that handsome face into awareness of her anger. But there was no point. She had tried that tactic before, and failed. Last time, he had—

Last time, he had kissed her.

The carriage slowed. Kit lifted the blind a fraction to

see where they were. Then he reached into a pocket and produced a lady's veil. 'I suggest you drape this over your bonnet, ma'am, just in case. One never knows who might be walking by. I would not wish your reputation to be sullied because you had omitted to wear a hat with a veil.'

Oh, how dare he? He was blaming her for what was about to happen. More than ever, she wanted to hit him, but she forced herself to drape the veil over her bonnet instead. It covered her face completely. It was unlikely she would be recognised, even by someone who knew her well.

He was already standing on the flagway, holding up a hand to help her down.

Marina hesitated. There was something about those lean hands... She was afraid to touch his fingers, afraid of what she would feel if she did.

'Come along, ma'am,' he said impatiently. 'Let us be done with this business of ours.' He looked narrowly at her, as if he could read her thoughts through the veil. 'Unless you wish to renege on our bargain?'

Marina rose, gathered her skirts and climbed down unaided, marching towards the door without once looking at Kit Stratton. She lifted the knocker and let it fall back on to the door with a hollow clang.

In the echo, a voice whispered in her ear, 'I was persuaded you were no coward.'

Marina shivered. She could feel his breath against her neck and the warmth of his body at her back. She could not escape. Oh, why did the door not open?

After what seemed an age, it did. The tiny housekeeper stood there, hostility writ clearly in the lines of her body. Even the black bombazine of her dress seemed to bristle. For several seconds she stood blocking the entrance, staring up at Marina with narrow, searching eyes.

'Thank you, Mrs Budge.' Kit's voice was cool but authoritative. His housekeeper stood aside to let the visitors enter.

Kit placed a hand—ever so lightly—in the small of Marina's back and guided her into the little sitting room where they had met before. Marina told herself to remain calm, to ignore the tingling of her skin and the sparks shooting down into her belly. She would find out all about them, soon enough. Soon, she would be in his bedchamber…in his bed.

He shut the door firmly on the housekeeper, giving instructions that they were not to be disturbed. Perhaps he wanted to— Oh, surely not here?

'No, Miss Beaumont,' Kit said laconically, 'I am not about to ravish you on this hideous Chelsea carpet. I hope you will grant me a little more finesse than that.'

He was reading her mind again!

'Pray be seated. May I offer you some refreshment?'

Marina shook her head dumbly. It would choke her.

Kit sat down opposite her, stretching out his long legs towards the fireplace. He seemed much too large for the tiny room.

'I must admit, ma'am, that I am surprised you have come.'

She sat up even straighter in her chair, but said nothing.

'You mean to keep your side of the bargain, then?'

Slowly, she raised the veil from her face and looked haughtily across at him. 'Of course. I would not break my word,' she said levelly. 'Even to you.'

He sat quite still, watching her. She was white and drawn. In the half-light of the small windows, she was not in the least attractive, apart from those huge, luminous eyes. A victim on the tumbrel could not have looked worse. How had it come to this? He had been so sure that she would break her word. Women always did. But this one had proved him wrong. He ought to let her go. So what on earth was he doing?

Collecting on a bargain, made and sealed. He had agreed to forgo twelve thousand pounds, and his revenge on Lady Luce, besides. Some recompense must be due for that. And there was something about this woman...

He sat silent, staring at her and wondering at his own perfidy. Was he truly about to allow an innocent gentlewoman to sell her virtue to him for twelve thousand pounds? In all his twenty-seven years, he had never paid a woman to share his bed. Never.

He had pursued them, certainly. Over many months, on occasion. Indeed, it had taken nearly a year to pluck his lovely Baroness from the arms of her husband. His friends in Vienna had called her unassailable. They had taunted him. In the end, he had been forced to prove that even she could be made to fall in love with him. Like a ripe plum, she had been ready to drop into a waiting, caressing hand. His hand. But, in truth, she had fully intended to fall...if not with him, then with another. That virtuous demeanour had been a façade, covering a lusty, passionate nature. She suited him; and he her. When she had come to London with her husband, it had suited him to follow. It had been time for him to return. And it suited him to have her here, whenever he wanted her.

That was not quite true. At present, he did not have his beautiful Baroness.

He had Miss Beaumont instead.

She was prepared to surrender herself to him. No doubt she thought she had made a bargain with the devil, but she would keep it, because she had given her word. A most amazing woman. If only she had the looks to match that remarkable character…

He ought to let her go. Now. But then that old harridan would have won. As she had done five years ago.

A second defeat was unthinkable. Miss Beaumont must be held to her bargain.

He should never have offered the bargain in the first place, for Lady Luce would be the gainer, while all the costs would fall on her hapless companion. Only a man sunk in the depths of infamy would take her. Was he that man?

Miss Beaumont was turning a ring around her finger under her glove. Or rather, she was trying to do so, with precious little success. Was she at all aware of what she was doing?

Kit rose and began to pace. There was too much furniture in the room. In the end, he gave up and went to stand at the window, looking out into the street. It had begun to rain again.

'Miss Beaumont,' he said into the heavy silence.

She started in her seat. The hand with the ring went to her mouth in an unconscious gesture of anxiety.

Kit came to stand over her. 'Miss Beaumont, you have kept your side of the bargain. I must admit that I did not expect you to do so. I honour you for your courage.' He paused for a few seconds. 'I must tell you, ma'am,' he began again, 'that I now have no desire to complete our mutual…business. I make it a rule never to mount more than one mistress at a time. Yesterday, as it happens, I was fortunate enough to…' He let the words tail off, watching her intently. 'I see that you take my meaning. If you permit, I will now escort you back to the park so that you may return home.'

'I...I do not understand. The debt... We agreed—'

'The debt is paid. You may deliver my letter to Lady Luce tomorrow. On Friday, I shall call and return her vowel, as I promised. The debt shall be cancelled.'

'I—'

Kit put his hands under her elbows and lifted her gently out of her chair. He could feel that her body was shivering. 'Do not be afraid, ma'am. I, too, keep my promises. You may be sure of that.' She looked quite bewildered. Her huge eyes were dark as she stared up at him. There was the beginning of a spot of hot colour on each of her cheeks, marring that beautiful complexion.

Slowly, he lifted the veil from the top of her bonnet and arranged it over her face once more.

'Come, Miss Beaumont,' he said softly. 'Your carriage awaits.'

She said nothing more while they mounted into the carriage and took their places as before. She said nothing throughout the drive back to the park.

Kit looked at her tense, shrouded figure. What was it about her? He was giving up a debt of twelve thousand pounds. And for what?

For a woman who was a worthy opponent, a woman who had as much courage as any man.

He smiled to himself as he watched her. He would make sure her honour was protected. She deserved no less. For Lady Luce, on the other hand, he had determined that there would be no protection. He would forgive her the debt, to be sure, but the whole world would learn that he had done it. He, Kit Stratton, would be seen to be thoroughly magnanimous. And she, the Dowager Countess Luce, would be publicly beholden to him for twelve thousand pounds of charity. The world would expect her to be exceedingly grateful to Kit Stratton.

She would be humiliated beyond bearing.

It was not the revenge he had planned for, but, on reflection, it might prove to be just as sweet.

Marina was very, very cold. The cracked leather at her back felt like sheet ice, reaching its freezing fingers through to her bare skin. That would account for the shivering that she could not prevent.

He was taking her back to the park. She had been in his house—at his mercy—and he was returning her, intact. She was not even worth an hour's distraction from his latest mistress!

She glanced across at him from under lowered lashes. She had not so far dared to look at him, even through the veil. She was afraid of what he would see in her eyes.

He seemed to be miles away. His face wore an expression of intense but distant concentration, as if he was solving a particularly knotty, abstract problem. How to checkmate a king, perhaps? Or overcome an attacking queen?

The rain had stopped. She had not noticed before. In Chelsea, it had been pattering half-heartedly on the roof, suggesting yet another muddy walk back to Lady Luce's house. Perhaps, now, it would not be quite so bad. She should be able to pick her way through the mud and the puddles.

A knowing smile started to play around Kit's mouth. Marina knew at once that he had solved his puzzle, and was now enjoying his anticipated victory. She never, for a single moment, doubted that he would win. He would always win, especially where women were concerned. He was the devil.

That lean hand moved the blind a fraction, just as before. 'We shall arrive in a moment or two, Miss Beaumont,' he said. 'You will be able to make your own way from here, I hope? You will understand that I dare not take you to your door, lest…'

Why was he suddenly so polite? It made Marina want to scream. An hour ago he had been set to ravish her in this very carriage. 'Thank you, Mr Stratton,' she snapped, unable to hide her burgeoning temper. 'I am quite able to manage without your…your services.'

Muffled laughter greeted her rather feeble sally. Marina felt she had achieved a small victory.

But it was short-lived. This time, he did not pull her on to his lap. He threw himself on to the seat beside her, tossed up her veil, and caught her gasp of alarm in a brutal, demanding kiss.

It was a kiss of possession. He was showing her that she was his, that he could have taken much more than her lips, that she would have been unable to resist. And to her eternal shame, it was so. She knew she ought to fight him, but her limbs were filled with a wondrous, glowing languor. His invasion of her mouth was no punishment, but a joy, tempting her towards delights that she could never have imagined. The warm scent of him seemed to surround her like a sun-filled arbour. She could have struggled free of his encircling arms, if her treacherous body had been willing to try. But it would not.

She slid her arms around his neck and yielded to an overwhelming desire to return his kiss.

It was Kit who broke it at last.

The carriage had stopped. Marina had no idea how

long it had been stationary. Her whole being had been drowning in the magic of her first truly passionate embrace. Now she was gasping for breath and her heart was pounding. What had she done? How had she allowed it to happen?

She gazed up into Kit's face, but his eyes were hooded and his expression blank. He was breathing quite easily. The kiss that had made such an indelible impression on her whole being seemed to have left him quite cold. Humiliation rose in her throat as if to choke her. Her face felt hot. She realised she must be quite scarlet.

She must get away from him!

Hastily pulling down her veil with one hand, she grabbed the handle of the carriage door.

Kit put a restraining hand on her arm. 'The path is on the other side, Miss Beaumont,' he said calmly. 'I would not have you descend into the mud.'

Marina's hands clenched into fists. Again, that incredible urge to scream like a demented fiend. She rose and pushed past him, not trusting herself to speak another word.

Unable to rise in the cramped interior, Kit bowed to her. 'You will understand that I may not alight to help you down, Miss Beaumont,' he said politely. 'I trust you will forgive me for that.'

Marina flung open the door and stepped down into the blessed freedom of Hyde Park. She half turned back to him. He was almost invisible in the gloom. 'For that, most certainly, Mr Stratton,' she said in a low venomous voice. 'But for nothing else.' Reaching up, she slammed the door on him with all the force she could muster.

She would almost have sworn that she heard an appreciative laugh from inside the carriage as she started to hurry away.

It was impossible to deal with such a man. Impossible for her. She must have nothing more to do with him.

Head lowered, she hastened towards the gate. Thank heavens there was almost nobody about. Only a single gentleman on horseback, taking his morning exercise.

She reached the gate just as the gentleman trotted up behind her on a fine bay mare. He pulled his horse aside politely so that Marina would not be splashed. Automatically, she looked up at him to nod her thanks.

Oh, no! Surely not! Please let her be mistaken!

He stopped in the act of raising his crop to his hat, a very strange look flitting across his features. Then with a tiny shake of his head, he completed the salute and walked his mare through the gate.

Marina looked after his retreating figure. It had almost seemed as if he recognised her. But that was impossible. They had never even been introduced, and besides… She reached up to straighten her concealing veil.

Part of it had caught on the top of her bonnet. Much of her face must have been visible from the moment she alighted from Kit Stratton's carriage. The rider of the bay mare had seen her step down, she remembered that clearly. He must have crossed her path deliberately just now, in order to get a closer look at a woman who was so obviously defying convention. By his expression, he had recognised her face, even if, please God, he did not yet know her name.

What would he do with the information he had acquired? Would he broadcast to the world that a very tall, grey-clad lady had emerged alone from a closed carriage in the early hours of the morning? He had only to describe her thus for her name to be forthcoming from many of Lady Luce's acquaintants.

Marina shuddered. The sheet of ice had returned to her back.

She would have to abandon her resolution to avoid Kit Stratton. He alone might be able to save her from public disgrace, provided she could appeal to him very soon.

For the gentleman on the bay mare was Sir Hugo Stratton.

Chapter Ten

None of it made any sense, Marina thought, throwing aside her bonnet and gloves and sitting down at her little writing table. The whole episode had been like a series of riddles, each more indecipherable than the last. First he had attacked her in his carriage. Next, he had spurned her, on the far from convincing grounds that he did not deal with more than one woman at a time. Finally, he had attacked her in his carriage all over again. So much for his claim of being faithful to his newest mistress.

For some reason, he had been toying with her. Men could be just as fickle as women, surely? And Kit Stratton was definitely that. In his Chelsea house, he could barely bring himself to touch her. In his dark and musty carriage, he had—

That must be it. It had been so dark in the carriage that he would not have been able to make out her features. He had probably told himself that he was kissing someone else, his latest mistress, perhaps.

She felt used. Could it have been worse if he had actually bedded her? As it was, she had screwed her courage to the sticking-place, and then he had rejected her, in the most obnoxious manner. Most humiliating of all, he had kissed her so beguilingly that she had responded—eagerly—in spite of the insults he had been heaping upon her. She burned with shame at the thought of what she had done, how she had felt... Her conscience reminded her that she had sinned, yet she knew that, given another chance, she would willingly sin again...

There must be no more chances.

Marina turned her ring round her finger, trying to devise a new, more terrible curse to throw at him. She was not very good at curses. Her mama had made sure that she learned none of the bad language used by the common soldiers. And what good would it do, anyway? She still had to ask—nay, beg—Kit Stratton to persuade his brother not to betray her to the world.

She dare not see him. She must write to him. Again. As before, her future would hang on his reaction to her request.

She pulled a sheet of paper towards her and steeled herself to write the most difficult letter of her life.

With a mischievous glance at her husband, Emma Stratton put a hand on Kit's shoulder to pull him down to her level so that she could plant a smacking kiss on his cheek. 'How lovely to see you, Kit,' she said, gazing flirtatiously at him through her long lashes.

Kit smiled indulgently at his beautiful sister-in-law. 'If the tabbies could see you now, Emma...' he warned, doing his best to inject a hint of menace into his words.

'And what do you mean by that remark, pray?' she replied, in mock outrage. The wicked sparkle in her eyes betrayed her.

From his stance by the window overlooking the busy street, Hugo wagged a finger at her. 'You know very well, you minx. They will never stop seeking scandal between you and Kit.'

Emma threw her husband a speaking glance and sank into her spindle-legged chair in a single, elegant movement. 'What, I? A respectable matron, the mother of three stout children? Fie on you, sir!'

Kit took her hand in his and raised it to his lips, grinning wickedly all the while. 'But who is to say they are all yours, Hugo? After all, we are so very much alike…' He left the thought unfinished. He did not need to remind Emma, or her husband, that she been compromised all those years ago as a result of mistaking Kit for Hugo in a midnight garden.

'You wretch, Kit,' she cried, rapping him hard across the knuckles with her fan.

'Seriously though, Kit,' said Hugo, strolling across the Aubusson carpet to where his wife sat and resting his hand gently on her shoulder, 'it would be wiser not to mention the likeness between us. You might just set them thinking. You know how easily rumours start.'

'I'd like to see how they would account for it, Hugo, when I have been in Vienna almost since the day of your wedding. I may have something of a reputation with the ladies—' Hugo raised an eyebrow, and Emma giggled '—but there are some things even I…'

Emma clapped her hands over her ears, but then she spoiled the moment by collapsing in gales of laughter. The two men were soon laughing, too.

Emma said, weakly, 'This is vastly improper. You are quite as bad as each other, you know.'

'Very true, my love, very true,' said Hugo, nodding. 'We shall now talk of subjects fit for my lady wife's drawing room. Will you not be seated, Kit? Tell me, did you see the lady who was with the Dowager Lady Luce at the ball t'other evening?'

'Why do you ask?' said Kit carefully.

Hugo grinned. 'Sparring for wind, brother? I ask, because I expect you to know every lady in London. You must have seen her. She is so much taller than all the other ladies that every eye must be drawn to her.'

'As it happens, Hugo, I did *not* see her at the ball, but I do know who she is.'

'Ah,' said Hugo, nodding expectantly.

'She is Lady Luce's companion. Her name is Beaumont.'

'Of course!' Hugo slapped his thigh. 'I should have guessed. The likeness was there all the time.'

Emma frowned across at him. 'Hugo, you are talking in riddles. What likeness? Who is Miss Beaumont?'

'I am not totally certain, Emma, but I think my friend, George Langley, was her uncle. You know he was killed at Ciudad Rodrigo, but I may not have said that his sister's husband, Tom Beaumont, died there too.'

'Oh, how dreadful!' cried Emma. 'A husband *and* a brother!'

Kit rose abruptly and strode across to the window.

Hugo nodded in sympathy. For a few moments he sat in silence, remembering.

Emma put a gentle hand on his arm. 'What makes you think she is related to them, love?' she asked softly.

'There can be no doubt. Not for anyone who knew Tom Beaumont. She has a great look of him. Same height, same build, same features. But what on earth is she doing as companion to that old harpy? Surely—?'

'I suspect her family is become very poor, Hugo,' said Kit in a harsh voice, turning back into the room. 'I take it the army did nothing for the widow?'

'I am afraid I do not know,' Hugo replied, flushing a little. 'You will recall that, after the battle, I was…in some difficulty.'

Kit nodded quickly. The last thing he wanted was for his brother to be forced to recall the accusations of cowardice that had been heaped upon him by his malicious commanding officer. They had long since been proved false, but the memories would still be painful.

'I had no chance to do anything for Mrs Beaumont at the time. I was not even permitted to write to her,' Hugo added bitterly. 'And when I eventually came home, it was years too late. I did not even know where to begin to look. Somewhere in the north, I fancy.'

Kit turned back to the window, his mind racing. He had so nearly done something thoroughly dishonourable to a lady who should have been under his family's protection. No wonder Miss Beaumont had shown such courage under his assault. She came from heroic stock. He clenched his fists in frustration and swallowed a groan. Miss Beaumont needed help, not harassment. But it was unlikely that she would accept anything from him. After all, she had said— Yes, of course, she had said he was not worthy to be Hugo's brother… The connection had been clear, almost from the start, if only he had thought to pursue it. And now…

Emma had been talking eagerly to her husband. 'And I shall certainly take her up,' she finished triumphantly. 'Lady Luce shall have nothing to say in the matter.'

Hugo gave a crack of unwilling laughter. 'That would be the first time, my love. Do you not agree, Kit?'

'What? Your pardon, Hugo, I was not listening. You asked…?'

'It is of no moment. Emma and I were just discussing

Miss Beaumont. Emma is determined to help her, yet I…I must admit I have doubts.'

'Oh?' Emma bridled visibly. 'Why?'

'Believe me, my love, I shall ensure that she and her family are not left in penury, but there is no need for you to become involved. She is only a companion, after all.'

'Hugo! What a wicked—!' Emma broke off, looking shrewdly into her husband's face. 'No. You would never say anything so unkind. Or so top-lofty. You are trying to hide something from me.' She clasped her hands in her lap, fixed her angelic blue gaze on his face and waited. A knowing little smile began playing round her mouth.

Kit waited, too. What on earth could Hugo know to Miss Beaumont's detriment? Unless—

'Emma, I am asking you not to take Miss Beaumont under your wing. At least, not immediately.' Hugo raised his brows, waiting for her response. His expression was grave. Eventually, Emma nodded, somewhat unwillingly, Kit thought. 'Believe me, I have good reason for my caution,' Hugo continued, unbending a little in the light of his wife's acquiescence. 'Suffice it to say that I saw her earlier today, somewhere no lady should be.'

Kit just managed to conceal a start of surprise.

'But she may have—' began Emma, eager to defend a possible protégée.

'Patience, my love, patience. Give me time to discover a little more about Miss Beaumont. I promise that if I find that she had good reason for her…actions, I shall positively insist that you help her.'

'Very well,' Emma said. 'I shall have patience, since you ask it of me. But do be quick about your enquiries, love,' she added with an impudent little grin, 'for I am already longing to meet your mysterious Miss Beaumont.'

In spite of his concern, Kit almost laughed. Emma was truly outrageous. She could play the part of the obedient wife to perfection, but underneath…!

Hugo was laughing, too, and shaking his head at his beautiful, wilful wife. 'So much for marriage vows, eh, Kit? Obedience, indeed!'

Rising quickly, Emma dropped a kiss on her husband's forehead, before he could move from his seat. 'Never fear, husband,' she said gaily. 'I shall not break my vows—or not today, at least—since I am promised to Lady Dunsmore and—' she glanced at the gilt mantel clock and gave a little shriek '—heavens, I shall be most dreadfully late.' She hurried to the door but Kit was before her, ready to open it for her. 'Goodbye, Kit. I leave you to my lord and master. No doubt you are well used to his imperious ways.' She left the room in a swirl of lemon muslin and jonquil ribbons. It seemed suddenly duller without her.

Hugo was still smiling when Kit came back to join him by the huge fireplace. 'An extraordinary coincidence, is it not, Hugo, that this young woman should be the daughter of your old friend?'

'Not quite that, Kit. Her uncle, Langley, was my friend. We served together for years. Her father was some years older and only recently transferred into the 95th, so I did not know him all that well. On reflection, though, I am not so surprised if the family is poor. Beaumont was always gambling and he very rarely won.'

'Ah,' said Kit. That could explain much about Miss Beaumont's attempts to protect her mistress from the evil consequences of gambling. Yet another reason to condemn his own behaviour, too.

'It sounds as if you know more about Miss Beaumont than you are prepared to say, Kit. I collect that I am right in thinking she is not a fit person for Emma to know?'

'No, Hugo,' said Kit immediately, 'you are not right. Miss Beaumont is most definitely a lady. What makes you think otherwise?'

Hugo glanced suspiciously at his brother, but Kit was still determined to give nothing away. He had schooled his features into a bland expression and simply waited, as Emma had done, until the silence forced Hugo into speech.

'Oh, very well, since you are so intent upon knowing. I saw her in the park, very early this morning. She was quite alone. She alighted from a carriage with its blinds drawn, apparently after having some kind of altercation with the person inside. I assumed her companion to be a man. And I can think of no acceptable reason for her being there. Certainly, when she saw me, she looked remarkably guilty.'

'You spoke to her?'

'No. We have not been introduced. I recognised her from the ball.'

'Through her veil?'

Hugo leaned back in his seat and eyed his brother sceptically. After a moment, he said, 'I shall not ask how you come to know that. But I am now more than ever sure that I should discover more about Miss Beaumont before I permit Emma to know her.'

Cursing himself for his stupidity, Kit flung himself out of his chair and strode across to the window, before his loose tongue could betray him even more. Was there anything he could say to retrieve the situation? If Hugo began to make enquiries about Miss Beaumont, rumours were bound to start to fly. And it would be Kit's fault. He must say something to buy a little time, if nothing more.

He turned back from the window and said, 'Hugo, I fully understand your desire to protect Emma's reputation, but you have no need to be concerned about Miss Beaumont. She is a lady, and a virtuous one.'

Hugo still looked unconvinced.

Goaded, Kit continued, 'I give you my word that I have not seduced her.'

'But you *have* met her,' Hugo said flatly. 'Alone, I take it?'

Confound it! Hugo had always been able to read Kit as no other could. He would not be satisfied with less than the truth...or some part of it. 'She sought me out to ask me to forgive Lady Luce's debt,' he said baldly.

'Ah, I see.' Hugo gazed into the fire for several moments, considering. Then he looked up again, and said, 'That is not, perhaps, surprising...given her background. And I can fully understand why she slammed the carriage door in your face. She would have been far from pleased by your refusal.'

'She was as mad as fire,' Kit agreed, smiling sardonically as he remembered how passionately she had responded to him, and how furious she had been at her own weakness. There was nothing to be gained by denying his involvement, but it would not do for Hugo to learn the whole. 'However,' he continued, 'given your revelations about who she is, I fancy I ought to grant her request.'

'Twelve thousand pounds? That would be remarkably generous, Kit. Especially given your feelings about the Dowager.'

'Nothing has changed there. It will please her not one

whit to have to admit that Kit Stratton has generously forgiven such an enormous gaming debt.' He nodded reflectively, watching his brother's reactions from the corner of his eye. Hugo's worried look had faded. 'Now that I come to think on it, it should be worth all of twelve thousand pounds to see the proud Lady Luce thus humbled.'

Hugo closed his eyes and shook his head despairingly. 'Having failed to dissuade you once before on that topic, I shall not interfere again. As to Miss Beaumont, I suppose I should—'

'You *are* satisfied, I hope, Hugo?' said Kit quickly.

'I accept your word, naturally. And since it appears that no one saw her with you except myself… Very well, Kit. I would not damage a lady's reputation without cause. I shall say nothing.'

'Even to Emma?'

'I shall suggest that she calls on Lady Luce.'

Kit choked. 'She would not dare!'

Hugo grinned, shaking his head. 'Of course she would. Emma will see it as a challenge. She will set about reconciling the two families, and taking up Miss Beaumont, just as she always intended. No doubt Emma will discover more about the virtuous companion in half an hour than I could do in a week of asking. I would say, Kit, that you should resign yourself to enjoying much more of Miss Beaumont's company than you had expected. Unless you wish to forgo your visits to Fitzwilliam House?'

'Certainly not,' Kit said promptly. 'If Miss Beaumont should happen to be here when I call, I dare say I shall learn to adjust.'

Checking yet again that the wafer was firmly affixed to Mr Stratton's letter, Marina let herself in to the Dowager's drawing room. She knew exactly what she was planning to say, having spent another sleepless night worrying about whether her ruse would work. Now, she was about to find out.

Marina walked quietly across to the window, and the Dowager's chair. Lady Luce's eyes were closed, but Marina did not think she was asleep. It was too early for that.

'Don't just stand there, girl,' snapped the Dowager, without opening her eyes. 'There is nothing wrong with my hearing, even when my eyes are shut.'

Marina fought back a nervous laugh. She must appear normal. Holding out the letter towards the Dowager's motionless figure, she said, 'A letter has been delivered for you, ma'am.'

Lady Luce half opened one eye. Then she sat up straight and took the letter, studying the handwriting. 'Don't recognise that fist,' she said, casting a suspicious look at Marina. 'Brought round this morning, was it?'

'I am not sure quite when it was delivered,' said Marina, who had decided to stick as closely as possible to the truth. 'Clearly, no reply is expected, since the messenger did not wait.'

'Hmph.' Lady Luce broke the seal and spread the sheet, then raised her glass to read.

Marina held her breath.

'The blackguard!' cried her ladyship almost immediately, throwing the paper to the floor and gripping the arms of her chair with her claw-like hands. 'How dare he? He *condescends* to make me a gift of twelve thousand pounds, because *my* intermediary has asked it of him! It is a foul lie! I would not send an intermediary to give him the time of day! And then he is pleased to inform me that he will call tomorrow to return my vowel. To laugh in my face, more like!' She paused to draw breath, temporarily exhausted by her tirade.

'May I read the letter, ma'am?' Marina asked as calmly as she could.

'If you must,' said the Dowager, with a dismissive wave in the direction of the paper on the floor.

Marina retrieved the letter and glanced at it, as if she were reading it for the first time. 'Perhaps one of your friends spoke to Mr Stratton without asking your leave, ma'am,' she suggested gently, watching for any signs of a further burst of fury. 'If so, he or she has saved you a vast deal of trouble.'

'Confounded impudence,' muttered Lady Luce. 'If I find out who has dared to interfere in my affairs, I shall—' She stopped and looked searchingly at Marina. 'Why are *you* defending this so-called intermediary? Mmm?'

'I know very few of your friends, ma'am, so I am hardly in a position to defend them. I was thinking only that, since the debt has caused so much difficulty with... between yourself and the Earl, it was a blessing that it no longer had to be paid.'

'Blessing? Believe me, my girl, it is no blessing to be beholden to Kit Stratton.'

With that sentiment, Marina was in total agreement.

'And if the price is to permit that young ne'er-do-well to lord it over me, I shall never accept—'

The door opened. 'Earl Luce, m'lady,' announced the butler.

Lady Luce uttered a very unladylike curse.

Heavens! Now I am truly in the suds, Marina thought.

The Earl strode into his mother's drawing room with a look of grim satisfaction on his face. The Dowager eyed him with disdain as he bowed over her hand. 'Good morning, Mama,' he said politely. 'I trust I see you well.'

Without waiting for a reply, he turned to Marina and looked her up and down assessingly. 'I did not expect to find you here still, Miss…er—'

'Beaumont,' snapped the Dowager. 'I will have you know, William, that Miss Beaumont is going nowhere at *your* behest. She is worth a dozen of those milk-and-water misses by whom you set such store. And I intend that she shall stay.'

Marina's eyes widened in surprise. Did Lady Luce really mean—?

'We will discuss that later, Mama. In private,' said the Earl, so angrily that his jowls shook. He paused, took a deep breath and tried to regain control of his plain features. 'We have weightier matters to discuss at present— your little…difficulty, Mama. I know you doubted my ability to raise so much money in so short a time. But you were wrong. I have brought you a draft for twelve thousand pounds.' He patted his pocket. 'At no small inconvenience to myself, I may add. I had to go into the City to conduct the final negotiations for this loan myself—' his distaste for the whole process was very evident '—but of course I had no choice. No matter how great the burden on my estate, I could not let it be said that my mother would renege on a debt of honour.'

Marina could see that the Dowager was grinding her teeth more and more with every word he said. She waited for the inevitable explosion of wrath.

Lady Luce looked up at her son's face. He clearly thought he had gained the upper hand at last. 'You have put yourself to a vast deal of trouble, William,' she said crisply, 'and without there being the least need. I do not

need you to lecture me about honour. I suggest you take
your twelve thousand pounds and put it to good use. Buy
Charlotte a new gown. Anything would be preferable to
that puce monstrosity she was wearing t'other night.'

'But you owe—'

'I owe nothing, William,' said Lady Luce, raising her
voice a little so that the sarcastic tone was very marked.
'I no longer have a debt to Kit Stratton. I can handle my
own finances perfectly well, without interference from
you. And now, if you will excuse me—' she rose from
her chair and began to make her way to the door, her
full skirts swaying as she moved past him '—Miss Beaumont and I have an engagement this morning.'

'But I went—'

'Good day to you, William,' said the Dowager firmly,
without turning round. 'No doubt you will find your own
way out. Come, Marina.'

Marina did not dare to meet the Earl's eye. He looked
as if he was about to suffer a seizure. And no wonder.
The Dowager, it seemed, would do anything to spite her
son. Anything. Even if it meant accepting a favour from
a man she detested as much as Kit Stratton.

Chapter Eleven

There had been no engagement, of course, though Lady Luce had called for her carriage and driven around the park in order to make good on her remark to her son. And she had spent almost every moment of their outing in berating, first, her son and then Kit Stratton. It was difficult to judge which of them she hated more. Marina had guessed that it was very much a matter of timing. The Dowager had used Mr Stratton's offer to outmanoeuvre her son, without thinking about the consequences. Those would come on the morrow, when Mr Stratton called on her to return her vowel.

Marina doubted that her ladyship would be able to control her temper in the face of such provocation, even though she now had no way of repaying the debt. It would have been quite amusing, had it not been so serious for Marina herself. The problem of Sir Hugo Stratton remained. Marina had had no reply to her latest letter to Mr Kit Stratton. Perhaps he would simply ignore her pleas? After all, why should he have any desire to oblige her? She had left him with the impression that she despised him—at least, that had been her intention.

She remembered, then, that low laugh as the door was

slammed in his face. That could not be the reaction of a vindictive man.

She would have to be patient and await his response. Somehow, she was now sure that there would be one. He was not a man who would simply ignore a cry for help, especially from a lady.

How on earth did she know that? She knew nothing about him, except that he was an out-and-out rake, and that none of the matchmaking mamas would trust their daughters anywhere near him, even though he was lately become very rich indeed. The Dowager was of the firm opinion that he would be a rake until the day he died, that, since the title was settled on Sir Hugo and his sons, there was no need for Kit to set up his nursery at all. Indeed, according to the Dowager, 'twould be better so, since a ne'er-do-well such as Kit Stratton did not deserve to inherit anything at all.

Remembering how her uncle had spoken of Hugo Stratton, Marina was not surprised that provision had been made for the scapegrace youngest son. Uncle George had always said that Hugo Stratton was the most honourable and upright of men, and that he cared for those who were less fortunately circumstanced. Strange, then, that Kit should be so very different in temperament. He—

Her musings were interrupted by a sharp tap on her door with a summons from Lady Luce. She required Marina's presence in her drawing room immediately. Company had arrived.

It could not be Kit Stratton. That was certain. He was not expected until the morrow and, given the animosity between him and the Dowager, it was highly unlikely that he would set foot in her house one moment before it was necessary.

* * *

'Ah, there you are, child,' said Lady Luce as the door closed behind Marina. Her ladyship sounded remarkably amenable for once, Marina decided.

Lady Luce turned to a visitor who was concealed by the back of the sofa. 'Come in, do,' said Lady Luce again, beckoning Marina forward. 'I wish to present you to Lady Stratton.'

Lady Stratton! Sir Hugo Stratton's wife—beautiful, elegantly clad in rich blue velvet with a feathered hat perched on her golden curls—sat perfectly composed on Lady Luce's damask sofa.

Lady Luce said formally, 'You will allow me to present Miss Beaumont, who is recently become my companion. She is related to the Blaines, but her family hails from Yorkshire. I dare say London is more than a little overwhelming after all those empty moors.'

Lady Stratton smiled up at Marina and extended her hand. 'Oh, I doubt that Miss Beaumont will allow a little dirt and noise to overset her,' she said. 'Miss Beaumont, I am delighted to make your acquaintance.' She pressed Marina's hand in a way that seemed significant.

Marina frowned a little, and stared into the loveliest pair of blue eyes she had ever seen. There was nothing to be read there other than innocence—and a hint of amusement. If Lady Stratton was come as envoy for her brother-in-law—and what other reason was there?—she was not about to reveal it. Marina could not help responding to that seductive smile and the friendliness in those beautiful eyes. Maybe—

'Oh, do sit down, child,' said the Dowager testily. 'I cannot be doing with you towering over us in that way.'

Lady Stratton laughed. 'I have often wished to be taller myself, ma'am,' she said, 'for my husband mocks my lack of inches. His brother is even worse, I have to say. But then, what else is one to expect from such a rogue as Kit?'

The Dowager snorted.

Marina had by now become well used to interpreting her mistress's eloquent snorts and grunts. This time, it betokened a cynical agreement with her visitor's comments.

Lady Stratton looked, with considerable amusement, towards her hostess. Then she said, perfectly politely, 'Our families have not been much in the habit of social intercourse, ma'am. That is partly because we spend so much of our time in the country. My husband is not much taken with London Society, as you may know. However, we are fixed here for a little time and I was hoping to persuade you, ma'am, to honour us with your presence at a small musical soirée we are holding on Saturday.' At the sight of the Dowager's visible hesitation, Lady Stratton leaned forward and said, 'Oh, do say you will come. And Miss Beaumont too, of course.'

Lady Luce hesitated still, but it was clear, to Marina, that she was not immune to her elegant visitor's enormous charm. Looking shrewdly at that lovely face, the Dowager said sharply, 'Will your brother-in-law be present?'

Lady Stratton's musical laugh filled the room. 'Oh, I doubt it, ma'am. I very much doubt it. Kit does not make a habit of frequenting the salons of respectable ladies, even those to whom he is related. Besides, his presence would be like to frighten off most of my guests!'

Even Lady Luce could not contain her amusement at that. Marina frankly laughed, inspired by their visitor's open gaiety.

'Yes,' said Lady Stratton, turning towards Marina, 'an outrageous thing to say, was it not? Even if it had the merit of being true. Have you met my brother-in-law, Miss Beaumont?'

'I fear she has,' said the Dowager acidly.

'Indeed? How very interesting.'

Marina closed her eyes for a moment, praying that Lady Stratton would not pursue the point. If she discovered that Marina had visited Méchante's gambling house, she would immediately withdraw her invitation.

'Tell me,' continued Lady Stratton, smiling in a way that seemed to envelop Marina with her charm, 'what did you think of my brother?'

'I...I...' For a moment, Marina was completely at a loss. 'He is...most striking,' she stammered. 'So very tall.' Good grief! What was the matter with her? She was rambling like an idiot. 'That is...he...'

Lady Stratton reached across and laid her hand on Marina's. 'You are very tactful, Miss Beaumont, and I thank you for it, but there is no need, I assure you. I am only too well aware of Kit's shortcomings, which are many. He is certainly both tall and striking. I have known impressionable young ladies who swooned at the mere sight of him. That was before he went abroad, of course. These days, innocent young damsels are usually forbidden to look on Kit at all, lest one glimpse of those handsome features should corrupt their morals completely.'

Marina could hardly believe her ears.

The Dowager chuckled wickedly. 'Quite right, too,' she said. 'Kit is a great deal too handsome. And, by all accounts, he has a most persuasive way with the ladies. Can't say I've seen it m'self. Seems an arrogant young puppy to me. Plays a fine hand of cards, though.'

That brought Marina back to earth with a jolt.

Lady Stratton rose, drawing on her fine kid gloves. 'I

must go. It has been a pleasure to talk to you, ma'am. Kit warned me that you were both forthright and honest. I only wish there were more in London of like mind. Society affairs can be so very dull, do you not agree?' She extended her hand to Lady Luce, who was nodding in agreement. 'I may expect you on Saturday, I hope? Both of you?'

Without so much as glancing at Marina, Lady Luce said, 'Yes, ma'am. You may. And if I should chance to see that brother of yours there, I promise you that I shall not permit our morals to be corrupted in any way. Who knows, if we really tried, we might reform him.'

Smiling, Lady Stratton shook her head. 'That, I fear, is most unlikely. All London knows that Kit Stratton is quite beyond redemption.'

Kit's Chelsea housekeeper had never before set foot in one of the grand houses in the west end of London. She was not altogether sure that she should be here now, but the Baroness had been very specific in her instructions and very specific about the rewards that Mrs Budge would receive if she carried them out.

The French maid who had brought Mrs Budge up the back staircase seemed to have a very high opinion of herself, almost as if the back stairs were not good enough for her. Mrs Budge knew better. A servant was a servant. A member of the nobility—such as the Baroness von Thalberg—would always have the power to order the lives of servants and to dismiss them on a whim. No wonder, then, that poor servants had to make a shilling or two in any way they could. How else would they live when times were hard?

Mrs Budge curtsied carefully towards the Baroness's back. She was attending to her toilet at the dressing table and appeared to be applying very skilful and almost invisible make-up to her beautiful features. Her sharp eyes were watching her visitor's every move in the mirror.

At last, she put down her brush and turned on her stool. 'So, Budge,' she said, in her pretty European accent, 'what brings you here, at this hour of the morning? I very much hope it is worth the inconvenience you are causing me. I am already late for a most important engagement.'

The housekeeper did not like the menacing undertone in that low, sensuous drawl. She curtsied again. 'M'lady,' she said, a little hesitantly, 'you wanted to know about any female who came to the house. There was a woman—a lady, I should say—who came to visit the master on Saturday last—'

'And today is Friday,' interrupted the Baroness silkily. 'You have taken a remarkably long time to bring me news of it.'

'Beg pardon, m'lady, but I did not think anything of it at the time. The young lady is no beauty. The master said she had called on business and I believed him. Couldn't see no other reason for him to entertain such a plain beanpole.'

'He took her upstairs?'

'No, m'lady, no. They were in the downstairs room. Only there.'

'And what did they discuss?'

'I…I don't know, m'lady. The door is very thick, and I—'

'Spare me your lame excuses. What else *do* you know?'

'She left alone. In a hackney. There was a letter came, shortly after. I think it must have been from her. Leastwise, the master gave instructions about dealing with letters, just after she left. We don't get his letters. Not as a rule.'

The Baroness frowned in annoyance.

'Then the master brought her back again. On Wednesday morning, very early, it were.'

'And they went upstairs?' asked the Baroness again.

'No, m'lady. They were in the downstairs room for only a few minutes. Then they left again.'

'Together?'

'Yes, m'lady.'

'I see. And what is this…person's name?'

'I…I don't know, m'lady. But she has written again. That is why I came. You said you…you said you would be grateful. I have brought you the letter.'

'Ah,' said the Baroness, extending her elegant white hand.

Mrs Budge took the sealed letter from her pocket and, after a moment's hesitation, gave it to the Baroness. 'I thought…once you have read it, it can be resealed and delivered to the master,' she said quickly. 'He will think it was delayed in the post.'

The Baroness was not listening. She broke the seal without any attempt to protect the paper beneath. Spreading the sheet, she quickly scanned the few lines it contained, before turning back to Mrs Budge. 'Unfortunately, there is no signature, only initials—M.B. I wonder…'

Frustrated by that news, Mrs Budge took a step towards the dressing table, stretching out her hand to retrieve the letter. 'I am sorry there is no name, m'lady, but I have brought you all the information I have. If you would please to return the letter, I—'

The Baroness picked up the single sheet and tore it to

shreds with careful precision. Then she screwed the fragments into a ball and threw them into the fire.

Mrs Budge gasped in horror as she saw her employer's letter twist and blacken in the flames. 'M'lady—'

'The letter was not delayed in the post. It was lost. Our mysterious M.B. will wait in vain for the succour she so desperately desires. And how well served she will be.'

Mrs Budge was more than a little puzzled by those enigmatic words. What on earth could have been in that letter? It was too late to find out now. She should have opened it herself before bringing it to the Baroness. 'What shall I say to the master?' she asked weakly.

'You will say nothing. No such letter ever arrived. Does anyone else in the household know anything of it?'

'No, m'lady.'

'Very well. I am indebted to you, Budge. Wait there.' She opened a drawer in her dressing table and fumbled among the contents.

Mrs Budge waited hopefully.

'Here,' said the Baroness, dropping a single guinea into Mrs Budge's waiting palm.

Mrs Budge looked at the coin in surprise. She had expected rather more for such valuable information, especially as she was risking her place by bringing it at all.

'Your face betrays you, Budge,' said the Baroness. 'I should have been much more generous, believe me, if you had provided a name or something of their conversation. I suggest you bear that in mind for the next occasion.' She picked up a silver bell from her dressing table and rang it vigorously. 'Now you may go. Make sure that no one sees you leave. And, if you find a name for this M.B., bring it to me at once. Then, you *will* be rewarded.'

Mrs Budge swallowed hard and curtsied, tucking that single guinea into the bottom of her pocket. It was too late to wonder whether she had been wise to accept the Baroness's bribe to spy on her employer. She turned to leave. The French maid had reappeared, ready to show her out.

'Wait.' The single word was very sharp.

Mrs Budge turned back obediently, but the Baroness was paying no attention to her. She had moved to her gilded writing desk and was already dipping her pen in the standish. The housekeeper assumed she was writing a note to the master, to be delivered when he next visited Chelsea. She waited patiently. Another service meant— or should mean—a further payment.

The Baroness wrote quickly, barely pausing to consider her words. Then she folded and sealed the letter with a plain wafer. 'You will deliver this immediately, Budge, if you please.'

Mrs Budge looked at it. It was not the Baroness's usual expensive writing paper. This was much coarser to the touch. Moreover— 'But I have never heard of this place, m'lady,' she protested, without stopping to think. 'How am I to find this Mr Johnson?'

The Baroness frowned her into silence. 'That is hardly my concern,' she said silkily. 'You will take the letter to that address and deliver it personally into the hands of Mr Johnson. No one else.'

Mrs Budge nodded, waiting expectantly. This sounded much more lucrative than waiting for the master to drop information about M.B.

'You will not wait for a reply. And you will tell Mr Johnson nothing—not one word—about the identity of the sender of the letter. And nothing about yourself, either. Do you understand?'

The housekeeper nodded again. She might do precisely as the Baroness ordered, but she would also do her best to find out the identity of the mysterious Mr Johnson. She might be able to sell the information later, perhaps to the master himself.

The Baroness handed over another guinea. Mrs Budge weighed the coin in her hand, letting it be seen that she thought the amount inadequate.

'There will be a further payment once the letter has been safely delivered.'

'But if I am not to wait for a reply, m'lady, how will you know that—'

The Baroness smiled very slowly. It was a little frightening. 'There is no need to concern yourself about that, Budge. I shall know for certain soon. Oh, yes. Very soon. And so, I fancy, will M.B.'

'Mr Stratton has called, m'lady.'

The Dowager, dressed very carefully in her widest and most imposing hoops, sat rigid in her chair. 'Show him in, Tibbs.'

Rising automatically, Marina discovered that her legs were shaking beneath her. She gripped the back of a chair with both hands until she had enough control to stand unaided. Kit Stratton must not see how much his presence affected her. She tried to fix a polite smile on her face.

'Mr Stratton, m'lady,' announced the butler, as he threw open the door.

Kit Stratton strode into the room, his tall, commanding figure seeming to dwarf everything around him. His bow to the Dowager was masterly. His bow to Marina—a little less deep, a little less slow—had a hint of irony in it.

The Dowager nodded slightly in acknowledgement of his salutation but she said nothing. She did not offer refreshments. Nor did she attempt to break the awkward silence that reigned in her drawing room.

He looked down on her tiny figure with the hint of a smile twisting one corner of his mouth. 'I am come in the matter of your debt, ma'am, as we agreed a se'enight ago. It was twelve thousand pounds, I believe?'

A slight blush began on the Dowager's scrawny neck. She looked away for a moment and then resumed her rigid stare. Still, she said nothing.

Kit Stratton withdrew a paper from an inside pocket of his beautifully tailored corbeau coat. He unfolded it, scanned it for a second, and then laid it on the table at the Dowager's hand. 'Your vowel, ma'am,' he said simply.

Lady Luce looked at him with distaste.

He was waiting for her answer. He might have decided to forgive the debt but he was clearly seeking a modicum of contrition from his opponent. Marina could see that his little smile was becoming more pronounced, as was Lady Luce's flush of embarrassment.

The Dowager reached out and picked up the vowel, crushing it into a ball with her wizened fingers. 'I am beholden to you, sir,' she said, with a tiny nod of acknowledgement.

Marina was willing the Dowager to say what was necessary to persuade Kit Stratton to leave. It would take only a few well-chosen words.

Say them, Marina prayed. Please say them.

Lady Luce said nothing.

Mr Stratton almost laughed. It was not a pleasant

sound. 'You are indeed beholden to me, ma'am,' he said. It was not exactly a threat, but…

'Twelve thousand pounds,' said Lady Luce at last, in strangled tones.

'Indeed,' he said, waiting.

'You are well aware that I do not have the money to pay you, sir.' The words sounded as though they had been forced from the Dowager's lips. The flush had vanished. She was now extremely pale under her heavy make-up.

Now he smiled. It was a very superior smile. 'I am perfectly well aware of that, ma'am, though I am pleased that you find yourself able to acknowledge it. I do not propose to demand payment from you. You have your vowel. The debt is at an end.'

Marina sensed that the Dowager was itching to strike his arrogant face. She seemed to be keeping her seat with difficulty.

He calmly turned away from Lady Luce and looked at Marina. 'I hope I see you well, ma'am, and that you are settling in since we last met—' Marina held her breath '—at Méchante's.'

'She will do very well,' said an acid voice from behind him. The Dowager had risen from her chair, clearly annoyed that he should even notice her companion. 'What I wish to know now, young man,' continued the Dowager, having regained his attention, 'is the identity of this *intermediary* you have the effrontery to mention. I gave no one leave to intervene on my behalf and I shall remonstrate with him at the first opportunity.'

'Shall you?' he said silkily.

Behind him, Marina quaked. Surely Mr Stratton would not betray her? Please.

'You will find that rather difficult, I fear,' he continued, 'because I have absolutely no intention of revealing his identity to you. I must have some recompense—must I not?—for the loss of twelve thousand pounds.'

The Dowager was so shocked that her mouth fell open in a most unladylike manner.

Marina felt a little bubble of laughter rising in her throat, but she crushed it before it could burst forth. So much for the Dowager's attempt to enter the lists against Mr Stratton. She had been unhorsed at the first pass and now lay winded at his feet.

'And now I must leave you, ma'am. No doubt we shall meet again at Méchante's.'

The Dowager seemed still incapable of speech.

He turned to Marina once more. 'Perhaps you would be so good as to show me to the door, ma'am?'

Marina's eyes widened, but the Dowager, recovering a little now, nodded angrily. 'Show him out, gel. Show him out, do. This ridiculous interview has gone on quite long enough.' Deliberately, she turned her back and marched across to her chair by the window.

He smiled knowingly and moved to open the door for Marina.

'Thank you, sir,' she said, a little breathlessly, waiting for the door to close behind them. She had only a few seconds to thank him for intervening with his brother to save her from disgrace—and no time at all to choose her words. 'Mr Stratton,' she said in a soft, urgent voice, 'I must thank you for responding so promptly to my letter. I am very much in your debt.'

Kit frowned. She was in his debt over the Dowager's vowel, but not over his response to her letter. That had been far from generous. What was she about, to say such a thing? Of course, now that he had formally forgiven the Dowager's debt, he no longer had any hold over the

companion, but it was the outside of enough for her to
take him to task about it with such sly, double-edged
words.

Kit looked down at her, hard. She had an air of innocence about her, which made him suddenly very angry. He had forgiven this debt out of regard for her courage…and perhaps her innocence. The words she had just
spoken were very far from innocent.

But he could not rail at her in Lady Luce's hallway,
however much she might deserve it.

Forcing himself to assume a bland, neutral tone, he
said, 'I am not in the habit of allowing ladies to remain
in debt to me, ma'am.'

Her immediate response was a fiery blush. And she
would no longer meet his eyes. Kit cursed silently. How
could he have made such a thoughtless remark? Not
even her devious words could justify what he had said.
He seemed to be losing his touch where Miss Beaumont
was concerned. She was bound to imagine he was referring to the crude price he had earlier demanded of
her. It would matter not a jot that he had told her, in
terms, that he had no intention of bedding her. And it
was even more unthinkable now that she was under his
family's protection. Surely she had the wit to understand
that?

'You need have no concerns on that score, ma'am,'
he said, rather more curtly that he had intended. 'There
are no debts between us. You should know that very
well.'

The blush had faded to a spot of heat on each cheek.
It reminded Kit that her skin was as flawless as a perfect
peach. His hand rose, almost of its own volition—

She stepped back smartly. His questing fingers met
only thin air.

'You are very direct, sir,' she said, her gaze fixed on a spot somewhere beyond his shoulder. 'And on certain points I fear we do not agree. As a gentleman, you must allow a lady to reach her own conclusions on indebtedness. Must you not?'

Kit bristled. 'I—'

The butler appeared at the foot of the staircase. Private conversation of any kind became impossible. Kit took her hand and began to raise it as if for a kiss, but then stopped with deliberate rudeness. 'You are too kind, ma'am. And now, I will bid you good day. The butler will show me out.' With a tiny bow, he walked nonchalantly down the staircase where he retrieved his hat and gloves, and left without a single backward glance.

Chapter Twelve

'Tell my woman to fetch down my plain evening cloak, Tibbs.' The butler bowed. 'And have the carriage brought round immediately.'

'At once, m'lady.'

Marina had risen from her seat on the stool by the Dowager's favourite chair.

'Where are you going, miss?'

'I thought to fetch my bonnet and pelisse, ma'am, since you have ordered the carriage.'

Lady Luce looked narrowly up at Marina. 'Sit down,' she said curtly. 'That will not be necessary. I shall not need you this evening.'

'Oh,' said Marina, wonderingly. It would be impolite to say anything more, however much curiosity she might feel.

The Dowager was not fooled. 'I congratulate you on your restraint, Marina. Unfortunately for you, your face is too expressive. Yes, I am going to Méchante's. And, no, I am not permitting you to go there again. It is not a fit place for a young lady such as you.'

'But a week ago—'

'A week ago, certain people required to be taught a

lesson,' she said forthrightly. 'I do not believe in be-labouring a point, once it has been taken. Even to William,' she added, perhaps a little untruthfully. Marina had noticed that the Dowager did not seem to mind how often she scored the same points against her son.

'There you are at last, Gibson,' said the Dowager sharply as her aged abigail entered the room, carrying the cloak which she immediately began to arrange around her mistress's shoulders. 'Now, while I am out this evening, I wish you and Miss Beaumont to work on the gown you were making earlier today. If it is to be wearable by tomorrow, you will both have much to do.'

'Yes, m'lady. I shall fetch it at once.' The abigail curtsied herself out, but not before the Dowager had added, to her retreating back, 'And do not forget what else I told you to do, Gibson. I am expecting to see a distinct improvement there, remember.'

Marina was following none of this. What on earth was going on?

It was too late to ask. Tibbs had arrived to conduct the Dowager to her carriage.

The abigail returned carrying her own workbox, and Marina's, too. 'I took the liberty of bringing this down for you, miss,' she smiled, the wrinkles on her cheeks very pronounced. 'Save you the trouble.'

'That was kind of you, Gibson,' said Marina, her eyes caught by the gown that was draped over the abigail's arm. It could not be one of the Dowager's. It was much too flimsy and stylish. And the colour was ravishing—a subtle shade of peach, shot with pale gold.

Gibson settled herself comfortably on the settee, clearly relishing the privilege of using the Dowager's drawing room. 'We can work here for the moment, miss, since the light is better. We can go up to your room later, so that you can try it on.'

Try it on? Marina had to swallow hard before she could speak. 'This gown is for me?'

'Why, yes, miss. Did her ladyship not tell you?' At Marina's shake of the head, she said, with a wry smile, 'Her ladyship does enjoy her little jokes.' She looked Marina up and down with her shrewd old eyes. 'I doubt it will take too long. Not with two of us to do the stitching. It wants but the setting of the sleeves and the flounce around the hem.' She opened her workbox and began to search for matching thread. 'Now, if it had been a gown in the old style, we should have been here for days. I know that these newfangled fashions can be very revealing, but they are much, much easier to sew.'

Marina could only nod.

'And with your figure, miss, this simple cut will be ideal. You wait and see. I promise you will be amazed at what I shall do for you.'

'Good evening, Kit.'

Kit was not surprised to be met by Méchante, almost on the doorstep. She had an uncanny knack of knowing exactly who was in her gaming house and where she was likely to be least welcome. After his last rejection of her advances, he should have known to expect a further assault, the moment he set foot in her house again. She was not a good loser.

He forced himself to smile down at her. 'My dear Méchante,' he said in a light, playful tone, 'how delightful to be welcomed by one's hostess. On the doorstep, no less. To what do I owe this singular honour?'

She smiled up at him with glowingly sensuous green

eyes. She was trying very hard to provoke a reaction. She seemed to need to prove that she could.

He continued to smile with the same studied friend-liness. She did not light even the tiniest spark of desire. She must know it, too. He caught the moment when her expression changed from seduction to calculation.

'Are you for Faro tonight, Kit?' she said abruptly. 'Your favourite opponent is here.'

Kit raised an eyebrow. 'Is she, indeed?' He did not need a name to know precisely who was meant by Mé-chante's remark. 'I must own I am a little surprised, considering…'

Méchante laughed. It was a rather brittle sound. 'Con-sidering that she has only just rid herself of last week's debts. Was that what you were about to say?'

Kit gave a tiny shake of his head. 'No. I was not about to say anything of the kind. If you wish for information about my dealings with the Dowager, you must address your questions to her, and not to me.'

Méchante tried again. 'Come, Kit. You can tell me, can't you? After all, it was in my house that the debt was incurred.'

He shook his head again, more forcefully this time. 'No. If she wishes you to know, she will—no doubt—tell you.'

'Oh, very well,' Méchante said testily. 'But if you wish to enter the lists against her in future, I shall insist on knowing everything. From now on, that is a condition of entry to my house—devised especially for you, Kit.'

He bowed slightly. 'I shall—of course—take note of your wishes, though I do not promise to frequent your house if you insist on such terms. As it happens, I have no intention of playing Faro tonight. It is a night for skill, I fancy. A simple hand of piquet will suffice. Will you join me?'

'Thank you, but no. Piquet is not my game. I wish you good fortune.' With an elegant curtsy, she led the way up the staircase to the landing and disappeared into the hubbub of noisy guests in the main reception room.

Kit strolled thoughtfully up the stairs, looking around him. There was no one about. The upstairs hallway was empty. The piquet room was beyond the main reception room. He looked towards the door to the Faro rooms. It was closed. He paused with his hand on the newel post. He might just stroll in to see how the game was progressing. If Lady Luce was there, he would resist the temptation to take a hand against her. She would be desperate to challenge him, and even more desperate to win, but it would not do to indulge her.

The first Faro chamber was empty. Surprising, Kit thought. Normally, both tables would be full. He strolled through to the inner chamber. There, every chair was taken. Lady Luce was seated immediately opposite the banker, a man Kit did not know. Judging by the pile of coin in front of her, she had been winning. She was not 'Lady Lose' on this occasion.

Kit propped himself casually against the side of the archway, watching the play. The game would soon be over.

As soon as the last card had been dealt, a player at the far end of the table hailed Kit with a drunken wave. 'Kit, old fellow. Won't you join us? Just the sort of man I like to play against. Generosity itself, what?'

Lady Luce's shoulders tensed visibly but she did not turn round. She seemed to be studying her fingernails.

Kit moved across to the table and leant a hip against it, spreading the fingers of one lean hand on the green baize, only inches from the Dowager's elbow. 'Not to-night, I thank you,' he drawled. He paused, watching Lady Luce's rigid figure. She seemed determined to ignore him. He would not permit that.

'Good evening, ma'am,' he said in a voice of the utmost politeness, but without altering his careless stance. 'I note that you appear to be rather more successful this evening than…on previous occasions.'

The Dowager raised her head a little and looked sideways at him through her lashes. 'Good evening, Mr Stratton,' she said sourly. 'You are not prepared to hazard your reputation at the Faro table, I collect?'

'I see no need, ma'am. I have nothing to prove there. *My* reputation is safe enough.'

'Indeed?' said Lady Luce with a tight smile. 'I had heard—' She broke off, looking round at each of the players in turn, gathering their attention. In the sudden hush, she said, 'I had heard that, in the matter of fidelity at least, reputations were becoming…just a little tarnished.'

What on earth did she mean by that? What could she have heard? The slight murmurings around the table suggested that the rumours—whatever they were—had already gone beyond the Dowager.

Slowly, Kit straightened, making her a tiny, mocking bow. She really was a very small woman. 'I have no doubt, ma'am, that the application of a sufficient quantity of gold will restore any lustre that may be missing. You need have no concern on that account. I will bid you good evening.' Before she could reply, he turned his back and sauntered out of the room.

On the far side of the archway, Méchante was standing, holding a glass of champagne and smiling with satisfaction.

Kit nodded towards her and continued on his way. He refused to let either of those confounded women see even a hint of weakness.

But underneath Kit's studied nonchalance, his fury was mounting. Lady Luce had suggested he was being unfaithful to Katharina. How dare she? It seemed that the old harridan would stop at nothing to inflict injury on Kit, even downright untruths. He had *not* been unfaithful to his Baroness, except— Miss Beaumont. That must be it. The Dowager must have learned about his clandestine meetings with Miss Beaumont and put her own interpretation on them. It was extraordinary, but what other explanation could there be? He would need to find a way of quashing the rumours before Katharina heard them, as she doubtless would. Lady Luce must be persuaded to—

No. Lady Luce was not the person most at fault in this case. Hugo had been sworn to secrecy on the subject of those meetings. Apart from him, no one knew that Miss Beaumont had visited Kit. There was only one possible source of the rumour that the Dowager had been spreading—Miss Beaumont herself.

If the woman had been naïve enough to confide in the Dowager, she would soon learn to regret her lack of discretion. And Kit would take the greatest pleasure in telling her exactly how foolish she had been.

'She is to play later. And to sing. She is not in the least retiring in that respect. I fancy she may be quite accomplished. She looks remarkably well this evening, too. Do you not agree, Hugo?'

Following his wife's gaze, Hugo murmured something that could have been assent. 'Something different about

her. Cannot quite put my finger on it. She looks…
younger.' His voice had a questioning note.

'Men,' said Emma with a laugh. 'Of course she looks
different. She has a new hairstyle. Much more flattering
than that tight knot she used to wear.'

'You are probably right, m'dear,' agreed Hugo. 'She
is not exactly handsome, but she looks like a woman of
breeding. Something to do with the way she holds herself, I fancy. She will turn heads, in spite of her lack of
conventional beauty. Pity she is so tall.'

Emma nodded slightly. 'I am too short, and she is too
tall. There is no pleasing you gentlemen. However, you
are right. There are very few gentlemen here who would
be tall enough to look her in the eye.'

Hugo chuckled wickedly. 'What you need, my dear,
is a visit from brother Kit.'

'Heavens, no! If Kit were to show his face here, half
the ladies would faint from shock and my reputation
would be in shreds.'

'Are you sure?' said Hugo softly.

Emma closed her eyes and nodded, as if the picture
was too painful to contemplate.

'In that case, my love, I suggest you prepare to be
shredded, for your brother-in-law has just walked
through the door.'

Emma's softly voiced cry of 'Oh, no!' was the only
sound to be heard in the sudden and complete hush per-
vading the huge white and gold reception room of Fitzwilliam House.

Kit Stratton stood in the open doorway surveying the
assembled company as if his arrival were the most natural thing in the world. He was wearing immaculate
black evening dress, with no jewellery save for a gold
pin in his intricate neckcloth. He looked bored. He did

not smile even when his eye lit upon his brother and his beautiful sister-in-law. He strolled easily across the crowded room, the guests standing aside to make way for him. Some of the older ladies stepped back very smartly indeed, as if afraid that his nearness might taint them. Kit appeared not to notice.

He bowed gracefully to Emma and then raised her hand to his lips. 'My dear Emma,' he said, 'my apologies for arriving so late. I trust I have not disrupted your entertainment?'

Emma frowned warningly at him, but Kit was not in a mood to accept her hints. 'I am surprised that you have chosen to attend such a dull affair, Kit,' she said smoothly as he let go of her hand.

Over her shoulder, Hugo added, in a voice intended for Emma and Kit alone, 'Especially as Emma definitely did not invite you, brother.'

Kit suppressed a smile. 'Perhaps you would care to introduce me to some of your guests, Emma?' He knew that her immediate reaction would be confusion. She would be well aware that many of her guests would be affronted to have Kit Stratton presented to them.

But Emma was more than ready to pick up the gauntlet that Kit had thrown down. 'I am sure, dear brother,' she said, 'that I shall be able to present you to some of my guests, at least.' She tucked her hand through his arm. 'Come.'

Kit glanced sideways to see that Hugo had a very knowing look on his face. He clearly believed that his wife would have the better of Kit in this encounter.

Emma led Kit directly to Lady Luce, whose tiny figure had been hidden by those around her. He had barely a few seconds to compose his features. After last night's

little encounter, it was unlikely that the Dowager would
be in the mood for exchanging polite nothings.

The grey companion seemed to be missing on this
occasion, which was a pity. Kit had hoped that Emma's
soirée would provide him with an opportunity to confront Miss Beaumont with what she had done. He had
determined that she would not learn just how furious her
indiscretions had made him. After all, she had probably
done more harm to her own reputation than to his. None
the less, he did not care for any woman to make free
with his name or to interfere in his private life.

'Ma'am, I think you are already acquainted with my
brother-in-law, Mr Stratton?'

Lady Luce frowned up at Kit's bland countenance.
'So, young man, you have decided to create another
scandal, have you?'

Kit bowed without a word.

'You should be ashamed of yourself,' continued the
Dowager. 'Half your sister's guests will be finding that
they suddenly have pressing engagements elsewhere.
You will ruin her party. You mark my words. Is that not
so, Lady Blaine?' she added, half turning to her companion.

Lady Blaine tried to look down her long nose at Kit.

'You will allow me to present Mr Kit Stratton,' said
the Dowager mischievously, visibly relishing Lady
Blaine's discomfiture. In normal circumstances, Lady
Blaine would never have permitted such an introduction.

Kit reached forward and impudently took Lady
Blaine's hand, raising it as if for a gallant kiss. He re-
stricted himself to another elegant bow. 'Delighted,
ma'am,' he said coolly.

'Mr Stratton,' said Lady Blaine, in the coldest, most
arrogant voice he had heard in years. 'Ma'am,' she went

on, turning back to Lady Luce, 'as it happens, I do have another engagement—'

'Balderdash,' said Lady Luce rudely. 'This is a musical soirée and the entertainment has barely begun. You cannot leave just because this young…ne'er-do-well has appeared uninvited.'

Kit was having difficulty in keeping his face straight. He did not dare to meet Emma's eye. Lady Blaine looked as if someone had placed a bad smell right under her nose.

'Besides,' continued Lady Luce, 'did you not say that your Tilly was about to perform? I do hope she is in good voice. Can't abide those screeching females who never know when to stop.' She looked round for the young lady in question. Everyone else followed suit.

Miss Blaine was standing by the instrument, dressed in a white muslin gown that was not in the least flattering to either her complexion or her thin figure. Her eyes were wide. She was absolutely immobile, as if she were transfixed by a beautiful vision. And her gaze was resting adoringly on Kit. It was a look he had seen too many times, on too many impressionable young females.

'Not sure that she looks capable of performing,' said the Dowager loudly. 'Looks to me as if she were about to swoon…or perhaps she is wandering in her wits.'

Lady Blaine choked and started across the room towards her daughter, but it was too late. Too many of the guests had heard Lady Luce's caustic words and had turned to look. A low murmuring had begun. In a few hours, the tale of Miss Blaine's infatuation would be all over London. Only the young lady herself seemed oblivious to what was going on in the room. She continued to gaze wide-eyed at Kit. Her lips had fallen open on a tiny sigh of delight.

Her mother took her by the shoulders, giving her a little shake. Her low angry words were inaudible but their effect on Miss Blaine was clear. She flushed bright red, hanging her head as her mother ushered her out.

Lady Luce snorted eloquently. 'Can't abide missish females with highty-tighty mothers,' she said, 'especially ones who never seem to lose at the card table.'

Emma quickly looked away, trying—Kit fancied—to hide her amusement. 'Excuse me, ma'am,' she said. 'I must find someone to take Miss Blaine's place. She was just about to sing.'

'Oh, Marina will do that,' said the Dowager airily, stopping Emma with a hand on her arm. 'She won't disgrace me, I promise you that. Where on earth has she got to?'

Marina? A most unusual name. Could she be referring to the grey companion? Kit had never learned Miss Beaumont's given name. But her initial was certainly M.

Emma was looking round the room. After a moment, she pointed with her fan. 'Over there, ma'am. If you will excuse me, I will go and ask her if she will favour us with some music now, rather than later.'

Kit watched Emma make her way through the press of guests, with a word here and a touch there to clear her path. She had the happy knack of charming everyone, almost without effort. Hugo was a lucky man.

Emma stopped beside a tall lady who was almost completely hidden by a pillar. She was dressed in a kind of filmy creation of pinkish-gold, with dark hair dressed high on her head, making her appear even taller. After a moment, she stepped out and, moving with exquisite grace, made her way calmly across to the instrument. Kit could not take his eyes from her. She seemed to be floating across the room.

It was only when she sat down at the instrument that the light fell full on her face. The Dowager's grey companion was not beautiful. But there was something about her that drew the eye. She looked…

Kit could not find the right words. He was seeing something in Miss Beaumont that, for all his experience, he had overlooked before. It was very strange.

And then she began to play.

Chapter Thirteen

Miss Beaumont played beautifully. Under her fingers, the instrument seemed to sing. Kit found her performance strangely moving, though he was careful to ensure that anyone watching him would conclude that he was thoroughly bored. It would do no good for Miss Beaumont's reputation if the polite world suspected that Kit Stratton had even the slightest interest in her.

It was rather more difficult to maintain that bland façade when she began to sing, for her voice was even more remarkable than her playing. He tried to remember whether her speaking voice had had that mellifluous, caressing quality. He did not think so. It had been low, cultured, pleasing—but it had not touched a chord in him in the way her singing voice now did. Was it because of what she sang? He was not sure. Both the words and the simple melody were new to him. She sang of the beauty of nature, of wild open spaces—like her home in Yorkshire, he supposed—and of the joy of being alive. He felt he could smell the heather on the moors as she sang. And she looked almost beautiful, too, seemingly transfigured by the simple act of making music. He would hardly have believed it possible. All thought of berating her vanished from his mind.

Emma took his arm as the first song ended. 'How can you, Kit? You are listening to the most ravishing performance you are ever like to hear, and you make no attempt to hide your boredom. Do you have a tin ear? Or are you merely a barbarian?'

Kit looked down into Emma's teasing face. He must not admit the truth, even to her. There were too many people around who might overhear. On the other hand, he was not prepared to lie about the beauty of Miss Beaumont's singing. That would be unworthy. 'Apologies, m'dear,' he said absently. 'I fear my thoughts were quite elsewhere. I was not listening. But if you tell me that Miss er…that the lady's performance was ravishing, I shall of course agree with you. It would be ungentlemanly to do otherwise.'

Emma rapped her fan across his knuckles. 'Ungentlemanly, indeed!' she said, trying not to laugh. 'The lady's name is Beaumont, Kit, since you appear to have forgotten. And you really should not attend musical evenings if you are not prepared to *try* to listen to the performances.'

Kit bowed, trying to appear suitably contrite.

Emma was not taken in. 'For your penance, brother dear, you shall stand by my side for Miss Beaumont's next song. And, at the end of it, I shall expect you to give me a considered opinion on both the music and its performer.'

Kit groaned theatrically but did not attempt to escape. He leaned back slightly against the pillar, feigning a lack of interest that he did not feel.

Miss Beaumont's second song was quite different from the first. It was an Italian ballad that had been much

in vogue in Vienna, though Miss Beaumont—Marina?—
adopted a considerably faster tempo than had been usual
in Austria. The added pace seemed to turn it into a different piece altogether—gay, infectious and bursting
with life. Kit wondered whether Miss Beaumont knew
how much of her inner self she was exposing by singing
as she did. Underneath the prim, proper and rather serious exterior of the companion, there was a completely
different person, a woman full of joy and laughter.

As he listened, rapt, Kit decided that this other Miss
Beaumont needed to be brought out into the light of day.
The stern Miss Beaumont appeared never to laugh. It
was time that she learned.

Marina bowed her head in acknowledgement of the
applause. She knew she had performed well, in spite of
her relative lack of practice since arriving in London.
She had been taking a chance on that first song, but it
was unlikely that anyone in polite Society would ask her
about it. They would not wish to admit that they did not
recognise it. Marina smiled to herself, just a little. It had
been Grandmama's favourite song, written especially for
her, and Marina had every right to sing it whenever, and
wherever, she might choose.

Lady Stratton came to join her as she rose to leave
the instrument. 'Miss Beaumont, that was delightful,'
she said, pressing Marina's hand. 'I cannot tell you how
moving it was. Even Kit was touched by the power of
your song.'

Marina followed her hostess's glance. Kit Stratton was
still leaning carelessly against a pillar, as he had been
throughout Marina's performance. He had looked anything but moved. Every time Marina had looked in his
direction—and she had tried very hard to resist the temp-

tation—he had seemed to be resigned to enduring a far from pleasurable experience.

Marina's doubts must have been obvious, for Lady Stratton said impulsively, 'You do not believe me? Come. You shall hear it for yourself.' She put her hand through Marina's arm and steered her across the room to where Kit was standing.

Marina swallowed hard and steeled herself to greet him with easy politeness. He straightened as the pair approached.

'Kit,' began Lady Stratton, 'I was just telling Miss Beaumont how much you had enjoyed her singing. I fear she was not convinced.'

Mr Stratton looked narrowly at his sister-in-law. Marina felt instinctively that he did not welcome her arrival at all.

'Miss Beaumont,' he said with a tiny bow, 'I congratulate you on your performance. I have never heard that Italian piece performed in quite that way before. Most…diverting.'

Marina had not truly expected effusive praise from Mr Stratton but, in this case, she would have preferred it if he had said nothing at all. His manner was more than a little condescending. She might owe him thanks for swearing his brother to silence about their meeting in the park, but she would not permit him to treat her with disdain. He acted in that way with all his other women— if Lady Luce was to be believed—but Marina was not prepared to become one of their number. Mr Stratton must be made to realise that.

Lady Stratton forestalled Marina's reply. 'Oh, dear. My Aunt Warenne is signalling to me. I fear that can only mean that she has detected something amiss with my arrangements.' She smiled warmly at Marina. 'Pray excuse me, Miss Beaumont. I am sure I can trust Kit to entertain you in my absence.'

An awkward silence ensued while Marina tried to think of an excuse to leave. It would appear unpardonably rude if she simply deserted him. Yet—

'May I ask you about that first song you sang, Miss Beaumont? My education must be much at fault, for I cannot say that I remember hearing it before.'

Oh, dear. What could she possibly say? If she told him that she was the composer, good manners would force him to compliment her on her talent, even though it would be a downright lie. She could imagine exactly how he would behave—in that insufferably superior way of his, assessing whether she merited the attention that the great Kit Stratton was bestowing on her, deciding whether she was worth bedding.

Heavens! What had made her think of that?

It was the way he was looking at her. His gaze was intent. His eyes were much bluer than she had remembered. In the gloom of the carriage, she had seen little. Here in the light of dozens of candles, it was different— quite, quite different. He could not attack her here, in the sight of all his sister's guests.

Marina found that she had raised her hand to her lips, as if reminding herself of how it had felt to be kissed by Kit Stratton. How could she have done such a thing? With all his vast experience of women, he was bound to be able to read her every move. Marina began to feel very hot, in spite of her low-cut gown. She hurriedly clasped her hands together, where they could do no more mischief. She felt the heat rising up her neck. She must…must think of some way of replying to him.

Mr Stratton was all chilly politeness. 'Are you quite well, ma'am?' he said evenly, ignoring her lack of response. 'It is very hot in this room. Perhaps you would like a little air?'

Was he proposing to escort her outside? Surely not. Publicly agreeing to a tête-à-tête with Kit Stratton would ruin her for ever. 'I…I am quite well, sir, I thank you.' She had regained control of her voice at last, thank goodness. 'And I do not think it will be necessary for me to take the air.'

'No?' He frowned briefly. 'I find myself wondering if it is the air or the company to which you object, ma'am.'

Marina's eyes widened. Surely a rake could not be insulted by a lady's refusal to be alone with him? But it seemed that he was. He had stiffened quite perceptibly.

Without thinking what she was doing, Marina reached out and laid a consoling hand on the smooth cloth of his evening coat.

It was as if her fingers had touched a living flame.

She jerked her hand away with a gasp. Under that silken exterior, there were tense muscles and warm, breathing flesh. She felt she had reached through to his naked skin.

This time, she blushed to the roots of her hair. Her whole body seemed to be on fire. She could hardly breathe.

He, of course, was fully in control. Confound him!

After a moment, he bowed with impeccable politeness and said, 'Will you allow me to fetch you something to drink?'

'I…I am a little thirsty after singing,' she said at last.

He nodded. 'Champagne?'

Wordlessly, she shook her head. Her fingers were twisting at her ring, as usual.

'No, perhaps not. Lemonade, then. Excuse me for a moment.'

Marina was left alone, trying to marshal her wayward thoughts. Being close to Kit Stratton was very dangerous. He was temptation. She could not stop thinking about the feel of his body, and the touch of his lips on hers. In spite of herself, she had wanted it to happen all over again. Here! It was madness. This was a man who had mistresses by the dozen, the most beautiful women in Europe. His only reason for kissing Marina had been to prove that he could, and that she could not help but respond to him.

It was not Kit, but his brother who came to join her. She tried to be glad of it. Kit Stratton was handsome, charming, but cold as ice. Ladies made fools of themselves over his perfect face, as Miss Blaine had done earlier. At least Marina had not done that.

'Miss Beaumont,' said Sir Hugo genially, handing her a goblet of cool lemonade, 'you will forgive me, I hope, for taking my brother's place. I wished very much to have a moment alone with you this evening, to tell you how much I valued your uncle's friendship. And your father's, too, though I did not know him so well. I had hoped to write to your mother after the battle but it…it did not prove possible. I hope you will believe that I am most heartily sorry for it. Tell me if you will, how does your mother go on? And you have a younger brother, too, I understand?'

'A most interesting evening—even without the Baroness. I must say, child, that you performed very well indeed. Everyone said so.'

Marina was not paying attention. The Dowager's remark provoked her into betraying her thoughts. 'Everyone except Mr Stratton,' she said sharply. In an attempt to retrieve her slip, she added hastily, 'I cannot think why he attended a musical soirée in the first place. He was obviously bored throughout. He did not even have the good manners to pretend to be entertained.'

The Dowager looked hard at Marina but said nothing for a moment. Then she changed the subject. 'I noticed you were deep in conversation with Sir Hugo. He was most taken with your performance. Heard him say so m'self.'

'He was most kind, ma'am. He spoke to me of my father, and of my uncle, who was his great friend. He said that he had always been sorry to have lost touch with Uncle George's family. He plans to write to Mama and—oh, ma'am, he says he should be able to offer Harry a living, once he is ordained. You cannot imagine how much that could mean to us. It is quite wonderful.'

The Dowager raised her eyebrows. 'Thought your brother already had the offer of a living,' she said flatly, 'from his London clergyman friend. His wife wrote to you, did she not?'

Heavens! Why had she ever told that stupid lie? 'The family have left London for the present. Did I not mention it, ma'am?' Marina began, cudgelling her brain for a plausible story. 'And it…it was not exactly an offer. There was no definite promise of a living, though there was a…a vague hope of something. Whereas Sir Hugo's offer,' she continued more confidently, 'is real. I have Sir Hugo's permission to write to tell Mama—and Harry—at once. I shall do so the moment we reach home.'

Emma sank into her favourite chair with a sigh of relief and closed her eyes for a brief moment.

Hugo smiled lovingly down at her. 'Your evening was a great success, my love,' he said. 'I am sure you could become one of Society's foremost hostesses if you chose.'

Emma looked sceptically up at him. 'That is not what Aunt Augusta thinks, I may tell you, Hugo. She blamed me for Tilly Blaine's outrageous behaviour. Insisted that I do something about it. Though what that was supposed to be, when the girl's mother was standing by, I cannot imagine.'

'Your Aunt Warenne was, no doubt, somewhat put out by Kit's arrival. You were lucky she did not insist on showing you the door, Kit.'

Kit turned back from the window where he had been idly watching the carriages below in the light of the flambeaux. He grinned at them. 'Emma's Aunt Warenne terrifies most men, I admit, but I have found that she mellows on closer acquaintance.'

Emma groaned. 'Even Aunt Augusta is not proof against your brother, Hugo. He should be locked up. He is a danger to womankind.'

Kit bowed ironically. 'I take that as a compliment, sister dear.'

Emma tried to look stern, but failed. 'Oh, stuff!' she cried inelegantly. 'Seriously, though, Kit, what am I supposed to do if chits like Tilly Blaine swoon at the very sight of you?'

'Ignore them,' he replied harshly. 'As I do. After a few moments on a cold hard floor, they tend to come to their senses.'

Emma shook her head despairingly. 'You have no heart, Kit Stratton. One day, perhaps, you too will discover how it feels to admire someone who does not return your regard. And you will be well served.'

'If I have no heart, as you suggest, my dear Emma, I will be unable to experience any such thing.'

Emma's response sounded remarkably like a growl. 'I never could abide logic-chopping gentlemen.'

Hugo grinned at his brother. 'I suggest you pour Emma a glass of wine, Kit. Perhaps if you present it to her on bended knee, she may be persuaded to forgive your impertinence.'

Kit laughed. 'The wine, by all means,' he said, pouring three glasses and carrying one to Emma.

She looked up at him, waiting, but he did not kneel. He gave her a dandy's exaggerated bow instead. She shook her head and took the glass from him. 'Hugo should have learned by now that you never take his advice, however good it may be.'

'Nonsense,' said Kit roundly. 'He advised me to attend your soirée, and I did so.'

'What? Hugo, you—!'

'And I am heartily glad that I did. It was a most entertaining evening. I found some of the music beautiful…in spite of my tin ear.'

Emma was looking daggers at her husband, who was trying to appear a picture of innocence.

Kit grinned wickedly. 'Come, dear sister, do not be angry. Hugo was only trying to reconcile Society to my outrageous behaviour. He appears to believe—I cannot imagine why—that they may be prepared to accept me if I do the pretty at gatherings like these.'

'Society will accept any single man with a good pedigree and a substantial income,' said Hugo cynically. 'Now that you are become so much more eligible, your notorious affairs will simply be viewed as youthful indiscretions.'

Kit said nothing, though he knew it was true. His recently acquired wealth had made a world of difference.

Emma sipped her wine thoughtfully. 'And do you plan to fulfil Society's expectations, Kit?'

'In the matter of a wife, do you mean?'

Emma coloured a little at his blunt reply. 'Yes, I suppose I do. You used to say—'

'I used to say that I had no intention of marrying. Displays like Miss Blaine's have done nothing to change my mind. How could any man wish to shackle himself to such a silly chit?'

'Perhaps you would not think so harshly of her if she were a beauty. It really is not her fault that she is thin and plain, you know.'

'That may be true, but she need not accentuate her lack of looks in the way she does. A woman may be thin and plain, and yet look remarkably well.'

Emma looked up at him with her head on one side. 'You are referring to the musical Miss Beaumont, I collect? And you are right. With that lovely gown and her more flattering hairstyle, she looked…not handsome, but…' She was searching for the right word.

'Striking?' put in Kit softly.

Emma paused before replying. 'Yes,' she said slowly. 'She was certainly striking. Particularly when she sang.'

Kit said nothing.

'I think,' said Hugo seriously, 'that there are hidden depths to Miss Beaumont. She did not say so in terms, but it appears that her family have suffered considerable hardship since her father was killed. Mrs Beaumont has been forced to take in pupils. And there is a son at Oxford, which must put a strain on her resources. It is no wonder, really, that Miss Beaumont has had to find a place as a companion. They probably need every penny she earns.'

'But you will help them, Hugo?'

'I have already promised to do so, my love. I told Miss Beaumont that I would be able to offer her brother a living, as soon as he was ordained. If you had seen the look on her face, Emma…'

'Which living did you promise her, Hugo?' Kit enquired politely.

'Why, Stratton Magna, of course,' said Hugo. 'It is the richest living in our gift, and the only one vacant, so—'

'I think you mistake, brother,' said Kit quietly. 'Stratton Magna is not in your gift. You may be head of the family, but Stratton Magna belongs to me.'

For a brief moment, Hugo looked nonplussed. 'You are right,' he said, with a thread of embarrassed laughter in his voice. 'But you know how we are placed with regard to the Beaumont family. We…I permitted them— my friend Langley's only kin—to live in penury for nearly ten years. Giving Harry the living of Stratton Magna would lift the family out of poverty—and without the appearance of charity. Would you have me withdraw the offer, Kit?'

Kit looked at his brother, and then at Emma, whose beautiful eyes were filled with concern. He permitted himself a little smile. 'No, Hugo. I would not. But have you considered how Miss Beaumont will react when she learns that she is beholden to me?'

Chapter Fourteen

En route to Fitzwilliam House once more, Marina leaned back into the velvet squabs of Lady Stratton's carriage. Such luxury for a mere companion.

She closed her eyes, relishing the moment. Lady Stratton, and Sir Hugo, too, were being so very kind to the penniless girl from Yorkshire. Not only had Lady Stratton persuaded the Dowager to permit Marina to visit Fitzwilliam House in the mornings, but she had also invited Marina to two of her evening parties. The Dowager had muttered a little at first, but had soon been forced to concede that she had no real need of her companion, since the evenings in question would be spent visiting the sort of gambling houses that were closed to gently bred young ladies.

Marina was not at all sure how Lady Stratton had done it. But the effect was that Marina's life in London was becoming more akin to that of a proper lady than a paid companion. And she had a wardrobe to match, for Lady Luce had gleefully made good on her threat to spend her son's money at the dressmaker's. She might exercise her scathing wit on the indecent modern fashions, but everything she had chosen for Marina was extremely flattering.

Looking down at the dark blue pelisse she wore, Marina smiled. It was so very satisfying to be dressed in glowing colours and beautiful fabrics, even though the dressmaker who had made them was far from top of the trees. That did not matter a jot. To Marina, it still seemed like a fairy tale. The Dowager had gone so far as to ban any garment in grey or brown, so Marina had quickly packed away her Yorkshire gowns before they could be despatched to the workhouse. That would be very wrong, for Mama had worked hard to produce the money to pay for those gowns. Besides, Marina might yet be forced to return home by a change in the Dowager's fickle temper.

Or by disclosure of her disgraceful meetings with Kit Stratton.

She gulped as his handsome face rose yet again in her mind. She could see him laughing with Lady Stratton like any normal gentleman, rather than like the wicked rake he was. She ought to despise him.

But she could not.

She wanted to condemn him out of hand for living a life of deep depravity and for attempting to lure her into it.

But she could not.

Everything that had happened between them had been her own doing, at least in part. She had gone to meet him—alone. She had visited his house. She had melted in his arms…

She was just as guilty as he.

And when she saw the laughing face he turned on his family, she had felt only envy. If only he would—

Marina dropped her head into her gloved hands. What on earth was happening to her?

She had been kissed by Kit Stratton. And she was lost.

'Why, Miss Beaumont!' Mr Stratton paused in the act of entering his sister's drawing room. 'What a... delightful surprise.'

Marina rose somewhat shakily from her chair. Oh, why did he have to appear now, as if she had conjured him out of her daydreams? And why had Lady Stratton not yet arrived? She was usually so very punctual.

He was waiting for her to say something. Waiting. He had cocked an eyebrow at her. Her obvious confusion seemed to be a source of amusement to him.

Marina straightened her back. 'I have leave to visit Lady Stratton in the mornings when Lady Luce does not require my services. Lady Stratton has been very kind.'

'So I should hope. She considers that the Strattons neglected your family after the death of your father.'

'Oh, no—'

'Miss Beaumont,' he said, in that deep, arresting voice that seemed to make her fingers and toes tingle, 'allow me to warn you that there is absolutely no point in disagreeing with Emma when she has made up her mind to something. If she has decided that our family owes a debt to yours, you would be well advised to accept it.'

How dare he? Marina knew he was arrogant, but this was the outside of enough. 'Indeed?' she said. She could not trust herself to say more.

'Indeed.' He looked her up and down then. It seemed that he had only just noticed her modish appearance, for his eyes widened a fraction. Did that signify approval?

Marina lifted her chin. She would not permit his presence to overset her. 'I am waiting for Lady Stratton, sir.

She suggested that we might practise our music together this morning. She had not mentioned that she expected any visitors.'

'No, she would not. Brothers, Miss Beaumont, do not count.'

Marina refused to react. He was clearly enjoying his attempts to bait her.

'As it happens, she did not expect me. I have come to take Hugo to Jackson's boxing parlour.' He looked shrewdly at her. 'You do not wrinkle your nose at the Fancy, Miss Beaumont. Emma would, I assure you.'

Marina returned his gaze frankly. 'I have a brother of my own, sir. I long ago learned not to notice such things.'

'Ah. Yes, of course.'

She felt as if he had just patted her on the head. Suddenly, she wanted to hit him, or kick him, as she had in his Chelsea house when he— Oh, God, why did that encounter keep pushing itself into her mind? Why were her thoughts for ever raging out of control? She—

'Oh, I am so sorry to have kept you waiting, my dear,' cried Lady Stratton, entering the room like a small whirlwind. 'I was— Kit! What on earth are you doing here at this hour?'

'Nothing of great import. I was planning on a visit to Jackson's boxing parlour. Promised to introduce a friend there this morning, but I wondered if Hugo might like to join our company. Some time since we have sparred together.'

Lady Stratton grimaced theatrically. 'It is one of the sad facts of life, Miss Beaumont, that ladies must put up with the singularly unattractive pursuits of their menfolk. I cannot, for the life of me, understand what pleasure they derive from using each other as punchbags.' She glanced at her brother-in-law. 'And you have no need to grin, sir! Oh, go away, do! You may continue your discussion with Hugo.'

He bowed to her with exaggerated care. 'Your wish is my command, dear sister.' He turned a fraction towards Marina. 'Miss Beaumont, you will allow me to say that I am delighted that the Dowager is permitting you a little time for yourself. Whether such freedom is best employed in the company of my quiz of a sister—' Lady Stratton only half succeeded in suppressing a shriek of outrage '—is a matter on which I am not qualified to pass an opinion. Day to you, ma'am.'

The door closed on him just as the book thrown by Lady Stratton reached the spot where his head had been. 'Wretched, wretched man!' she exclaimed, but she was almost laughing as she spoke.

It was not possible for a lady in Marina's position to make any comment. She tried to force a smile. Lady Stratton might laugh at her brother's wit, but Marina knew it hid his cold, ruthless heart. She had seen him at his most dangerous, drawing the Dowager towards financial ruin and Marina herself towards...

Towards what?

Hugo shook his head. 'I'm afraid not, Kit. I have an engagement this morning that I cannot break, though I should be happy to accompany you on another occasion. Jackson will tell me I am sadly out of condition. And he would be right, too. Haven't been in the ring for weeks.'

'In that case,' Kit said, 'I am glad you cannot come. What is the use of a brother who cannot provide a decent level of opposition?'

Hugo grinned. 'Let us make an appointment to meet

in a week's time, brother. Then I'll show you opposition.'

Kit stretched out his hand. 'Agreed,' he said. 'Five guineas to the winner?' They shook hands on the deal.

'Kit, there's something I have been meaning to ask you.' There was a noticeable hesitation in Hugo's voice suddenly. 'I… Have you heard any rumours lately?'

Kit's brows rose. 'Have to be more specific, I'm afraid, Hugo. I hear rumours all the time. What sort of rumours?'

'About…your Austrian lady friend.'

Not Marina, then. Katharina. What on earth could Hugo have heard? Kit permitted himself an exaggerated sigh. 'Ah, I see. No, I have not. But I trust you will tell me what they are.'

'I would not do so ordinarily, but she… You deserve better, Kit, than to be made to look a fool by that… female.'

Kit knew instinctively what was coming. He felt an instant surge of anger, first—and unfairly—against Hugo for being the bearer of such tidings, and then against Katharina for being the cause of them. But he refused to allow his bruised pride to show. Even to his brother.

'You may tell me the whole, Hugo,' he said evenly. 'Do not attempt to spare my feelings. In this case, I have none, believe me.'

Hugo stared at him for a second before continuing, 'It is rumoured that the Baroness has taken another lover. No, I do not have a name, I'm afraid, but I have heard it now from a number of sources. They could be wrong, of course, but…'

'But you do not think so.'

'No. Especially as it… You ought to be aware, Kit, that one of those infernal scandal sheets is making much of your affairs, and of the fact that the Baroness is known to have strayed.'

'You have seen it?'

'No. No, I have not, though others have. Do you want me to try to—?'

'Thank you, Hugo. No. I am grateful for the information. There is nothing more for you to do now. I shall deal with matters in my own way. I trust that Emma knows nothing of this?'

'I am not aware that she does,' said Hugo carefully, 'but her Aunt Warenne is always one of the first with the latest *on dits*. I should think it is only a matter of time…'

'In that case, I had better be on my way. It seems I shall be…sparring with more than one opponent today. Wish me luck, Hugo?'

'With your experience, shall you really need it?'

The Baroness was white with anger but she did not raise her voice. 'So you have the impudence to come to me for payment, do you, Budge?' Her foreign accent was becoming more pronounced with every word. She waved a paper at the housekeeper. 'After this?' she hissed.

Mrs Budge quailed, but stood her ground. 'I carried out your orders exactly, m'lady, I promise you. It has been almost a week now and you said—'

'I gave you clear instructions to say nothing about the writer of that letter. Do you deny that you disobeyed me?'

'No, m'lady. I mean, yes, I…' She shook her head slightly, trying to regain control. 'M'lady, I said nothing about you to Mr Johnson or anyone else. I simply delivered the letter you gave me.'

The Baroness spread the paper she held and glanced down at it. 'Are you telling me that you had no conversation with Mr Johnson?'

'Er…no, m'lady, not exactly. We…we exchanged the time of day, so to speak.'

'Quite,' said the Baroness sourly. 'I should have known better than to trust an English servant. Especially one who dares to ask for payment after betraying me.'

'M'lady, I swear—'

The Baroness thrust the paper towards Mrs Budge. 'Read it, then, Budge. Read it. And then tell me that you are not responsible. If you dare.'

Mrs Budge scanned the paper, her hand shaking a little at the violence of the Baroness's onslaught. Then she lifted her chin and looked resolutely at her accuser. 'M'lady, this is nothing to do with me. I did not tell Mr Johnson that you and the master are… And I certainly said nothing else about you.' At the Baroness's snort of anger, she added, daringly, 'How could I have done so, when I knew nothing about your other affairs?'

'How dare you?' spluttered the Baroness. 'Get out of my house before I have you thrown out. Get out, I say!'

Mrs Budge almost ran out of the room before the Baroness could make good on her threat. Clearly she would receive not a penny more from the Austrian woman.

What would happen now? The Baroness might well betray her treachery to the master, who would be bound to dismiss her if he found out. And Mrs Budge could not afford to lose her place, or the income it provided.

Yet there might be another way of earning money, at least for now. The Baroness had accused her of betrayal and was treating her as if she were guilty. So…she might as well reap the rewards.

She would pay another visit to the well-informed Mr

Johnson and, this time, she would not be nearly so circumspect about what she told him. The next edition of Mr Johnson's little scandal sheet would give the haughty Baroness a seizure—she hoped—besides making the woman the butt of London gossip for the rest of the Season.

She pursed her lips and nodded at her own cleverness. Good. Very good.

And, just in case that did not do the trick, she would ensure that a copy of Mr Johnson's interesting history would find its way to the Austrian Embassy, for the personal attention of the noble Baron von Thalberg.

Instinctively, Kit ducked back into the shadows. He had no desire to be seen in the vicinity of Katharina's house. There were quite enough rumours flying already.

Then he recognised the black-clad woman who had emerged. It was his own housekeeper.

Now, that was very interesting. What possible reason could Mrs Budge have for visiting Katharina at her home? He had given the woman no message to deliver. In truth, he had had no communication at all from Katharina for over a week, which was not surprising if his little Austrian was indeed playing him false, as Hugo had suggested. Clearly, it was time they parted. He had made it plain enough, throughout their liaison, that he was always faithful to his mistresses—while they lasted—and that he expected the same courtesy from the ladies in question. Since Katharina appeared to have ignored his warning, their rupture could not now be delayed.

For a moment he toyed with the notion of entering the Baron's house and giving Katharina her *congé* face to face. What a scandal that would create! The diplomat's wife receiving one of the greatest rakes in London—alone in her drawing room, too. Did he dare?

Yes, he did. He would do it—were it not for the scandal that would then descend on Emma and Hugo, as well as himself. That would be mightily unfair on them. Kit would have to find another means of dealing with the duplicitous Baroness. A lesser man might do the deed by letter, but Kit had no intention of adopting such a cowardly tactic. He would confront her with her deceit and leave her in no doubt of why she was to be banished from his bed.

His eye was caught by Mrs Budge's raised hand. She had walked only a few yards from Katharina's door and was trying to hail a hackney. Even more interesting! Where could she be going that justified such expensive transport? No doubt Katharina had paid her, but what was her errand? It made no sense for Katharina to employ Mrs Budge to take messages to her new lover. There were plenty of other servants in the household who could be bribed to do that. What was the service that only Kit's housekeeper could perform for the faithless Baroness?

He looked around rapidly for another cab, but there was none in sight. He cursed roundly. A passing gentleman looked at him in surprise and disgust, hesitated, and then walked on.

Kit grinned ruefully at his own loss of control. The housekeeper's hackney was out of sight. It would be impossible to follow her now. He might as well continue with his original errand and call at his friend's house, next but one to Katharina's. He would be waiting to be taken to Jackson's boxing parlour for his introduction to the great man. A turn in the ring was even more necessary now, Kit decided. He really needed to vent his wrath on someone this morning, or he would explode.

Mrs Budge would not escape scot-free, however. At some point convenient to Kit, the housekeeper would be faced with an interview that she would find more than a little uncomfortable.

Chapter Fifteen

'I did not come here to be insulted,' hissed the Baroness, rising indignantly from her seat in the cramped parlour.

'No, Katharina, you came here to see if you could cozen me into believing that these rumours were a pack of lies.' He fixed her with a stern gaze. 'Well? Did you not?'

She did not reply. She tried to meet his eyes, but failed. To cover her confusion, she began to pace around the room.

'Spare me these theatricals, my dear. You should know they will achieve nothing. I asked you here to tell you face to face that our…understanding is at an end. You know why.'

She threw a sharp glance at him and deliberately turned her back.

'Does your husband know that you are playing him false yet again?'

She spun on her heel. 'How dare you say such a thing! You, of all men! As if you were blameless!'

'My dear Katharina, it was but a simple question. I ask because I have a warning for you. Once, you were discreet. Now, it appears, you are not. If these rumours should reach the Baron's ears and he should be minded to defend his honour—it is not impossible, you know, since he is neither as old nor as blind as you would like to believe—I shall refer him to your latest *cher ami*. I have no intention of facing a bullet at dawn for Cullen's—' He stopped abruptly, waiting until she looked him in the eye once more. 'I am sure your English is quite adequate to supply the appropriate word.'

He smiled coldly at her, before striding across to the fireplace to pull the bell. 'Mrs Budge will show you out.' He folded his arms and leaned casually against the mantel until the door opened.

'Show my visitor out, Mrs Budge,' he said sharply.

The housekeeper curtsied and took her stance by the open door.

'Goodbye, my dear. Be grateful that I did you the courtesy of a meeting. It is more than you deserve. A woman who uses servants to spy on their own master deserves no consideration of any kind.'

The Baroness threw him a look seething with hatred, before marching through the open door.

'I hope you paid her well,' he called after her, relishing the housekeeper's suddenly ashen face, 'for she is most certainly going to lose her place.'

The Dowager smiled grimly. 'Splendid. Absolutely splendid,' she said with satisfaction. 'It will be delightful to see that woman get her just deserts.'

Marina had no idea what her mistress was talking about, but it must have something to do with the scandal sheet that lay in her lap. What woman could she be referring to?

'Kit Stratton has excelled himself this time. I should

not have believed that he had it in him. And his Austrian…er…mistress will be mad as fire. I wonder…' Her smile broadened. 'I wonder if someone will see fit to show this to her husband. We might have a real diplomatic incident then. Oh, it is famous.' She chortled nastily, enjoying the thought. Then, seeing Marina's puzzlement, she threw the paper across to her. 'Read it, if you wish. But don't come over all missish when you do. It's the way of the world.' She nodded to herself. 'And when the world pauses to think about it, they will soon work out the identity of the mysterious M.B.'

M.B.! Marina felt as if all the blood had suddenly drained from her body. She barely had enough strength in her fingers to spread the cheap paper. She was betrayed! Now that her initials had been printed in a scandal sheet, it would take no time at all for her identity to be discovered. She had been a fool to depend on Kit Stratton's aid. And much too quick in thanking him for ensuring his brother's discretion. Sir Hugo must have spoken of what he had seen…or perhaps the culprit was Kit Stratton himself. She had been mad to think him a gentleman.

She felt as if a black cloud had settled around her. It was only a matter of time now until she was completely disgraced.

She glanced furtively at the Dowager who was still smiling in grim satisfaction. Why? She had hinted that she knew the identity of M.B., but that was impossible. If she had known the truth, she would not be talking to Marina in this odd way. She would be telling her to pack her bags.

There was something very strange about all this.

Marina bent to the paper.

The piece was short but devastating. A certain Mr S.

had been seen to have an assignation with a mysterious
tall lady. The scandal sheet, drawing on its private
sources, was not in the least surprised to learn of that,
since the gentleman's 'close friend,' a foreign lady of
exalted position, was known to have been seeking solace
in other quarters of late. The mysterious lady was known
to the editor (he said) but he would not injure her reputation by naming her at this stage. Her initials, however,
were M.B.

Marina swallowed hard. She looked across at her employer. For a second, everything became hazy, as if she
were about to faint, but then her vision cleared again.
She did not dare to say a word. She was sure her voice
would crack.

Lady Luce seemed to have noticed nothing. She was
totally caught up in her enjoyment of the scandal to
come. 'I shall not drop any hints for a day or two,' she
said, 'for I wish to see how many are astute enough to
work it out for themselves. And to see how Kit Stratton
will react. If he has an ounce of common sense, he will
take himself off to Vienna again, before the axe falls.
But then, he always was a stubborn, arrogant man.
Thinks he can talk his way out of anything.'

She rose from her chair, chuckling, and made for the
door. 'I dare say it will be better than a play.'

Marina expelled a long breath as the door closed behind the Dowager. She must think! What was she to do?
Should she warn Mr Stratton of what the Dowager was
about? But how could she? She did not understand it
herself. Besides, he would accept no advice from a mere
female, especially one like Marina, whom he clearly despised.

The Dowager seemed to think that the axe was about

to fall on Kit Stratton. If Marina had an ounce of sense, she, too, would simply stand by and watch.

The horse stumbled. Automatically, Kit gathered him up, mentally upbraiding himself for his failure to pay attention to his mount, or the terrain. The last thing he wanted was an injury to his favourite bay.

'Sorry, Caesar, old fellow,' he said soothingly. 'Your master is not worthy of you today.' He reined the huge stallion back to a gentle walk. At this pace, Caesar would now look out for himself, and, since they had the park to themselves at this early hour, Kit could indulge himself in a little reflection.

It was now two days since he had parted from Katharina. He had no regrets. Indeed, it was surprising how little impact her absence was having on his life. He had enjoyed her beautiful body—what man would not?—but he did not *need* her. He never had. It was unusual for him to be without a mistress, to be sure, but he was in no hurry to replace her.

In truth, none of the women in London Society attracted him in the least. They lacked beauty, they lacked wit, they lacked—

He shook his head. What on earth was the matter with him? The ladies in London were easily the equal of those in Vienna. Why was he suddenly so difficult to please? London offered mistresses a-plenty to choose from, married ladies who presented no threat to his independence, who would be more than willing to share his bed in return for an expensive bauble or two...and the chance to boast of having captured the handsomest rake in London. Kit grimaced a little at the thought. He knew only too well how Society spoke of him. Sometimes, his looks were a curse.

He began to review the potential candidates. Méchante, for example, would not hesitate, even now, in spite of the way he had insulted her. She had been an accomplished lover, once. And he could not deny that she was coldly beautiful. But, like all the rest, she cared only for herself. She had no redeeming qualities. There was absolutely nothing there to admire.

The same was true of all of them.

He frowned. All except—

Miss Beaumont was the only woman who had anything in the least admirable about her. She did not have looks, but she did have courage. It was a pity that she appeared to have duplicity, too. He should have taxed her with it, when he had the chance. At Emma's party, for example. Why had he not?

Because he had been so bewitched by the way she sang that he had not been able to bring himself to shatter the spell. She was no beauty, it was true, but in that simple shimmering gown, with her chestnut hair falling in loose curls about her face, she had stirred something in him that had given him pause. What kind of woman could make music like a female Orpheus? He had wanted to begin to understand that—and other things about her, too. He had been quite incapable of taking her to task, no matter how justified his criticism might be.

But was it?

He tried to remember precisely what she had said on the landing of Lady Luce's house. He could not. Something about his letter, but what exactly? He had been sure at the time that she was intending to insult him, but what if he was wrong? Women were sometimes so very difficult to read.

Except in bed, of course, he thought with a smile,

remembering the many neglected, resentful wives who had come to purr under his hands. There, he had never had any difficulty at all.

'Mama, I must speak to you.'

Lady Luce raised a questioning eyebrow. 'Indeed, William? And what, pray, is so urgent?'

'I have news about Kit Stratton, ma'am.'

'Very well. I am listening.'

'I think I should speak to you alone, Mama.'

Marina rose immediately.

'Tush!' said the Dowager. 'Miss Beaumont is my companion and knows a great deal more than you give her credit for. Sit down at once, Marina. Anything that my son wishes to say to me, he may say in front of you.'

The Earl looked both uncomfortable and angry. His neck had turned an unbecoming shade of purple. 'Very well,' he said in a strained voice. 'If that is what you wish, ma'am. But I warn you that what I have to say is not for the ears of a gently reared young lady.'

The Dowager threw him an eloquent look. It suggested that, in her opinion, her son's views on what young ladies should and should not know left much to be desired. However, she said nothing. She merely nodded at him, impatiently.

He cleared his throat and began rather pompously, 'You will know, I suppose, ma'am, that Mr Stratton has had a number of...er...liaisons.' He glanced furtively towards Marina and then looked hurriedly away. 'It is rumoured that his return to England was simply to follow his Austrian mis—er...his Austrian, when her husband was sent here. For all I know, it may be true. However, you will be interested to know that she has tired of him and that he—a man who has always prided himself on being the one to end these little…affairs—appears to be on the point of receiving his *congé* from the lady. It will be the first time, I dare swear.' He smiled down at his mother. 'I was sure you would relish the news.'

'And I did relish it, William…the *first* time I heard it. That was several days ago. Where on earth have your wits been all this time? Or is it that you have been relying on Charlotte for your information? She is always the last to know.'

The Earl's colour mounted once more. 'If you are not interested in what I have to say, Mama, I shall take my leave.'

'Stuff!' said his mother sharply. 'Stay where you are. Now, *I* shall tell *you* about Kit Stratton.'

Marina held her breath. What more did the Dowager know? She had been smiling to herself almost non-stop since the moment she had first read the scandal sheet's wicked tale. It looked as if she believed every word of it. And she seemed to be firmly convinced that she alone knew the identity of Kit Stratton's latest mistress, the elusive M.B. She was wrong, of course, but how was she to be set right? Did she really know another M.B.? So far, she had not chosen to share her secret with Marina. Would she reveal it now?

'While it may suit the lady in question to put it about that she is giving Mr Stratton his *congé*, it is certainly not true.'

'What? Mama, you—'

'Allow me to finish, William. As I said, it is not true. Mr Stratton ended the relationship himself, as soon as he discovered her perfidy. That was several days ago, William. Can't say I blame him. Was there anything else you wished to tell me?'

Lord Luce seemed incapable of speech.

'Then, since you do not appear to have seen it, I will give you a little light reading matter.' She took the scandal sheet, now rather ragged, from her pocket and handed it to him. 'I suggest you share it with your dear wife. Then you may puzzle together over the identity of M.B.'

Her son was rapidly scanning the sheet. His jaw had dropped open.

'Interesting, ain't it?' said the Dowager with something approaching a gleeful cackle. 'Let me give you a word of advice, William. Don't look too far afield for the mysterious M.B.'

'I beg your pardon, ma'am? I cannot think what on earth you can possibly mean.'

'That is because you refuse to use what little sense you were born with.' She was looking very hard at him. He seemed to be genuinely puzzled, as well as indignant. 'Oh, very well. I am becoming tired of waiting, in any case. At this rate, I shall be carried out in my box before anyone else discovers who she is.'

Holding her breath, Marina began to study the toes of her slippers.

'M.B.,' said the Dowager. 'It should not be so very difficult, especially for you, William. Think— No. Consider, if you will, the number of ladies of your acquaintance with surnames beginning with B. And then think, very carefully, about a family that is…allied with your own. That is where you will find M.B. Indeed, you yourself have been almost as close to the lady in question as Kit Stratton is rumoured to be.'

'What? Mama, I—'

The Dowager rose angrily. 'Do you never listen to a word I say, William? I told you to *think*, not to talk drivel. Oh, go away. Go away before I lose all patience with you.'

Patience was the last virtue that Marina would have attributed to the Dowager, but she was too full of anxiety to be able to appreciate the joke. The Dowager's description could fit Marina—pretty well, at least—but she was almost sure now that she was not the intended target. Lord Luce had never been close to her, not in any way. So who?

The Earl had risen automatically with his mother, good manners overcoming his wrath. He was refusing to acknowledge Marina's existence in any way, which was not surprising considering that she had just witnessed yet another humiliating scene between them. 'I will take my leave, then, Mama,' he said, bowing. 'I'm afraid I can make nothing of your riddles. I cannot think of any family of my acquaintance that would permit such disgraceful behaviour. A young woman alone with Kit Stratton? It would be scandalous.'

The Dowager nodded, smiling maliciously.

'I am sure no such person would be tolerated by my family. And as for your hints… Why, there is only one family that would fit your description, and the Blaines are quite above reproach—'

The Dowager snorted eloquently. 'Are they, indeed? You, obviously, do not stop to wonder why her ladyship always wins when she holds the Faro bank. Tongues are starting to wag about your precious Blaines, William.'

The Blaines? Oh, good God, was that what the Dowager had meant? Why did all Marina's problems seem to stem from the Blaines? Marina began to feel a little sick.

Her reaction was nothing to William's, however. He was gasping like a stranded fish. And his colour was mounting, yet again. Marina had never seen an apoplexy, but she was beginning to wonder whether she might be about to.

The Dowager made for the door, ignoring her son's plight. 'Come, Marina,' she said, beckoning. 'We have matters to attend to. Remember what I have said, William,' she added with affected geniality. 'M.B. A lady that you, too, have held in your arms. Intriguing, ain't it?'

In her haste to make up for her lateness, Marina did not really look where she was going. 'Oh, I beg your pardon,' she said quickly, automatically reaching out a hand to steady the young lady against whom she had stumbled. 'How clumsy of me.'

The young lady smiled a little vacantly, but it animated her plain features. It was the eldest Miss Blaine. 'No harm done,' she said. 'Why, you must be Miss Beaumont.' She suddenly blushed bright red. 'Forgive me,' she continued, in a tumbling rush of words, 'but since you are the only other young lady who is as tall as I am, I could not help but guess at your identity, even though we have not been introduced. We were both at…at Lady Stratton's party, but Mama and I had to leave because…because I—'

'Because you felt unwell,' Marina improvised, automatically trying to put Miss Blaine at her ease. 'It was not in the least surprising. I found it very hot myself.' She glanced up the stairs towards Lady Stratton's drawing room. 'Have you been calling on Lady Stratton?'

'Oh, yes. She is usually at home to visitors on Mondays. We called on Monday last, because Mama said I must apologise for…for making a scene. But Lady Stratton would not hear of it. She insisted we should call

again. She is so kind and charming, do you not think?
And so very elegant.' There was no mistaking the envy
in Miss Blaine's voice.

'Yes, indeed,' Marina agreed, trying unsuccessfully to
warm to the awkward young woman. 'She has been immeasurably kind to a mere companion, too.'

'But I thought…I understood that you were…related
to Papa?' There was something about her tone. It suggested that, if Marina had been a mere companion, Miss
Blaine would not be prepared to converse with her at
all.

'Ye…es,' replied Marina, a little hesitantly.

'Well, in that case, I shall call you Marina. And you
must call me Tilly.' She gave an embarrassed giggle.
'Dreadful name, is it not? But since ''Mathilda'' is even
worse, I fear I have no choice in the matter. I often wish
Mama had called me something more poetic—'

'Tilly!' Lady Blaine's voice thundered from the landing above them. 'Why on earth are you dawdling there?
I expressly asked you to order the carriage. Do it immediately, if you please.'

'I was just about to do so, Mama, but I encountered
Marina, and—'

'Miss Beaumont,' said Lady Blaine, with emphasis,
looking down at Marina with profound dislike. 'No
doubt she is here on an errand for her employer. Pray,
do not let us keep you from your duties, Miss Beaumont.
You will find Lady Stratton in her drawing room.'

Marina glanced at Tilly, but the girl was already hurrying off down to the hall to carry out her mother's
orders. And it was unlikely she would ever again dare
to address Marina in Lady Blaine's presence. The
woman seemed to enjoy inflicting humiliation on others,
even on her own daughter.

Picking up her skirts once more, Marina slowly mounted the rest of the stairs until she stood on the landing alongside Lady Blaine. From her greater height, she looked down into the older woman's face, registering the depth of dislike and contempt in her hard eyes.

An imp of mischief prodded Marina into a pert little curtsy and an insolent speech. 'How kind of you, Cousin. As it happens, I know my way.' Then she hurried along the corridor before the astonished Viscountess had time to utter a single word in reply.

'Miss Beaumont!' Lady Stratton was alone. She rose from her chair as the door opened. 'What a pity! Lady Blaine and her daughter have only just left.'

Taking a couple of deep breaths, Marina forced herself to behave as normally as she could. This was the wrong time, and the wrong place to turn her mind to—

'Do sit down, my dear. You look a little flushed. Are you perfectly well?'

'Perfectly, ma'am, I thank you. It was just that I was a little late and so I was hurrying.'

'There was no need, I assure you. Do remove your bonnet. I will ring for some fresh tea. You look as though you need a cup.'

Marina watched her hostess move elegantly across to the bell. Everything seemed so very normal. She was a guest in a lady's drawing room. They were about to take tea.

And Marina had at last discovered the identity of Lady Luce's M.B.! After three days of racking her brains, the answer had been dropped into her lap.

She closed her eyes in horror for a moment. There could be no doubt. The Dowager's hints had been clearly directed at the Blaines, even though she had never actually pronounced the name. The Dowager's M.B. was part of a family allied with her son's. She must have been referring to the close friendship between Lady Blaine and William's wife. It was just possible that, at some time, William had held the child Mathilda in his arms. The Dowager had probably been making mischief, as she so often did, by telling her son he had held the *lady* in his arms. She would enjoy taxing his rather weak intellect.

But could it really be true?

Yes. In the Dowager's eyes, at least. She seemed to detest the Blaines almost as much as she detested her own son. And it had been the Dowager who had drawn everyone's attention to Tilly Blaine's obvious infatuation with Kit Stratton.

A hint or two more from Lady Luce—or from that wicked scandal sheet—and the whole of Society would quickly identify Tilly Blaine as the mysterious M.B., the woman who was reputed to be Kit Stratton's new lover. Miss Blaine would be ruined.

It must not be allowed to happen.

It would be a monstrous injustice to an innocent girl whose only fault had been to betray her feelings for London's foremost rake. And it would be Marina's fault.

Something must be done to save Tilly Blaine, even if—

The door opened. She had not heard a knock.

Marina turned, expecting to see Lady Stratton's butler with the tea tray.

'Afternoon, Emma,' drawled that well-known voice. 'Have I arrived too late to greet your visitors? How very remiss of me.'

Chapter Sixteen

Marina was a mass of warring emotions. The sight of Kit Stratton's handsome, elegant person made her heart race and her mouth go dry. But she knew that she had every reason to be furious with him. Was he not, ultimately, responsible for having betrayed her—or at least her initials—to the world at large? Was he not responsible, at least in part, for the potential disgrace that was hanging over poor Tilly Blaine?

Given the slightest opportunity, she would have no hesitation in taking him to task. She rather doubted that anyone had ever done so before, particularly a woman, but in this case, she had cause. And she would not permit his overpowering masculinity to prevent her from doing her duty. She refused to give in to the disturbingly seductive memories that plagued her dreams. Dreams where Kit's strong hands had gently—

She forced herself to look coldly on him.

He bowed slightly. 'Forgive me, Miss Beaumont. For a moment, I thought Emma was alone. It had not occurred to me that you might be here at this late hour of the day.'

Marina bridled but said nothing. Of course he had

overlooked her. She was only a poor, plain companion, was she not?

Lady Stratton had crossed the floor to take her brother-in-law by the arm and draw him into the room. 'You do not fool me, brother dear,' she said archly. 'I know precisely why you have arrived at this late hour. You are deliberately avoiding my other guests, while allowing yourself to claim that you have done the pretty by your brother's wife.'

He grinned down at her. 'I make no attempt to deny it—especially as I recognised the arms on the carriage that was driving away. I must admit that the society of Lady Blaine is not at all to my taste.'

'But I thought the Viscount was a member of your club?'

'Yes, but so are many gentlemen. It does not mean that I seek out his company. Besides, he has been abroad since just after I returned to England. Visiting his plantations, or some such, I understand.'

'Oh,' said Marina, before she could stop herself. Her disapproval must have been apparent from her tone, for Mr Stratton threw her a very strange look. She felt she must be blushing, at least a little. But, on the other hand, she knew that she had right on her side on this occasion. She looked challengingly back at him. 'Are you surprised, sir, to learn that some people do not approve of the exploitation of our fellow men? The Church teaches us that we are all brothers. It cannot be right to enslave our brothers.'

Mr Stratton looked at Marina with frank curiosity. 'A follower of Wilberforce, I collect?'

She nodded.

'Most laudable,' he continued. 'But the slave trade is ended. Your battle is won, is it not?'

'No, indeed,' she countered hotly. 'We may no longer transport the poor souls out of Africa, but, in the plantations, they are still in chains. And—'

The door opened to admit the butler. 'Tea, at last,' breathed Lady Stratton, sounding relieved. 'You will take a cup, Kit?'

'Beg pardon, m'lady,' said the butler, setting the tray down on the pie-crust table, 'but Sir Hugo asked if you could spare him a few minutes, on a matter of urgency. He is in his bookroom.'

'How very awkward,' she said, but moved to the door with a little shrug. 'Miss Beaumont, I must ask you to forgive me for a moment. Might I prevail upon you to do the honours in my absence?'

'Of course.'

'And Kit will be on his best behaviour, I promise you.' She glared a warning at him, but it seemed to produce no reaction. 'I shall return shortly. Pray excuse me.' She hurried from the room.

Marina's heart had begun to beat very fast. She told herself to ignore it. As the door closed on the butler, she lifted the silver teapot and looked up at Kit Stratton with as much coolness as she could muster. 'Cream and sugar, Mr Stratton?'

'Thank you.'

He took the seat opposite Marina. His biscuit-coloured pantaloons were so tightly moulded to his body that Marina could see the flexing of his every muscle when he stretched out his long legs. She tried to concentrate on the sugar basin and then on handing him his cup.

'Thank you,' he said again, reaching out with one strong, lean hand. He did not touch her, but at that moment Marina's hard-won control began to crack, and her hand wavered slightly. If he had not taken the cup just then, the tea would have been spilt.

I must be going out of my mind, she thought. Why am I concerning myself about serving tea, when this man is about to bring utter disgrace upon me? And upon Tilly Blaine?

She took a deep breath and folded her hands in her lap. Her tea sat untouched on the table. 'Mr Stratton, I must ask you if you are aware of the rumours that are circulating about you and...about our meetings.'

His eyes narrowed. 'I collect that you are about to tell me, Miss Beaumont,' he replied non-committally.

That was almost too much. 'I should not need to do so, since you must be the cause of them.'

He raised an eyebrow.

That was the last straw for Marina's increasingly fragile temper. 'How dare you?' she raged. 'You led me to believe that you had done as I asked. I was fool enough to think that you were a true gentleman, that you would ask your brother not to betray what he had seen. I should have known not to trust you. Tell me, pray, was it you who betrayed my indiscretion to the scandal sheets? Or did you merely disclose it to your friends? I am sure they must have been vastly amused.'

Very slowly, he replaced his cup on the table. Then he leaned back in his chair and surveyed Marina through half-closed eyes. She could feel his contempt, but she would not be cowed, not by a worthless rake. She straightened her shoulders and returned his blatant stare.

'Very good, Miss Beaumont,' he said softly. 'And now, perhaps you would be good enough to explain these accusations of yours. I may add that I am not in the habit of betraying confidences.'

'Then why did you betray mine?'

'I did not,' he said flatly.

She barely heard him. She was now so angry that the words were tumbling out. 'You and Sir Hugo were the only people who knew I had been in your carriage. No one else saw me in the park that morning. It was obvious that your brother had recognised me. Why else would I write to you as I did? You allowed me to believe that all would be well, while—'

'You wrote to me? When?' He was leaning forward now, his whole body alert.

'You know when,' she responded tartly. How dare he pretend not to remember?

'Miss Beaumont,' he said slowly, 'I received no letter from you.'

'But—'

'No letter,' he repeated firmly. 'It is true that my brother recognised you in the park. I assure you that he has spoken of it to no one, not even to his wife. He felt he owed it to your father and your uncle to preserve your good name.'

'Then—'

'And I have spoken of it to no one except my brother, Miss Beaumont. If your name is circulating in the scandal sheets, it is none of my doing, I promise you.'

'Oh.' Marina let out a long breath and dropped her head into her hands. A moment ago, she could easily have flown at him; now her strength had evaporated. It could not be true. Could it? 'I do not understand,' she whispered at last. 'If neither you nor Sir Hugo spoke of it, how is it that—?' She did not finish the sentence. What did it matter who was guilty? Her shame would be just the same. She could not bring herself to look at him. She could not move.

Kit reached out and gently removed her hands from

her face, holding them in a comforting clasp. 'Miss Beaumont,' he said, trying to convey his sympathy in the tone of his voice, 'Miss Beaumont, look at me.'

It seemed a very long time before she obeyed. Her huge eyes were full of horror, as if she could see a terrible fate awaiting her.

'You believe the Strattons have betrayed you. I promise you we have not done so. But, from what you say, it appears that you have been betrayed. Tell me of this letter. When was it sent? Who delivered it?'

Miss Beaumont lifted her chin an inch. 'I wrote to you as soon as I reached home. I took the letter to the receiving office myself.'

'You are sure the direction was correct?'

'Yes, of course. I could not mistake it. After all, I had only just come from your house.'

'You directed it to me in Chelsea?' At her impatient nod, he said slowly, 'I see. That was unfortunate, I think.' It was unfortunate, too, that she had entrusted her letter to the post, rather than to a messenger, but it would not do to tell Miss Beaumont what he was beginning to suspect. She was distraught enough already. He must treat her with great care from this point. But he had very little time. Emma might return at any moment.

He tried to smile reassuringly at her. She had not withdrawn her hands, but he doubted there was anything to be read into that. He was not sure that she was aware that he held them. 'I did not receive your letter, ma'am. Would you be kind enough to tell me what was in it?'

'I…I cannot remember exactly, sir. I said that I thought your brother had recognised me. I…believe I asked you to intercede with him, in hopes that he might say nothing.'

'That was all?'

'I may have mentioned alighting from your carriage…to explain how it was that Sir Hugo saw me. I am not sure.'

Kit frowned. Worse and worse. There was one last question. It had to be asked. 'Miss Beaumont, did you sign your letter?'

'Oh, no,' she replied quickly.

He breathed a sigh of relief.

'I used only my initials.'

Kit looked quickly down at the floor, trying to hide his obvious dismay. Her letter was lost—and it contained all the information needed to ruin her. She—innocent and unworldly as she was—had thought she would be safe as long as she did not sign her name. Confound it, how many women did she think there were with the initials M.B.?

'Miss Beaumont—'

'Mr Stratton, I…I apologise for my hasty words a moment ago,' she said stiffly, avoiding his eyes. With a sudden movement, she pulled her hands from his and hid them in her skirts. She was blushing now, terribly conscious that he had been holding her hands.

He was reminded yet again that she had a flawless complexion. He found himself wishing that she would look at him again. She had beautiful eyes, even if the flecks of gold were now hidden by the depth of her hurt.

She spoke to her skirts. Her voice was so low that it was difficult to make out her words. 'Mr Stratton, I think it is worse than you know. A scandal sheet is circulating. It says that you have a new m…mistress, a tall lady with the initials M.B. There is much speculation about my…about the lady's identity.'

Kit nodded. This was very serious—for Miss Beaumont. 'Do you have any reason to believe that you have been identified as M.B., ma'am?' he asked softly.

'Oh, no,' she cried, dropping her head into her hands once more. 'No reason in the world.'

Kit thought she was beginning to sound a little hysterical. It made no sense. She must know she was safe as long as M.B. remained unidentified.

'Lady Luce is certain that the lady in question is Tilly Blaine.'

Kit stared in total disbelief. Miss Blaine? Tilly Blaine?

'Her real name is Mathilda, you see, but everyone knows her as "Tilly" so the connection is not obvious at once, and—'

Kit began to laugh. He could not help it. The thing was just too absurd. Tilly Blaine! A gushing beanpole of a woman who talked—once started, she was almost impossible to stop—of nothing but poets.

Miss Beaumont shot to her feet, rattling the teacups in her haste. 'How dare you laugh, sir? Have you no thought for what Miss Blaine may be made to suffer? You—'

Rising politely, Kit calmly lifted the tea table out of range of her wrath. 'My dear Miss Beaumont,' he said smoothly, 'I have not the least doubt that nothing will come of it. For who would believe that I would ever—?'

'You conceited coxcomb!' she spat. 'You think of nothing but yourself. You say no one would ever believe that you—the great Kit Stratton—would have secret meetings with a plain girl like Tilly Blaine. May I remind you, sir, that you had two such meetings with me?'

Kit took a deep breath. What on earth had possessed him to say something so arrogant? A cock crowing on a dunghill showed more humility than he. Miss Beaumont would never listen to a word he said after this. He reached out to take her hand once more, but she pulled away as if she had been burnt.

At that moment, the drawing room door opened.

Emma had returned.

'Are you for Faro tonight, ma'am?'

'Perhaps,' said Lady Luce. 'Worries you, don't it, Méchante, to see my run of luck?' She allowed the lackey to relieve her of her dark evening cloak. 'Be grateful I am not Lady Blaine. After all, I *do* lose—sometimes. I fancy I might see whether my luck still holds tonight.'

Lady Marchant bowed her acknowledgement. 'As you wish, ma'am,' she said. 'My rooms are always open to you.'

The Dowager snorted and turned towards the staircase.

'What do you think about this latest rumour?'

'What rumour?' said the Dowager sourly, pausing on the step.

'Why, about Kit Stratton's latest mistress, the mysterious M.B.'

The Dowager looked narrowly at her hostess. 'You do not know who she is,' she said flatly, and with obvious satisfaction. 'How very frustrating for you.'

'Am I to understand that you do?' Lady Marchant's voice dripped venom.

'Naturally,' said Lady Luce evenly. She looked Méchante over for a long moment. 'But I do not propose to share that information. Not yet.'

Lady Marchant made to speak, but the Dowager forestalled her. 'I know there is no love lost between you and Kit Stratton. So I will give you a hint, for we are surely allies in this little charade. This time, Kit Stratton has gone much too far. This time, he might even find himself riveted. And I doubt he will enjoy the experience.' She laughed nastily. 'But I most certainly shall. I would gladly have paid him his twelve thousand pounds for this. Pity he will never know it.'

Méchante's eyes gleamed with malice. 'M.B. is a *lady*? A *single* lady?'

Lady Luce nodded. 'We should perhaps look forward to dancing at his wedding.'

'Oh, it is famous! I doubt I shall dance at his wedding, however. On his grave, more like.'

The Dowager's eyebrows shot up.

'My dear ma'am,' said Lady Marchant, 'I may not have succeeded in identifying M.B.—I admit my sources have been useless there—but I have not been idle, I assure you.' She continued confidingly, 'You will have noticed the increasing rumours about Kit and the Austrian Baroness? I fancy her husband is finding it…somewhat difficult of late to overlook her adventures. What is more, I have made it my business to ensure that most of the foreign diplomats—and especially the French Ambassador—are laughing at the Baron's inability to keep his wife in his own bed. His stiff-necked pride will never tolerate that, especially from a Frenchman. There must now be a good chance that Kit Stratton will have a bullet in him before he gets near the altar.'

'Balderdash! Kit Stratton is a crack shot.'

Lady Marchant beamed at the old woman. 'I do not believe that I said anything about a duel, ma'am. You must know there are other ways…'

The Dowager paused assessingly. 'Indeed there are. I thank you for the information, Méchante, and I shall watch developments with…interest. As it happens, I am holding a large party on Wednesday evening. Everyone will be there—the diplomats, the Strattons, the cream of Society… It could be very entertaining. Such a pity that I cannot extend an invitation to you, my dear, but I am sure you understand…'

Marina had just reached the end of her second page of notes about the arrangements for the Dowager's party on the morrow, when the butler entered with a letter.

'Lady Marchant's man brought it, m'lady,' said Tibbs, offering the salver to the Dowager. 'He did not wait for a reply.'

Lady Luce nodded a dismissal. She sat for a moment, weighing the letter in her hand. 'I wonder…' she said softly. Then she broke the seal.

From her seat on the low stool, Marina watched anxiously. She was quite certain that Lady Marchant was out to make mischief in any way she could. The Dowager had hinted that Méchante was become Kit's enemy. And what better way to attack Kit than by attacking M.B.?

The letter contained an enclosure. The Dowager lifted it fastidiously with the very tips of her fingers and laid it aside.

Oh, God, it looked like— Please, no! Not another!

The Dowager cackled gleefully. 'My alliance with Méchante! I had not expected it to bear fruit so soon. But so it is.' She took up the second paper again, more eagerly this time, and unfolded it. After a moment, she looked up and said, 'The Baroness will be furious. And as for the Blaines… You will enjoy this, Marina, after all the insult that their family has inflicted on yours. Listen. ''We have, in the past, been reticent about the identity of M.B., out of proper regard for a lady's reputation. But we now learn that her conduct does not merit such restraint. We have learned, with horror, that M.B. is known to have visited Mr S. at his house in Chelsea on at least two occasions and to have been quite alone with him there. We can only deplore such laxity of morals in the young females of today. Their parents should reproach themselves—'' So they should,' said the Dowager, dropping the paper into her lap and putting aside her reading glass. 'Much too high in the instep, in my opinion, for an upstart Viscountess. Time she was brought down a peg or two.'

Marina's mind was in a whirl. Her only thought was that someone had betrayed her visits to Chelsea. It must have been Kit Stratton. No. It could not have been Kit Stratton, for he had denied it. Not Sir Hugo either, for he was sworn to secrecy. But someone had done it. Someone… If only she knew who it was, she could perhaps—

No. There was nothing that she, a poor companion, could do. In any case, it was too late. Her conduct was known to the world. It wanted only the revelation of her identity to complete her ruin. And that could not be long delayed, for—

'Earl Luce, m'lady.'

The Earl strode in, carrying another copy of that infernal scandal sheet!

Marina felt her heart shrivelling within her like an autumn leaf. There was no hope now. The Earl detested her. When he found out what she had done—as he soon must—he would make quite sure that the whole world learned of her disgrace.

'Mama! I have brought you the latest news. I fear you will be greatly shocked. It is scandalous—'

Lazily, the Dowager picked up her own copy of the scandal sheet and waved it in her son's direction. 'Save your breath, William,' she said acidly. 'I learned of it long ago.'

The Earl let out a long, exasperated sigh.

Marina wished that the floor would open and swallow her up. Her blood was pounding so loudly in her ears that she felt as if her head would burst.

'Oh, sit down, do. Tell me,' the Dowager continued, with poorly feigned concern, 'how is Charlotte taking the news?'

'I have not told her. She is… You must understand, Mama, that Charlotte is in an…interesting condition.'

'What? Again? For heaven's sake, William, you cannot afford to support ten children, far less eleven. What on earth were you thinking of?'

'Let me remind you, Mama, that marriage was ordained by God for the procreation of children.'

'Hmph! Even you are not required to populate the earth all by yourself. You are a fool, William. Sometimes I wonder if—'

'Mama,' interrupted the Earl, with a sharp glance towards Marina, the unwilling witness of his humiliation, 'I came to ask your advice about this…this…' He waved his scandal sheet in the direction of the copy on his mother's lap. 'You say that you know who M.B. is. So, you must also know that it falls to me to take action in the matter.'

Lady Luce raised an eyebrow.

'Someone must do so, Mama. Her father will not return for at least another month and her brother is only a schoolboy. I cannot ignore my responsibilities. Remember that I am her godfather.'

Tilly's godfather! Marina closed her eyes and dropped her head. Her hands were tightly clasped to stop them from shaking. Automatically, she felt for her ring.

'So you have decided that I was referring to Tilly Blaine, have you, William?'

'Are you telling me that you were not?'

'I am telling you nothing at all. It is for you to draw your own conclusions.' The Dowager pursed her lips for a moment. 'I must say, however, that I should not be surprised at anything that family might do.'

The Earl stared hard at his mother but she said nothing more. She looked, Marina thought, like a cat who had just caught a live mouse and was waiting for it to attempt to escape, so that it could be caught all over again. Why did one old woman get so much pleasure from tormenting her only son?

'Very well. You leave me no choice, Mama. I shall go immediately to consult Lady Blaine. She will be profoundly shocked, of course, but I must have her agreement before I take the...necessary steps.'

Necessary steps? What on earth could he mean? What was he going to do?

The Dowager relaxed back into her chair. A tiny smile flickered at one corner of her thin mouth. She said nothing at all.

The Earl waited a moment. Then he said, 'As you wish, ma'am. I bid you good morning.'

A quick bow and he was gone.

The moment the door closed on him, the Dowager began to laugh. It was a hard, brittle sound, and to Marina's ears, it was filled with malice.

'Pompous ass,' said the Dowager at last, straightening her back once more. She lifted her lorgnette and turned her gaze to Marina. 'What is the matter with you, child? You look as white as a sheet. Do you tell me you are not enjoying this little tragedy? I told you it would be better than a play, did I not? Pity that William has proposed himself for the leading role, for his acting ability leaves much to be desired. I doubt there will be many curtain calls.'

'Ma'am.' Marina's voice was barely audible. She cleared her throat and forced herself to try again. 'Ma'am, may I ask what the Earl meant…about taking the necessary steps? I did not—'

'Lud! You really are a country mouse,' said the Dowager, shaking her head. 'I had not thought that Yorkshire was so very far from civilisation. Why, he will insist that Kit Stratton marries that gel. What else did you think he would do?'

Marina felt a chill of fear settling round her body. She could neither move nor speak. Kit Stratton would be forced into a totally loveless marriage. It did not matter that Tilly Blaine worshipped him, for she would soon discover that her new husband despised her. No doubt, she would learn to hate him. Oh, it was a terrible fate for both of them.

And it was Marina's fault.

She closed her eyes. Her anger at Kit Stratton's outrageous behaviour had melted away as if it had never been. Now she could see his handsome face looking down at her with sympathy in his eyes. She could almost feel his hand on hers, gentle and comforting, when he should have been accusing her of betrayal. Nothing he had done could possibly merit such a lifelong punishment. A woman who truly loved him would sacrifice herself to save him. A woman who truly loved him— and Marina could no longer pretend to herself that she did not—was bound to tell the truth, no matter what the cost to herself.

Oh, dear God, how had it come to this? She was in

love with the blackest rake in London. If anyone discovered it, she would be ruined.

Marina willed a shell of ice to form around her heart. It was the only way. She sat immobile, allowing it to grow. She had fallen in love with Kit Stratton, in spite of herself. If he so much as guessed her weakness, he would use it against her. She did not think she could bear that. She must lock her feelings away where not even the strongest flame could melt a path to them.

Otherwise, she was totally lost.

The Dowager was paying not the least attention to Marina. She was totally absorbed in her own train of thought. 'He will never succeed,' she said emphatically.

Marina was shocked back to the present.

'Kit Stratton will never agree to an alliance under duress. He went into exile five years ago to avoid marrying Emma Fitzwilliam—and she was both beautiful, and an heiress. He will certainly refuse to marry a plain, empty-headed ninny like Tilly Blaine. Especially when it is William who demands it. He will laugh in William's face.'

'But Miss Blaine—'

'Balderdash! Think, Marina. Everyone knows that Kit Stratton's mistresses are always diamonds of the first water. If Tilly Blaine was alone in his company, it would have been at *her* instigation, not at his. Can't say I'm at all surprised, after the exhibition she made of herself at Lady Stratton's. She will be responsible for her own ruin. And for making William look the fool that he is. Dare say the whole Blaine family will have to go abroad.' She nodded happily at that new thought. 'You and I will have our revenge, miss, and London Society will be well rid of them all.'

Chapter Seventeen

'And so she berated me, Hugo. You've never seen such fire, I tell you. Her eyes were ablaze. She looked to be about to launch herself at me, claws unsheathed like a tawny lioness. It was a pity that I had to quench the flames…and so callously, too.'

Hugo gave him a rather strange look, but said nothing.

'She must have thought me totally devoid of feeling but, in truth, the idea that I would have anything to do with Tilly Blaine was so absurd… However, I should not have laughed. I freely admit my fault, but—'

'That is all very well, Kit, but did you admit your fault to Miss Beaumont?'

'I… No, I could not. Emma returned just then, and it was impossible for me to say anything more. As it was—'

'As it was, Emma was well aware that something…out of the ordinary had taken place in her absence. She told me that Miss Beaumont seemed quite distressed. That is why I am here. You know well enough that I feel in some degree responsible for Miss Beaumont's welfare. So I must ask you, Kit, did you take advantage of her?'

'No. Of course not. I would not do such a thing. Not to Miss Beaumont. I held her hands, nothing more. And my aim was only to comfort her. She was distressed, but more for Miss Blaine's sake than for her own.'

'She is a remarkable woman, I think,' said Hugo.

Kit nodded thoughtfully. He had long since reached the same conclusion. She was in some considerable danger of losing her reputation, but she seemed more concerned for others than for herself. He had never encountered a woman like her. In that instant, he resolved to do what he could to protect her. It would be little enough. He should have found out precisely where his housekeeper had been and what she had done, but he had been so incensed by the woman's treachery that he had dismissed her the moment the Baroness was out of the door. He would never find her again now.

Kit's butler knocked and entered, carrying a letter on a salver. 'Excuse me, sir, but this has just been delivered. The messenger says it is urgent. He is waiting for a reply.'

'Very well,' said Kit, ripping open the seal. 'Take him to the kitchen. I will ring when I am ready.'

'Very good, sir.' Soundlessly, the butler bowed himself out.

Hugo had quietly taken a seat beside the fireplace. He was smiling. 'You have your servants very well trained, Kit.'

Kit looked up and grimaced. 'Here, perhaps,' he said, his voice full of self-reproach, 'but not in all my establishments. Good God!'

'What is it?' asked Hugo, rising.

'This letter. It is from Katharina…the Baroness. She writes that her husband knows about her affairs and that he is threatening her.'

'What does she want from you? Did you not warn her to refer her husband to her latest lover? Cullen, ain't it?'

Kit nodded. 'Apparently, I am the only one who can help her. She asks me to meet her but—' he looked again at the letter, to make sure that he had missed nothing '—she specifies neither time nor place. She says only that she dare not go to Chelsea.'

'Sounds smoky to me.'

'And to me,' agreed Kit. 'I have never been moved by impassioned pleas. "Do not fail me," she writes. What am I supposed to make of that?'

'Something underhand, I should guess. Shall you ignore it?'

'No.' He went to his desk and sat down. 'For the moment,' he said, beginning to write, 'I shall humour her. When she has stated her terms…'

'When she has stated her terms, Kit, you will not go alone to meet her.'

Kit glanced up and grinned briefly. 'Protecting my back still, brother?'

Hugo grinned back. 'You used to say that was what brothers were for, as I recall.'

Kit did not respond. He merely shook his head ruefully and continued with his letter. Hugo, well used to his brother's ways, returned to sit in his chair, seemingly content.

The butler returned just as Kit was sanding his letter. Odd. He had not rung. 'You are become a mind-reader, it appears?' he said, looking sideways at the man.

'No, sir,' said the butler impassively. 'Lord Luce has called. He insists on seeing you immediately.'

'Ah, that explains it.' Methodically, Kit sealed his letter and handed it to the butler. 'See that the messenger has that. And now…I suppose you had better ask my latest visitor to come in.'

Lord Luce entered the room like a ship in full sail, seeking an enemy to blast with his cannons. But he stopped short when he saw that Kit was not alone.

'You are acquainted with my brother, Sir Hugo Stratton, are you not, sir?' said Kit with withering politeness.

'Indeed,' said the Earl through gritted teeth. 'However, my business, sir, is with you. Alone, if you please.'

Hugo, who had risen to bow to the Earl, resumed his seat with calm deliberation. Kit tried not to smile. Hugo could be mighty stubborn when he chose and, in this case, he had clearly decided that Lord Luce's visit required a witness.

'My brother has my full confidence, sir,' Kit said. 'You may discuss any business in front of him. Pray be seated.' He waved the Earl towards a stout chair. 'How may I serve you?'

The Earl did not sit. He looked as if he were about to explode. 'You may serve me, sir, by making an offer of marriage to my goddaughter, Miss Mathilda Blaine! I need not demean her, or myself, by giving you reasons. You know them well enough.'

So that was to be the way of it, Kit thought. In the absence of the father, the godfather came to demand satisfaction. Pity that Luce lacked the necessary dignity to play the role of the wronged parent.

'I fear you are mistaken, sir,' Kit said, very deliberately. 'I have given Miss Blaine no reason—no reason at all—to believe that she might expect an offer from me.'

'You…you lying devil, Stratton! Two private meetings in your Chelsea hide-away. Is that not reason enough? Eh?'

Kit pursed his lips. 'Has Miss Blaine told you, in terms, that she was there?' Seeing Luce's hesitation, Kit continued, 'I take it that she has not.'

'Didn't need to. Her mother taxed her with it. She didn't deny it. How could she? You were seen together, dammit!'

'Might I ask, by whom?'

The Earl began to bluster. 'Don't matter who saw you. Whole of London will know. The gel will be ruined if you don't do right by her. And I intend to see that you do!'

Kit clasped his hands casually behind his back and began to pace slowly up and down in front of the hearth. 'How very unfortunate,' he said at last, shaking his head, 'that we find ourselves unable to agree on that point.'

'What? You—!'

'I have absolutely no obligation to Miss Blaine. Pray convey that message, with my respects, to the Viscountess. My respects to your lady wife, too, of course. Good day to you, sir.'

Kit moved to open the door. Hugo rose politely.

The Earl finally exploded. 'By God, I'll see that you suffer for this! Every door in London with be closed to you. To every last one of you!' He stomped out, muttering.

Calmly, Kit closed the door on the Earl and shrugged his shoulders. 'Nasty,' he said. 'I am sorry you had to be witness to that, Hugo.'

Hugo chewed at his lip for a moment. 'He means mischief, Kit. You must see that. What do you mean to do? I don't believe for a moment that you will allow that clown to blacken your name all over London.'

'Our name, Hugo. His threats were directed at us all, you and Emma included.'

'I will consult Emma, of course, but I do not take kindly to threats.'

'Nor I,' agreed Kit. 'And in this case, a lady's honour is involved.'

'Miss Beaumont's?'

Kit nodded. 'I cannot disprove Luce's allegations without compromising Miss Beaumont. And that I will not do.'

'Do you have a choice?'

'Certainly. I shall do nothing. I have absolutely no desire to be legshackled, Hugo. Even if I had, Miss Blaine is the last woman I should choose. Let Luce do his worst—if he dares. No one in his right mind would believe that I willingly sought an assignation—no, two assignations—with Tilly Blaine. Luce will be laughed to scorn.'

'That's a pretty risky tactic, Kit. And Miss Blaine could be ruined. Have you no thought for her?'

'Miss Blaine has brought it upon herself, Hugo. You heard what Luce said: the girl had a chance to deny the allegations, but she did not. She must *want* to be ruined.'

Hugo shook his head a little sadly. 'Wants to seize the faintest chance of marriage to you, more like.'

'More fool she,' retorted Kit harshly. 'I should make her the devil of a bad husband, Hugo.'

'Now that, I fancy, is the first sensible remark you have made all morning,' said Hugo with a fleeting grin. He made for the door. 'You will send to me at once if you hear from Luce again? Or from your Baroness? Good. Do not forget that Emma is expecting you this afternoon. And she will not accept excuses!'

Kit maintained his nonchalant pose until the door had closed behind Hugo. Then he sank into the chair behind his desk and distractedly ran his fingers through his thick hair. Hugo had been remarkably restrained, Kit concluded, particularly as the Stratton name was bound to be sullied by Kit's decision to ride out the coming storm. What a coil! First, Katharina—and then, this Blaine woman. She must be mad! No woman could believe—surely?—that she could blackmail a man into marriage on the basis of a few mistaken rumours. What kind of marriage did she think it could be?

She probably did not think about it at all. Most women were incapable of thinking beyond the altar and their bride-clothes. Tilly Blaine must have spun herself some mad fantasy based solely on his handsome face. Truly, his looks were a curse!

Kit shook his head despairingly. Hugo had said—and he was right—that inaction was a dangerous course to follow. Luce would not have the sense to keep his mouth shut. And there would always be those who would quote the old adage of 'no smoke without fire'. Even while they admitted that Kit Stratton had never been known to trifle with single women, particularly plain ones, they would wonder. And they would gossip. In the end, Kit would be forced to offer for Miss Blaine.

He would have to go abroad again.

Would that not be an admission of guilt in the eyes of Society? And what about Hugo and Emma? His disgrace would also be theirs.

If Kit left England, the scandal would be soon forgotten.

His choices were stark. He could flee. Again. Or he could betray Marina Beaumont. That he would not do.

Marina hesitated by the steps. She was not sure that she dared to enter Fitzwilliam House again after yesterday's altercation with Mr Stratton. She had been so dreadfully embarrassed when Lady Stratton walked in on them. She had covered up her anger as best she could, but Lady Stratton was no fool. She must have been aware that her guests were at outs. It had been a relief to escape from the house.

Marina wondered how Mr Stratton had accounted for their quarrel. Perhaps he had simply pretended that nothing had happened? Perhaps Lady Stratton was too polite to ask?

It was impossible to know. Just as it had been impossible not to respond to today's urgently worded request that Marina call on Lady Stratton as soon as possible. Her ladyship had even sent the Stratton carriage to sit at the Dowager's door, to await Marina's convenience.

She was in no doubt about why she had been invited. The request had come in the name of Lady Stratton, to be sure, but it must have originated with the lady's brother-in-law. Kit Stratton knew—as did his brother— that Lord Luce's allegations about Kit and Miss Blaine were totally without foundation. The Earl had no grounds for demanding that Kit should marry Miss Blaine. But Marina was the only person who could prove it.

Marina took a deep breath and mounted the steps. The door swung open just as she reached for the knocker. She was expected. Replying mechanically to the butler's greeting, she followed him up to Lady Stratton's drawing room without another word. Her brain was too full of questions. What could she say to Lady Stratton, who had been so very kind to her? What about Sir Hugo, who knew the real truth? Lady Luce might be absolutely sure that Kit would not be forced into marriage with Tilly Blaine, but what if she were wrong?

Marina lifted her chin resolutely when she reached the

upper landing. She had been taught to be honest and to have consideration for others. In this situation, however, such simple rules would not suffice, for she could not save one party without harming the other. She was sorry for Tilly Blaine, but the only way to save the girl's reputation would be to sacrifice Kit. And Marina was not prepared to do that. It was not a matter of love. Absolutely not, for love was buried. It was a matter of honour.

'Miss Beaumont, m'lady.'

Lady Stratton hurried forward to take Marina's hand. She looked less composed than usual, but at least she was alone. Marina had been expecting—and dreading— a meeting with one or other of the Stratton men.

'Thank you for coming so promptly, my dear. The Dowager made no difficulty?'

'No, ma'am. She…she is much absorbed in domestic matters at present. And she is promised to a card party this evening. She said that she had no need of me.'

'Good. I would not wish to inconvenience her in any way. Will you not be seated? Do take off your bonnet and be comfortable. I will ring for some tea.'

Marina did as she was bid, wondering what was coming next.

She did not have long to wait. The tea tray was delivered by an impassive butler—followed by Mr Kit Stratton.

'Miss Beaumont,' he said formally, bowing.

Marina's throat was so dry that she could not speak. She managed to incline her head.

'Miss Beaumont, I trust you will forgive me,' said Lady Stratton, colouring a little, 'but I find that I am again required to leave you to consult with my husband. So very tedious, is it not? But I know that I can depend on you to do the honours on my behalf.' She whisked herself out of the room almost before Marina had time to draw breath to reply.

She was alone with Kit Stratton. Again! And he was looking down at her with eyes full of accusation.

'Cream and sugar, Mr Stratton?' asked Marina. Her voice was a croak.

'Indeed, ma'am. I have not changed my habits since yesterday.'

He was not about to make this interview an easy one, but Marina did not feel she had grounds for complaint. He probably wanted to strangle her for what she had done. Being a gentleman, he would confine himself to wounding her with words.

She handed him his cup. She did not smile. Nor did she speak.

The silence was broken at last when he said, 'I take it that you are aware, ma'am, that Lord Luce called upon me today?' He waited for her nod before continuing. 'And you are aware of the details of his errand?'

She nodded again. There was nothing she could say.

'Good. That makes our discussion that much easier.' He paused, replaced his cup carefully on the tray and turned in his chair so that he could look directly into her eyes. 'I need to be sure, Miss Beaumont. You do not intend to intervene in any way in this matter?'

That sounded very much like an accusation to Marina's ears. Did he really believe that she would remain silent while he was forced into a loveless marriage? Was that what he thought of her? How could it be that she loved a man who believed her to be so base?

She stared back into those blue eyes, refusing to drop her gaze. She would prove that she was no coward. 'Mr Stratton,' she said in a low, determined voice, 'I may be poor, but I am not without honour. It was not possible for me to reveal the truth to Lord Luce this morning—' she fancied she saw a momentary gleam in his eye at that '—but I have every intention of telling him at the first opportunity. The Dowager—I have no doubt—will ensure that this scandalous rumour is exposed for the falsehood that it is.'

His eyes narrowed. That fleeting gleam—if it had ever been there—was long gone. He now looked absolutely furious. Marina fought against her natural desire to shrink from him.

He reached out and clasped her wrist in a grip so tight it was almost painful. 'Miss Beaumont, you will allow me to tell you that you are a fool. You would announce to the world that you had private meetings with the worst rake in London—twice. Just what do you expect to achieve? Mmm? Other than your own ruin, of course.'

Marina felt as if his words were blows, battering her defenceless body.

His merciless attack was not over. His grip tightened on her flesh. 'Do you think to save Miss Blaine from disgrace by your admission? You are too late for that, my girl. She has all but announced to the world that she is M.B.'

'No! She could not have—'

'I have it from her godfather's own lips, Miss Beaumont. Would you have me call him a liar?'

'No, but—'

'I am glad you spare me that, at least. Now,' he said, pulling her a little closer, 'you will listen to me. I have given Lord Luce my answer. The matter is decided. You will not say a word about your part in it, neither to the Dowager nor to anyone else. Your story would change nothing, but it would certainly brand you as yet another of Kit Stratton's misguided mistresses.'

'But—' She tried to struggle free. He must not be allowed to go through with this.

He reached out his free hand and placed a finger gently across her lips. 'Be quiet, Marina, and listen to me. Do you never do as you are told?'

That single touch changed everything. She could not utter a word. Though his strong hand gripped her frail wrist bones as fiercely as ever, that finger was resting on her mouth with the delicacy of a butterfly. She felt a sudden overwhelming urge to taste his skin.

Something must have shown in her face, for his hold on her wrist relaxed a fraction. His free hand left her mouth to stroke a stray curl away from her cheek, but his finger did not return to her lips. She closed her eyes to hide the longing that filled her at the loss of his touch.

'You will return to Yorkshire quite soon. In a week or so. You will say that you no longer need to be employed as a companion, since your brother is to receive a rich living. That is true enough, though it cannot now be at Stratton Magna. I could not allow— It might give rise to…difficulties if you were living on my estate.'

'*Your* estate! It is *your* living?'

'I shall arrange for it to be exchanged for another,' Kit said coolly.

In that moment, all Marina's longings were overtaken by a desire to strike his haughty face. He was calmly arranging her life—and her family's—without permitting her to say a word. And it was quite obvious that he was determined to allow himself to be blackmailed into marriage with Tilly Blaine. Stupid, arrogant—

'I see,' she said angrily. 'I collect that I am now permitted to speak? How very kind of you, Mr Stratton.' She jumped to her feet, wrenching her wrist from his grasp with a tiny mew of pain. 'Then you will allow me

to tell you that I have absolutely no intention of taking
orders from you, sir. Tilly Blaine is a fool, and dishonest,
to boot, if she thinks to secure a husband by such lies.
I shall tell the truth, to anyone who will listen. And if it
should ruin my reputation…I have only myself to blame.
Everything that happened was my own doing. And I am
more than prepared to face the consequences of my actions. What is more—'

She was given no chance to continue. Kit seized her
by the shoulders and shook her, hard. Her eyes widened
in shock. Then he took her into his arms, and looked
deeply into her eyes. 'Marina, you are, without doubt,
the most courageous, and the most exasperating woman
I have ever met.'

And then he kissed her. It was a kiss of anger, and of
ruthless power. She knew it was intended to prove how
weak she was, to show her that she could not stand
against him.

She knew it. And yet she wanted to yield to him. The
touch of his lips renewed the encounters of her dreams,
when he had come to her in love and gentleness. Her
body yearned for him. In spite of everything.

She was a fool!

'No!' she cried, pushing him away with all her
strength as he raised his hand to her hair. 'No! I will not
be a pawn in your games, Mr Stratton! Even a plain
companion has a conscience, sir, and I intend to obey
mine. Good day to you.' She grabbed her bonnet and
ran out of the room without giving him the opportunity
to say another word.

For perhaps the first time in his life, Kit was completely at a loss. At first, he could think of nothing but
the proud set of her head as she fled from him. He had
abused her…again. Where Marina Beaumont was con-

cerned, his vaunted powers over women seemed to vanish. He had brutally restrained her, he had shaken her almost until her teeth rattled, and then he had kissed her as if he wanted to punish her. For what? For daring to stand up to him? For offering to sacrifice herself to save him from marriage to the dreadful Miss Blaine?

He must do something…or Marina would be ruined. She was a paragon, a woman in a thousand, and she would be cast down into the mire for trying to defend him.

He must find a way of stopping her.

His flight would not save her. Only her own silence could do that. And she would not remain silent while she believed she could stop him from marrying Tilly Blaine.

He slumped down into his chair and tried to think rationally. It took a long time, but eventually an answer came. It was far from palatable.

Marriage.

Society required him to offer for Tilly Blaine. Once their forthcoming marriage had been made public, nothing—nothing—could prevent it. Marina could surely be brought to realise that her confession would be useless. She was bound to agree to keep silent.

Provided his marriage had already been announced.

He shook his head despairingly. A week ago, he would not have believed it possible. He, Kit Stratton—the rake who had sworn he would never be shackled to any woman—no longer cared whether he was forced into marriage or not.

Kit crossed to Emma's little writing desk in the corner of the room. He would swallow his stiff-necked pride and demand—no, request—an urgent interview with Lord Luce.

And at that interview, he would offer marriage to Miss Tilly Blaine.

Chapter Eighteen

Almost tripping in her haste, Marina hurried down the stairs in response to the Dowager's summons. Lord Luce had called on his mama yet again, probably to gloat about his meeting with Kit Stratton. Now was Marina's chance to convince the Earl that he was wrong about his goddaughter and Kit Stratton. There might still be time to prevent the announcement of the engagement.

The Earl glanced up in annoyance when Marina entered the room but, for once, he said nothing. Perhaps he had realised, at last, that his protests would merely inflame his mother's temper more than ever.

'And so I was right,' said the Dowager with satisfaction, paying no attention at all to Marina's arrival.

'Not precisely, Mama,' said the Earl. 'It is true that young Stratton acted just as you predicted when I called on him yesterday. Refused point blank to recognise his obligations to the gel. Challenged me to do my worst. Dam…dashed impudent, too.'

The Dowager began to look very pleased with herself.

Marina could not believe her ears. He couldn't have! He was going to marry Tilly Blaine. Had he not said so, just yesterday? Lord Luce must have misunderstood… somehow.

'After discussing the matter with Lady Blaine, we…I decided to give the fellow a little time to reflect before I took any action.'

'Hmph! You mean Lady Blaine told you not to say anything. She has the sense to see that there is no point in trumpeting the ruin of her daughter's reputation. She knows that the rumours will start soon enough by themselves. While you—'

'While I have been proved right, ma'am,' he declared. 'Young Stratton has now written to me requesting the favour of an interview at my earliest convenience. He is to call on me this morning. I have no doubt that he will make an offer for Tilly.' He allowed himself a very superior smile. 'Lady Blaine is delighted, as you may imagine. When I left her, she was writing to her husband, telling him the good news and how fortunate the family had been to be able to rely on such an invaluable intermediary as myself. She told me that no godfather could have done more. Of course, I always knew I had diplomatic skills, but—'

'Your only skill is in deluding yourself,' retorted the Dowager. 'You think that you will be applauded by the Blaines and all their set for this great *coup* you have brought off, do you? I tell you it will not happen.'

'Excuse me, ma'am,' began Marina, trying desperately to attract the Dowager's attention. This wicked charade must be stopped.

'Not now, Marina. I am talking to William.'

'But, ma'am, it is vital that you listen to me. Mr Stratton has been wronged. Miss Blaine was *never* alone with him.'

There was an astonished silence. Lord Luce stood goggle-eyed.

'I beg your pardon?' exclaimed the Dowager at last, turning to stare at Marina.

'Miss Blaine is not M.B. I am.'

'Impossible—'

'Be silent, William. Marina? Explain.'

'It is quite true, ma'am. It was I who visited Mr Stratton at his house in Chelsea. Twice.'

'I warned you not to keep this…this hussy in your house, Mama. You should have—'

'I asked you to be silent, William. I have no doubt that Marina had good reasons for her actions—'

It was only then that Marina realised she would have to explain what she had done, and why. Her horror must have shown on her face for the Dowager continued quickly, 'We will speak of that later, my child. For the moment, we must concentrate on William's little escapade. So much for your great victory, eh, William? You cannot hope to marry her off now.' Marina was at a loss to understand why Lady Luce sounded so pleased.

'Nonsense,' said the Earl. 'I do not believe what Miss…what this person says, not for one moment. Come, come, Mama. Tilly has admitted that she was with Stratton. Are you suggesting that she lied? A Viscount's daughter? To her own mother?'

'Tell me, William,' said Lady Luce softly, 'what *exactly* did your precious Tilly say?'

The Earl looked a little self-conscious. Then he said, 'I was not present, of course. Lady Blaine said she taxed Tilly with being M.B. and…and Tilly would not deny it. So it must be true.'

'Balderdash! Tilly Blaine has the brains of a flea as well as the face of a horse. I'd wager a king's ransom she said nothing at all. Probably just stood there, looking guilty, with her mouth hanging open at the very idea of having been alone with Kit Stratton. Well?'

The Earl began to pace. His mother sent a conspiratorial glance towards Marina.

His pacing stopped abruptly. 'It is of no moment whether Tilly was with him or not. What matters is that he is prepared to offer for her. His letter leaves me in no doubt about that.' He patted his pocket. 'We'll never get a better offer for Tilly. She's well enough dowered, but for the rest... Can't pass up a chance like this. Her father will be delighted that I've caught her such a rich husband.'

If Marina had not heard his words, she would not have believed that any gentleman could be so wicked.

The Dowager did not attempt to mask her outrage. 'You are a blackguard, William. Your only interest is in being able to boast about your famous victory over Kit Stratton. I tell you I will not permit it. Kit Stratton may be a rake, but he is worth ten of you.'

'But you hate Kit Stratton, Mama!'

The Earl had voiced Marina's exact thoughts. Why should the Dowager take Kit Stratton's part against her own son? No matter how much she despised him, he was still her own flesh and blood.

'Not nearly as much as I hate you. And the family of the man who sired you.'

'What? But my father provided for you...this house, the—'

'Your father disowned you and rejected me. Did you never notice how little you resembled the family portraits?' She shook her head. 'No. I suppose you did not. A strong intellect has never been much in evidence among the Blaines.'

The Earl's jaw had dropped open. Deflated, he sank into a chair.

'I will not allow that accursed family to triumph over me again—even if I have to side with Kit Stratton to do it. I warn you, William. If you persist in trying to force this match, I will announce to the world that your father was the late Viscount Blaine.'

'You…you will only bring scandal on yourself,' he protested weakly.

'What of it? I am an old woman now. Everyone who mattered—my husband, our son—is dead long ago. Why should I care a rap what they say of me now?'

'I am still your son, too, Mama,' he replied, with surprising dignity, 'and my children are your grandchildren. You will ruin their lives for your petty revenge.'

'Petty, is it? Your father—your real father—seduced me and then threw me into the gutter. My family was about to disown me. I could have died if it had not been for Lord Luce. He married me and saved my reputation. And when our own darling son was killed in India, and my husband soon after, Lord Blaine—your *father*— came to gloat over my distress. Said your brother was a weakling, of weakling stock. Said I should be glad that a real man had sired *you*.' She glared at him. 'You are no son of mine. Look at you, with your tyrant's ways and your broods of children. You're a Blaine, all right.'

'No, Mama. Under the law, I am the rightful Earl Luce.'

She almost groaned. 'The title should have gone to Roland. He was the only true Luce.'

'My brother is dead, Mama. No amount of revenge will bring him back to you.'

'No, but the Blaines shall suffer as I have suffered. I mean what I say, William. If you force Kit Stratton to marry that Blaine chit—*your niece*, I should say—I'll denounce you at the altar if I have to.'

He rose from his seat and shook his head at her. 'Think carefully before you do anything so rash, Mama. Remember that you are known to be…unconventional. They will take it as the ravings of a lunatic.'

'Balderdash!'

'And nothing you might say will influence Lady Blaine, in any case. What will she care if you had an affair with her father-in-law? He is long dead. Whereas her daughter—and the prospect of imminent disgrace— is very much alive. No, Mama, your pitiful little black-mail will not serve.' He bowed abruptly. 'Good day to you, ma'am,' he said, and marched out.

Marina could not believe what she had just heard. It explained much, but it was like…like the plot of a Gothic novel. Such things did not happen in real life, did they?

The Dowager looked at Marina with defeat in her eyes. 'Shocked, child?' she said quite gently. It sounded nothing like her normal, robust delivery. 'I dare say your grandmama could have told you much about her family and their wicked deeds. The Blaine men have always been wild with women. Not their own women, you un-derstand. Blaine women, both wives and daughters, must be totally beyond reproach in that regard. Dare say that's why your grandmother was cast out. She challenged her father. And her brother. They would never tolerate that. Never.'

'Is that…forgive me, ma'am, but is that why you let me stay? Because of what the Blaines did to my family?'

Lady Luce gave a wan smile. 'The Blaines have done enough harm already, to your family and to mine. Couldn't let William revert to his father's ways. He's already a bully. And he longs to be a tyrant. He'd be a womaniser, too, if he had the money or the looks.'

'He is *your* son too, ma'am,' ventured Marina, expecting one of the Dowager's bruising snubs for her pains.

'Perhaps, but I can't say I've ever seen any of myself in him. Always backs away from a fight.'

'He did not do so this time, ma'am. He seemed… determined to give you your own again.'

She snorted. 'Only because he thinks he is on safe ground.' She paused. 'This time, I fear he may be. The Blaines could win. Again.' Her thin hands were curled into fists.

'Ma'am…I think I should leave London.'

'Why? I need you here.'

'But Lord Luce is bound to tell Lady Blaine about… about what I have done. She…she despises my family. She will find a way to brand me as Kit Stratton's mistress, I am sure of it…though I promise you that I am not. You would not want a companion with such a reputation, ma'am. I should go now, before the rumours start.' And before Kit's betrothal is announced, she added silently to herself. If she was taxed about her dealings with Kit, she would be unable to conceal her feelings for very long.

'Certainly not. You will stay here. Lady Blaine cannot slander you without giving up all hopes of forcing young Stratton into marriage with her daughter.'

Marina knew that the Dowager was wrong. Lady Blaine did not have to say that Marina was M.B. She had only to say that Marina had allowed herself to be seduced by Kit Stratton. The tabbies would be only too happy to spread the scandalous rumour, especially when it came from such an impeccable source.

'Besides,' continued the Dowager, 'I think my threat may give her pause. William is much too sure of himself. The Blaines would not wish it known that the late Viscount was given to seducing innocent young ladies…and then abandoning them. Mark my words, Marina, I shall not allow them another victory.' She drummed her fingers on the arm of her chair. 'They are all promised for my party this evening. I think that a short private interview will be in order.' She smiled, in very much her old way.

'And now,' she continued blandly, 'perhaps you ought to tell me about the real M.B. and her dealings with that handsome young rake?'

Marina gazed at herself in the glass. She was still thoroughly agitated. If it had not been for Gibson's help, she would have been unable even to fasten her gown. And as for her hair…

She looked dreadfully pale, almost ghastly, in spite of the glowing pink of her new evening gown. She viewed herself with something approaching horror. She was about to be exposed as a harlot. And she would have to watch, from the sidelines, while the man she loved was forcibly betrothed to the daughter of a wicked, scheming family. There was nothing she could do to prevent any of it.

She made her way along the hallway and down the stairs, reminding herself to keep her head high and her back straight. The Dowager had summoned her to join her makeshift conference in the bookroom on the ground floor. Marina hated that place. It was the room in which the Earl had interviewed her on the day she arrived— and again on the day he had sought to dismiss her. It all

seemed so very long ago. For it was before she had
learned to love Kit Stratton.

She tried not to think about him, but it was useless.
She had only to hear his name for her heart to start
pounding and her skin to tingle in anticipation of his
touch. It was unlikely she would ever see him again—
in spite of everything the Dowager had said, she was
sure to be banished to Yorkshire very soon—but she
found herself longing for one more glimpse, one more
touch of those strong fingers…

Foolish, foolish girl, even to think of such a thing!
She had tried to save him. And she had surely failed.
This interview would prove it.

Tibbs was standing guard by the bookroom door. He
nodded at Marina and opened it.

'Miss Beaumont is here,' declared the Dowager.
'Good. We may begin.'

'I do not see why I should have to tolerate the presence of a woman like that,' snapped Lady Blaine, looking to Lord Luce for support. 'If you will excuse me,
ma'am—'

'I will not. I would remind you, ma'am, that you are
a guest in my house. I decide who shall go and who
shall stay.'

Marina tried to hide her clenched fists in her skirts.
Terrible though it was, this interview would have to end
soon. The Dowager's guests were arriving. If only there
were something she could do…

'I take it, ma'am,' continued the Dowager firmly, 'that
Luce has told you the gist of our discussion this afternoon?'

Lady Blaine looked down her nose at the old lady.
Eventually, she gave a tiny nod.

'Let us have the truth with no bark on it. You and

your family are proposing to use falsehoods to catch a rich husband for your daughter. You do not need me to tell you how dishonourable that is. Your daughter is no better than a slut!'

Lady Blaine was shocked into a protest. 'How dare you say such a thing? My daughter is innocent of any wrongdoing. She—'

'Your daughter allowed the whole world to see her behaving like a mooncalf over Kit Stratton. I don't call that innocent!'

'Of course it was!' retorted the Viscountess, who was now becoming extremely angry. 'With those remarkable looks, he seemed like a hero to Tilly, the sort of man who belonged in the settings of her favourite poems. She was daydreaming, nothing more!'

'Perhaps you should take her off to see some of the exotic locations she is so fond of,' said the Dowager quickly, 'instead of forcing her into marriage.'

'Her husband can show them to her,' said Lady Blaine flatly. 'After they are married.'

The Dowager nodded to herself. 'You are determined, then, ma'am? Very well. So am I. If you go ahead with this, I shall announce to the world that your dear friend, William, is the illegitimate son of the late Viscount. He is, in fact, your husband's older brother.'

'Half-brother,' corrected Lady Blaine.

The Dowager waited for her to continue, but she did not. 'Have you nothing more to say?'

Lady Blaine glanced at the Earl and then drawled, 'The whole world knew that my father-in-law sired children on the wrong side of the blanket. If you wish to add yourself to the list of his mistresses, ma'am, please do so. It will not affect my family—or our decisions— in the least. And now, if you please, I should like to join your other guests. I came here on the promise of Faro and I have every intention of playing.' She bowed her turbanned head a fraction and then swept across the room and out of the door.

The Earl made to follow.

'A moment, William.' When he turned back, the Dowager said, 'I take it that Kit Stratton has made an offer for Miss Blaine?'

'Yes. This afternoon.'

'And it has been accepted?'

'Yes. Nothing can be announced until the Viscount returns, naturally, but we expect him very soon now. Lady Blaine received a letter from him this very afternoon.'

'How very fortunate for her,' said the Dowager acidly.

Her son did not attempt to reply. He bowed politely to his mama, looked with loathing on Marina, and strode out of the room.

'Ma'am,' began Marina, putting a hand gently on the Dowager's arm.

Lady Luce turned a strained face to Marina. This time, she appeared to be completely defeated.

'Ma'am, I have had an idea. The other day, you said…you implied that Lady Blaine cheats at Faro. Are you sure of it?'

The old eyes gleamed. 'Absolutely sure,' she said firmly.

'We may yet outwit them…if…if you are sure that is what you want to do?'

The Dowager nodded immediately. 'Absolutely sure,' she said again.

'Then…then I must ask you to trust me, ma'am, and to follow my lead, however strange my actions may seem. I do not know precisely what I shall have to do—

I must gauge the lie of the land first—but I shall certainly need your help. I can explain that later. Upstairs.'

The Dowager had started to move towards the door. Her guests would be wondering why she had not yet appeared. 'My help?'

'Lady Blaine is going to play Faro. And—with your help, ma'am—so am I!'

'Good evening, ma'am.'

'Mr Stratton!' Marina stopped in her tracks. What on earth was he doing here in Lady Luce's house?

He reached for her hand but she whipped it behind her back. She dare not let him touch her now. She dare not even think about him. She must focus only on what she was about to do.

He looked quizzically at her. 'I don't bite, Miss Beaumont. You are quite safe, you know. And I *was* invited.'

She nodded, wide-eyed. 'I beg your pardon, sir,' she said in a strained voice, and then stopped. She could think of nothing more to say.

'My brother and his wife are here, too. It seems that the Dowager has decided to offer the Strattons a truce. I wonder why?'

Marina was in no doubt that he understood perfectly. It was simply that he enjoyed baiting people, especially Marina herself. She tried to frown him down. 'Excuse me, if you will, sir. I am needed in the Faro room.' She turned to go.

'How very interesting,' he drawled, taking her arm and slipping it through his own. 'I was just on my way there. We can go together.'

'No! I—'

He put his free hand firmly on top of her fingers. She

could not escape from his grasp. 'Marina,' he said softly,
'you are exasperating…and you are beautiful—'

She gasped. That was a downright lie.

'And, on this occasion, you will do as I say. Come.'

He started towards the card room, forcing her to follow. What else could she do? The warmth from his body
seemed to be spreading out from the spot where his fingers clasped hers. She could feel it coursing through her
veins like fiery spirit, burning a track towards her heart.
The Dowager's brandy had been nothing like this. From
this, she did not think that she could ever recover.

He had said she was beautiful.

Kit knew perfectly well that he should not have done
it. He was telling himself so, even as he pressed her
hand.

It might be his last opportunity to touch her soft skin.

Soon she would be gone from his life. Settled and
comfortable—he would see to that—but gone. He would
not be able to keep up the necessary pretence if he continued to see Marina Beaumont.

He loved her—more than he had ever thought possible.

Hugo had been right, as he always seemed to be. Kit,
the rake, the man who cared for no member of the female sex, had fallen in love with the bravest, the most
infuriating, the most wonderful woman in the world. But
he could not marry her. If only it could have been otherwise. If only Marina were—

There was no point in brooding over such a mad fantasy. He could never have married Marina. Not while a
belted earl was publicly accusing him of seducing his
goddaughter. A marriage between Kit and Marina would
have made her an outcast. She would have been labelled

a harlot—or worse. A man might learn to cope with exile and public humiliation. A gently reared lady never would.

And so he was betrothed to Tilly Blaine—an empty-headed chit who lived in a world of poetry and make-believe. He had never given the girl a moment's thought. Not even once. But now—or as soon as her father came home—he would be required to dance attendance on her, to squire her to parties, to play the part of the happy bridegroom-to-be. It would take every ounce of his self-control to play the part, but he would do it.

He would do it, provided Marina Beaumont was gone from his life.

He looked down at her. She was avoiding his eyes, but he could see the slight flush on her neck and feel the tremble in her fingers. She knew! She must know!

'Why, good evening, Kit.'

At the sound of that sultry voice, Kit felt an almost irresistible urge to utter the foulest curses known to man. He gritted his teeth. His muscles tensed, ready for the conflict to come.

'And it is Miss…the Dowager's grey companion, is it not? Will you forgive us for a moment?' The Baroness put her hand possessively on Kit's arm. He wanted to shake it off, to berate her for her rudeness to Marina, but it was too late. Marina had pulled away from him and disappeared without a word. Out of the corner of his eye, he saw that she had found the Dowager and that they were whispering together.

'Is she the best you can do, Kit? Really, I should have thought—'

'What do you want, Katharina? I came here to play cards, not to pull caps with you.'

'Why—' She broke off, looking suddenly concerned.

'I cannot talk now,' she whispered, nodding towards the stairs where her husband had just appeared. 'Later. I will think of something.' She whirled away.

Kit turned to watch the Baron's ramrod-straight figure ascend the stairs. He was in his prime, in spite of his prematurely greying hair. The gold-braided dress uniform sat well on his spare frame. He strolled past Kit without so much as a glance. Kit, conscious of the humour of the situation, bowed briefly from the neck. He had always believed that cuckolded husbands deserved some slight acknowledgement, even if only on the duelling field.

Having made sure that neither the Baroness nor her husband was before him, Kit strolled into the Faro room. He might as well play. He had lost the only thing that would ever matter to him. Perhaps if he lost his wealth tonight, the Blaines would be less eager to have him as a son-in-law.

He settled down to play with reckless abandon.

Chapter Nineteen

Kit had been playing for over an hour, and losing heavily. He had not cared a jot—in fact, he had been rather pleased—until Lady Blaine had taken over the bank. Against her, he felt a need to win.

The Dowager, on Kit's immediate right, had been remarkably polite to him, almost as if there had never been a feud between them. She was an unpredictable old woman, but she played a fine hand of cards. He would have sworn she could track the cards as well as he could himself.

The place on Kit's left hand had been vacant for a while. He had found himself wishing that Marina would take it, but he knew she would never do that. It would seem much too forward. She was sitting at the far end of the table, occasionally placing a small wager with a shaky hand. He supposed that the Dowager must have provided her with the stakes. Soon they would be gone. She was losing too often.

The bank's first deal was over. Lady Blaine had won very heavily throughout. Too heavily? Had Kit missed something? He had heard rumours…

Lady Blaine smiled nastily at the Dowager, sitting im-

mediately opposite her. 'The luck would appear to be
with the bank tonight, ma'am,' she said, pulling the heap
of winnings towards her. 'Shall you attempt to recover
your losses?'

To Kit's enormous surprise, the Dowager pushed back
her chair and rose. 'No point in chasing your luck when
it don't intend to be caught,' she said sharply. 'Don't
worry, ma'am. I shan't leave you without an opponent.
Marina! Come and take my place. Your luck cannot possibly be worse than mine.'

Marina rose obediently from her seat and came round
the table. She appeared hesitant and concerned. 'Ma'am,
I—'

The Dowager put her hand on Marina's shoulder and
forced her to sit. 'Play,' she said shortly. Then she fixed
her gaze on Lady Blaine and issued a clear challenge.
'Miss Beaumont takes my place and plays with my
stakes. You will accept that, I take it, ma'am?'

Lady Blaine went rather red, but she nodded. She
could not do otherwise in the Dowager's house. Kit
found he was rather enjoying the old woman's mischief-
making. Perhaps she was not such a harridan after all.

Marina did not look at him or acknowledge his presence in any way. Kit was not really surprised, but the
devil in him decided that she should not be permitted to
ignore him. He would make her do or say something,
even if it was only to tell him to mind his business. It
would be good to see the fire in her eyes again.

Lady Blaine had broken a fresh pack and was shuffling it rather absently; all her attention seemed to be
focused on the other players at the table. No doubt she
was hoping that more would come to fill the empty
places. The greater the number of players, the greater
her winnings would be.

Kit looked sideways at Marina. Her hands were lying loosely on the green baize. She was staring down at them, apparently lost in thought. 'Have you played Faro often, Miss Beaumont?' he asked quietly. Once the play began again, it would be much more difficult to converse with her. He must make the most of this one chance. She might not be beside him for more than one game.

She did not look at him. For a moment, it seemed that she had not heard him or, at least, that she was not going to reply. Had he really offended her so grievously?

Finally, she spoke. 'I have rarely been in the kind of company that could afford to, sir,' she said in a low voice.

From the far side of the table, Lady Blaine was straining to overhear their conversation. 'I take it that you are experienced enough to shuffle the cards, Miss Beaumont?' she sneered.

At that, Marina looked up at last. A little uncertainly, she stretched out a hand to take the pack. 'I can try, ma'am, if you permit.'

Rather than put the pack into Marina's waiting hand, Lady Blaine put it down on the table. Then she smiled knowingly at one of the gentlemen.

Ignoring the snub, Marina simply picked up the pack and began to shuffle the cards. It was obvious that she was no card player. At one point, she almost dropped the pack.

'Perhaps you would cut, Mr Stratton, once Miss Beaumont has finished?' asked Lady Blaine condescendingly.

Kit nodded. He could not trust himself to speak civilly to the woman.

'May we join you?' said Hugo's voice from the back of the room.

Kit turned and rose from his chair to greet Emma. She

was looking decidedly pleased with herself. Was that a result of yesterday's successful scheming? He was almost sure that Emma had deliberately left him alone with Marina on the previous afternoon, though he had been unable to fathom just what she was trying to achieve. Women!

'Would you like to sit here, Emma?' He indicated the vacant place on his left.

'No, thank you. I prefer to sit at the end, next to Hugo. He counts the cards better than I do. You would never tell me how to bet, Kit. You enjoy watching me lose.' From any other woman, it would have sounded like an insult, but not from Emma. There was always that enchanting glint of humour in her eyes.

'As you say, ma'am.' Smiling, Kit made Emma an extravagant leg, before resuming his seat. Miss Beaumont did not seem to have moved an inch. She was still struggling to finish shuffling the pack.

He waited patiently, watching her hands. He would never have believed that she would be quite so clumsy. It did not sit with the elegance of all her other movements, but—

'If you have finished, Miss Beaumont?' Lady Blaine sounded decidedly testy.

Marina coloured a little and abruptly stopped shuffling.

'May I, Miss Beaumont?' Kit held out his hand for the cards.

Without raising her eyes, she placed the pack on his palm. She did not touch him by even a fraction.

'Thank you, ma'am,' he said softly. He cut the cards swiftly and pushed the pack back across the table to Lady Blaine.

'At last,' she said. 'I was beginning to think we would

never be able to play.' She looked round at the players.
There were now seven of them. 'Stakes, ladies and gentlemen, if you please.'

Mechanically, Kit placed his bet. Marina did not move
at all. 'Do you not wish to play, ma'am?' he asked quietly, hoping the noise at the table would prevent the
banker from hearing his words.

She shook her head slightly. 'In a moment, sir,' she
said. Her hand was toying with the little pile of cash that
the Dowager had left behind. Then she pushed a bank-
note on to the three.

The game was unusually noisy. When Emma won, she
exclaimed about her good fortune. When she lost, she
groaned aloud. The second lady player followed suit.
Marina, however, did not. She watched the banker win
her stake from the three and simply replaced it, without
a word. She lost again, and replaced it again. Why was
she playing that single number, over and over?

Kit was waiting to see what she would do if she lost
a third time, when he felt a touch on his left side. Katharina! Automatically, he started to rise, but she stopped
him with a hand on his arm.

'Please do not let me disturb your game, sir,' she said
in that husky drawl that he had once found so attractive.
She slid into the seat and began to fiddle with the reticule
on her wrist.

He tried to ignore her. She was probably trying to find
her money so that she could join the game. If she had a
little more consideration for her fellow-players, she
would have done that before sitting down.

Another three was turned up. But this time, it was the
carte anglaise. Marina had won. Kit felt absurdly
pleased for her. He bent towards her, with a whispered
word of encouragement.

From the other side, he felt a hand slip something into his pocket.

No one else was paying any attention at all to Katharina. They were too engrossed in the game. Soon, it would be over.

Marina allowed her winnings to ride on the three. So she was not a total novice, then. She knew enough about Faro to understand that she could win seven times her stake. Pity she did not also know that the odds were so much in favour of the banker.

Lady Blaine looked round once more, waiting for stakes to be placed. Then she turned over her next card with a snap.

'Lurched again,' said Hugo, with a laugh. 'I should never have listened to your advice, my love.'

Lady Blaine faced the *carte anglaise*. Nobody won.

'You never do,' Emma retorted, 'except when you are looking for someone to blame. It was not I who suggested you should put your money on the five.'

'Well, there will be no more now,' he said. 'I think that they have all been played out.'

'Are you sure?' said Emma, her hand still hovering over the livret.

'Almost,' Hugo replied with a twisted grin.

'When you are ready, ladies and gentlemen,' said Lady Blaine testily. She sounded like a bad-tempered schoolmistress.

Emma hesitated for a second more, then dropped her stake on to the six.

On Kit's left, Katharina rose. All the gentlemen at the table stood up politely. Lady Blaine looked furious that her deal was being interrupted.

Katharina's smile encompassed all the men, but ignored the ladies. 'I do not think I am in the mood for Faro, after all,' she said with a pout. 'Excuse me.'

Kit patted his pocket surreptitiously as he resumed his seat. No, he had not been mistaken. She had definitely slipped a note to him. Clever. If her husband asked, all those present would say that Katharina had barely spoken to Kit. She was being very careful indeed. Could it be that the Baron really was threatening her? She had always said that he had a fiery temper.

Lady Blaine had just dealt the final *carte anglaise*. Again, none of the players won.

There remained only one card to be played. It must be a three. And it would win for the banker. Kit felt a little sorry for Marina. She had not staked much on her threes, but she would have lost three times and won only once.

Lady Blaine faced the last card. It was a five! Kit could not believe his eyes. He was certain he had not miscounted, even though he had been distracted a little by the Baroness. The last card should definitely have been a three.

'I knew I should not have relied on you to count the cards for me, Hugo,' protested Emma somewhat archly, giving her husband a playful rap with her fan. 'You said all the fives had been played, you wretch.'

'I was sure that they had,' Hugo replied slowly. 'I must have made a mistake. However, it is of no moment. If you had bet on the five again, you would have lost on the banker's last card.'

'True,' agreed Emma.

Lady Blaine began to gather up the used cards and her large pile of winnings. As banker, she had done very well indeed.

Marina raised her head and looked straight across at

the Viscountess. At the same moment, the Dowager appeared in the doorway. All the gentlemen rose politely.

'I thought…' Marina stopped and frowned. She looked puzzled. 'Beg pardon, ma'am, but should there not have been another three?'

Lady Blaine gaped.

All the players round the table stopped dead and stared.

Lady Luce strode forward and stood behind Marina's chair, with her hand on the companion's shoulder to prevent her from rising. 'What was that you said, child?'

Marina turned her head to look over her shoulder at the Dowager. 'I…I…must have been mistaken. It could not have been… It seemed to me that there were only three threes played, but—'

'Of course you were mistaken, Marina. Not surprising, I should say, considering how little you know about cards. However—' she paused and directed a narrow-eyed stare at the Viscountess '—there have been too many instances of cheating at Faro recently, especially at private parties. Some hostesses, I know, will no longer permit it to be played in their houses. I will not allow any suspicion of impropriety to hang over mine.' She stretched out her hand imperiously. 'The cards, if you please, ma'am.'

Lady Blaine still sat immobile.

'If you please, ma'am,' said the Dowager again, louder still. 'You would not wish to be classed as one of those bankers who cheats to win, would you?' she added pointedly.

Kit leaned on his chair and stared at the floor so that no one would see his face. He had thought that Marina was clever, but this…this was brilliant. Unfortunately, it was also very dangerous indeed. In fact, it was madness.

Lady Blaine had no choice. She handed over the pack. Her face was ashen and her fingers were not quite steady.

'Thank you,' said the Dowager curtly. She marched to the end of the table and began to lay out the cards. The players crowded round to watch. No one spoke.

The cards spoke for themselves. A three and a seven were missing. There were two extra cards—a five and a ten.

Lady Blaine began to bluster. 'The pack must have been wrongly made up. I did not—'

The Dowager picked up the fives and tens and compared them with the rest of the deck. 'I fear not,' she said grimly, picking out two cards. 'These cards did not come from a new pack. They are slightly worn. And I fancy—' she held one of them towards the candelabrum '—I fancy there are pinholes in this one.'

Everyone gasped. Everyone except Kit. And Marina.

She was hanging back, trying not to be noticed. And she was refusing to meet his eyes.

The Dowager appeared to be outraged. 'I cannot believe that you dared to do such a thing as a guest in my house,' she said angrily to the speechless Viscountess. 'I will thank you to leave immediately. You will understand if I do not recognise you, or any of your family again. I may say that I do not expect that any other respectable members of Society will do so either.'

Lady Blaine rose to her feet, though she needed to lean on the back of the chair to do so. Her guilt was written on her face. None the less, she protested, 'It must have been a mistake. No other explanation is possible. You may choose to believe the worst, ma'am, but my true friends will not.' She made for the door, straightening her back as she went. She had not once looked at the pile of money lying on the table.

The Dowager looked round at her remaining guests. 'I cannot tell you how sorry I am,' she said.

Her tone was an odd mixture of regret and ill-concealed triumph, Kit decided, wonderingly. Was it possible…? Had she known all along? But how could she have made sure—?

It had to have been Marina. A three had been removed. And Marina had played only threes.

Either Marina had deliberately set out to expose Lady Blaine's cheating or…or she herself had fuzzed the cards in order to entrap the woman. In either case, it was breathlessly daring.

And his Marina was nothing if not bold.

Lady Luce shook her head sadly. 'I had heard the rumours, of course. I knew she had been winning often—perhaps too often—when she held the bank, but I never dreamed…' She sighed. 'However, so it is.' She moved round the table to the banker's place. 'What am I to do with all this?' she said, indicating the pile of money. 'Perhaps you would like it to be returned to you?'

'Certainly not,' said Hugo firmly. 'We lost it. We might well have lost it anyway. Perhaps you have a favourite charity, ma'am? A foundling hospital, or some such?'

'I have a better idea,' Kit put in, deliberately concealing his mounting fury under a veneer of mild amusement. 'Why not give it to the anti-slavery campaigners? After all, Lady Blaine's husband is due back from his plantations any day now. I am sure he would appreciate the gesture.'

That made Marina raise her eyes to his, at last. She was looking daggers at him.

'Splendid!' said the Dowager with a crack of harsh laughter. 'We shall see what the scandal sheets make of that!'

Kit did not miss the momentary glance of triumph that Lady Luce directed at Marina. His worst suspicions were confirmed. And now his anger threatened to overwhelm him.

The Viscountess Blaine was most definitely a cheat. But Marina Beaumont had risked everything in order to ensure that the woman was publicly exposed.

'My dear, you excelled yourself,' whispered the Dowager as soon as they were out of earshot of the others.

Marina shook her head. She had replaced the three, to be sure, but not the seven. Nor had she inserted the marked card. Lady Blaine had added that after the pack had been shuffled. Marina was at a loss to understand why the woman had taken such a stupid risk—she could fuzz the cards with such extraordinary skill that the players had no chance of winning, except when she permitted it. Without those missing cards, she would never have been exposed. But one would have been enough. Marina need not have cheated at all…

'You must have a remarkable way with the cards, child. Nobody suspected anything. That woman will never be able to lift her head again.'

'Kit Stratton knows.'

The Dowager's smile vanished. 'How can he know? He said nothing when you were shuffling the cards, did he?'

'No, ma'am. But he knows. I saw it in his eyes.' She would never forget that look, a mixture of shock and disgust. He knew she was a cheat. How could she ever face him again?

'That's as may be,' said the Dowager gruffly, 'but he will do nothing, even if he does suspect you. Why should he? Lady Blaine's guilt was obvious to everyone. And her disgrace will remove his obligation to marry their wretched daughter. Kit may be a rake, but he's a gentleman. No gentleman could be expected to maintain an offer for the child of a proven cheat. He should be calling down a blessing on your head!'

'But what of Miss Blaine? She is the innocent party in this. She will be ruined by his public rejection of her.'

'No, my dear, she will not,' said the Dowager, patting Marina's arm soothingly, 'for the betrothal was never announced. What is more, you are forgetting that Tilly Blaine lied in order to ensnare Kit Stratton. She knows she was never alone with him. She told her mother that she was.'

'But she—'

'No, Marina. Do not try to defend her. Even if her first reaction was misinterpreted—and I take leave to doubt that, myself—she has had two full days to tell the truth. She has not done so. She is a true Blaine.'

Marina did not try to argue. The Dowager was right. Lady Blaine and Lord Luce had conspired together to entrap Kit Stratton, and Tilly had done nothing to stop them. Her motives did not matter. The deed was wicked, worse by far than anything Marina had now done. Tilly was fortunate that the betrothal had not been made public. Her disgrace would stem only from her mother's.

'I think I should like to retire now, ma'am, if you would permit it.'

'Certainly not! What are you thinking of? You must

stay and you must be seen to enjoy the party. Play a hand or two of cards.'

'I could not,' breathed Marina, horrified.

'Of course you could. Not Faro, I agree—I shall permit no more Faro tonight—but a rubber of piquet, perhaps.' She looked hard at Marina. 'Just make sure you do not appear too expert,' she added in an undertone.

That should not be difficult, Marina thought, for her brain was in such turmoil that she would probably forget everything she had ever known about card playing.

'Come, let me find you an opponent,' said her ladyship, leading Marina towards Sir Hugo and Lady Stratton. 'I am trying to persuade this gel of mine not to dwell too much on that unfortunate incident with Lady Blaine. Can't seem to get it out of her head. What she needs is something to occupy her mind, like a rubber of piquet. Do you play, Sir Hugo?' The Dowager was being extremely direct.

'I do,' began Sir Hugo a little uncertainly.

'He does, ma'am,' interrupted Lady Stratton, 'but he has promised to take me down to supper. However, I am sure that Kit will be happy to oblige you.' She turned and beckoned.

No! Please, no! Marina wanted to run, but her legs were made of lead.

Kit bowed with his usual elegance. When Lady Stratton explained the Dowager's request, his expression remained totally impassive. Then he turned to Marina. 'I should be delighted to give you a game, ma'am,' he said, offering her his arm.

The Dowager beamed.

Inwardly, Marina cringed. This could not be happening.

But it was.

In a matter of moments, they were seated at a small table and Kit was breaking a new piquet pack.

'You will understand, ma'am, I am sure,' he said silkily, 'if I choose to take charge of shuffling this pack myself.'

They had been playing, in total silence, for nearly half an hour. Marina had lost almost every hand. Her discards had been weak and her card play even weaker. It was pitiful to watch.

But Kit was still furious with her. He feared that if she spoke a word to him, he would lose his temper. It was barely under control, as it was. More than anything, he wanted to take her in his arms and shake the life out of her. Set a cheat to catch a cheat. What on earth had possessed her to do something so foolhardy?

He gritted his teeth and led another card. She failed to follow suit. It was the last straw. 'If you wish to play piquet,' he snarled, 'you should learn the rules. You are required to play a club, if you hold one. And I am perfectly well aware that you do.'

Her hand trembled. She looked up at him with those huge eyes. They were full of guilt.

His anger vanished instantly.

'Marina,' he said softly, 'I should like to beat you. How could you do such a thing? You—'

She threw down the remainder of her cards. 'What I do, sir, is my concern alone. And since I am such an unworthy opponent for you, I will not trouble you further. How much do I owe?'

Her guilt had been replaced by indignation. She obviously thought he deplored what she had done. He did, of course, but only because of the risks she had been taking. He wanted to protect her, but every time he tried to get near her, she bristled like a porcupine.

'You owe me nothing,' he replied. Then, almost as an afterthought, he said, 'We failed to agree any stakes at the outset. However, since you have conceded defeat, I ought, I suppose, to exact a forfeit of some kind. Will you allow me to take you driving tomorrow?'

'No.' The word was quietly spoken, but it was final.

'Why not?'

She almost squirmed in her chair. She was clearly surprised by his question. Did she think he would take a dismissal so easily?

She clasped her hands on the table and fixed her gaze on them. 'You forget my position, sir. I am a companion, a servant. I know my place—and it is not in a gentleman's carriage.' She rose from her chair and walked calmly out of the room. Even in defeat, she still held herself like a duchess.

No, Kit thought, your place is not in my carriage. It is in my bed. And that is where you are going to be, my sweet Marina, even if I have to abduct you into it.

Chapter Twenty

'I thought I heard a carriage half an hour ago. Who was it?'

'It was Lady Stratton's carriage, ma'am,' said Marina, avoiding the Dowager's eye.

'Would she not step inside?'

'She…she was not *in* the carriage, ma'am.'

The Dowager said nothing. She simply stared at Marina and waited.

'She… I… She sent a message, inviting me to call on her at Fitzwilliam House. I declined.'

'What? Why on earth—?'

'Ma'am, I cannot become intimate with Lady Stratton. She is a great lady—as you are—and I am a nobody.'

'I should have thought,' retorted the Dowager, 'that, after last night's escapade, Lady Stratton would be extremely grateful to you.'

'But she does not know—'

'And you are certainly not a nobody. You are a Blaine.' She stopped short and gave vent to something that was almost a giggle. 'Then again, perhaps not,' she added ruefully. 'It might be unwise to make too much of your links to *that* family. The rumour mills are already working. Lady Blaine may have spoken of her ''true friends'' but they seem to be deserting her in droves.' She chortled. 'And I understand that another edition of that nasty little scandal sheet is in preparation.'

'But how can that be? There has not been time—'

'There is always time, Marina, if one makes it one's business to use it.'

It was worse and worse. The whole episode would soon be all over London. And it seemed that the Dowager was conspiring to make that happen. Marina really must escape from it all. She could not bear it any longer. Kit had been saved, but at the cost of Marina's peace of mind. She yearned for him, but she knew she must never set eyes on him again. He would now remain in London—its foremost rake—and so she must leave.

The butler entered. 'Lady Stratton is below in her carriage, m'lady. She presents her compliments, and asks if Miss Beaumont may be permitted to accompany her on her drive this afternoon.'

'No,' breathed Marina.

'Of course,' declared Lady Luce roundly. 'Fetch your bonnet and pelisse, Marina. And be quick about it. Her ladyship will not wish to keep her horses standing.'

'You look pale, my dear. Are you quite well?'

'A…a little tired, ma'am, that is all,' Marina lied. 'Her ladyship's card party finished very late.'

'And you, of course, were required to stay until all the guests had left. The role of a companion is not an easy one. And I doubt that Lady Luce is an easy mistress.'

'No, ma'am, you are wrong!' protested Marina. 'The Dowager has been immensely kind to me…and…and…'

Lady Stratton patted Marina's hand. 'Forgive me for

speaking out of turn. It was wrong of me. Especially as her ladyship has been so generous in sparing you to me. What made her change her mind this afternoon?'

Oh, dear. Now what could Marina say? 'It…it was not Lady Luce who declined your invitation earlier, ma'am. I…I thought she would need me and so I took it upon myself to—'

'Very commendable, my dear. But you are here now. And is it not a beautiful day for a drive in the park?'

Marina nodded gratefully.

'I must tell you,' continued Lady Stratton, lowering her voice, 'that last night's scandal has done us a very good turn. Kit had engaged himself to Lady Blaine's eldest daughter—not with the blessing of his family, I may add—but there can be no question of a marriage now. Not with *that* family. No one will receive them in future, and— But you must know all this. Is not Lord Luce godfather to Miss Blaine?'

Marina was forced to admit that it was so.

'Then you must be aware of the methods that Lord Luce employed to entrap Kit. I have a great deal of respect for the Dowager, Miss Beaumont, but I find it very difficult to think well of her son. He has not behaved like a gentleman.'

There was nothing Marina could say. Everything Lady Stratton said was true.

'Hugo tells me that the Blaines will be going abroad as soon as the Viscount returns. It will be something of a shock to him, I expect.'

A wave of guilt hit Marina. She had never once considered the Viscount in all this. She had cared only for Kit. She was wicked, thoroughly wicked.

'I cannot say that it worries me overmuch,' continued Lady Stratton. 'Lord Blaine is a reprobate—just like his father was. His fortune stems from his sugar plantations, and it seems he don't much care what he does to increase it. Some of the tales I have heard are…upsetting. Kit thinks— But you are not interested in listening to my ramblings. Tell me, did you enjoy the party last night? After the Faro ended, I mean.'

'I…I hardly remember, ma'am. It was all so unsettling. If I had not mentioned the missing card—'

'If you had not mentioned your missing card, Lady Blaine would not have been unmasked for the cheat she undoubtedly is, and I should still be contemplating the nightmare of having Tilly Blaine for a sister. You will never know how grateful I am to you.'

Marina felt herself blushing.

'It seems that Tilly Blaine is the only member of that family who views it all with equanimity. She, apparently, is so delighted at the prospect of travelling in Europe that she is quite unmoved by her mother's disgrace. Strange girl. Her head is so stuffed with poetry that there is no room for common sense.'

It was quite late by the time Marina returned to the Dowager's house. She would have to hurry to change for dinner. Lady Luce frowned on a lack of punctuality.

Marina threw off her day gown and began to splash water on her face. There was no time to do more. Her hair… Oh, dear, her hair was beginning to come out of its pins. She would have to—

'May I help, Miss Marina?' The Dowager's maid had come in without a sound.

'Gibson,' said Marina thankfully. The old abigail was always wonderfully deft with hairpins. 'How thoughtful of you. I am desperately late, I fear. Do you think you could help me with my hair?'

'Not to worry, miss. Her ladyship said as I was to help you, since you had been delayed with Lady Stratton. Sit down here. It won't take but a moment.'

Marina did as she was bid and watched, entranced, as Gibson turned her dishevelled locks into a smoothly elegant style. 'Gibson, you are a marvel,' she said, and meant it.

The abigail coloured a little. 'That's enough of your nonsense, miss. Come, let us find you an evening gown. What about the green silk?'

'Well... Have you any idea, Gibson, what her ladyship's plans are for this evening? Are we going out?'

'I believe so, miss. Her ladyship did not say precisely, but she is wearing one of her fine gowns.'

'In that case, it had better be the green silk,' agreed Marina. 'And the matching slippers, too.'

By the time the dinner gong sounded, Marina was walking sedately down the stairs as if she had all the time in the world.

The Dowager, however, was not deceived. She looked Marina up and down. Then she gave a nod of approval. 'I must say that that gown is particularly becoming,' she said. 'It is perhaps a little low-cut, but at least it is not as flimsy as some of the gowns the gels are wearing nowadays.' She led the way into the dining room and took her seat. 'Pity that you will not have a chance tonight to display how well you look.'

Oh. It seemed that she was not to go out after all. Marina felt a pang of disappointment for which she was soon reproaching herself. What right had she to expect evening engagements?

'I am going to a card party. Alone,' said the Dowager flatly. 'After last night's performance, you would attract far too much attention.'

Marina had to admit that Lady Luce was right.

The Dowager then proceeded to talk incessantly throughout dinner. Marina found she was grateful, for she was not in the mood for conversation. Her mind kept reverting to images of Kit Stratton, no matter how hard she tried to banish them. He was not to marry Tilly Blaine after all. He—

It was not her business. Kit Stratton was nothing to do with Marina. Not any more. Her thoughtless actions had given rise to a great deal of grief but, thanks to the card playing skills her father had taught her—and a lot of luck—she had succeeded in undoing the harm she had caused. To Kit, at least. As for the Blaines… She must learn to live with what she had done there. Lady Stratton's artless revelations in the carriage suggested that the family's downfall was well merited. It even sounded as if Tilly had recovered from her passion for Kit. Remarkably quickly, too. Perhaps she would fall in love with an Italian poet…

'If you are ready, Marina…' The Dowager had risen, ready to leave the dining table.

Marina sprang to her feet. 'I beg your pardon, ma'am. I'm afraid I was wool-gathering.'

'Hmph,' snorted the Dowager, leading the way up to her drawing room.

'Excuse me, m'lady. A note has just arrived for you.'

Lady Luce did not respond to the butler until she had reached the landing. 'Bring it up here, man,' she said sharply. 'Can't read it at that distance.'

Marina tried not to laugh. The Dowager was on top form again.

The note was from Lady Marchant. And it produced a crack of laughter from the Dowager.

'Oh, don't look so downcast, Marina. This is priceless.

I promise you will enjoy it.' She sat down in her usual chair and glanced towards the decanter.

Marina had long ago learned to recognise the signals. She filled a glass and placed it on the table by the Dowager's hand. Then she took her usual seat on the low stool alongside.

'Very good, my dear, very good.' She spread Lady Marchant's note and raised her lorgnette to read it again. 'Yes, excellent. It seems that young Kit Stratton will not be the handsomest rake in London for much longer.'

'He is going abroad, too?' Marina was more than a little surprised. Lady Stratton had mentioned nothing of the kind.

'Oh, no. Nothing so simple.' She raised her glass and sipped slowly, smiling with pleasure. 'I may have forgiven you, child, for interfering in my debt to young Stratton, but I have certainly not forgiven *him* for his impudence when he returned my vowel. Arrogant young puppy....' She frowned at Marina. 'After the way he treated you, I should imagine you will be pleased to see him brought down a peg or two.'

There was an iron band around Marina's heart. With every word the Dowager spoke, it was tightening, until she could hardly breathe. 'What…what do you mean, ma'am?' she whispered hoarsely.

'Why, the cuckold's revenge, of course. It appears that the Baroness's husband does not take kindly to being made to look a fool. He has arranged—with the willing help of Méchante, I have no doubt—to change Kit's pretty face a little.'

Horror, and outrage, gave Marina back all her strength. She jumped to her feet. 'You must stop him!' she cried.

'Why? No one is going to murder young Stratton. Not

in Green Park. I dare say it will be just a discreet little mill…a few cuts and bruises, nothing more. Kit will soon mend.'

'But, ma'am, you cannot—'

'Stop fussing over nothing, Marina. You are too soft-hearted by half.' She rose and swept out.

Marina was left alone. She could call on no one but herself. There was no time to change, or to send a message, for the attack might take place at any moment. In any case, she had no idea where to find Kit.

Except in Green Park.

'You are not going alone, Kit.'

Kit raised a weary eyebrow. Hugo was in one of his stubborn, elder-brother moods.

'You accept that?'

'Yes, since you insist.'

'Good,' said Hugo. 'Now, this could be a clandestine meeting with your Baroness, as she suggested, though I doubt it. Since she insisted that you go alone, I shall be your…coachman.'

Kit gave a crack of laughter.

Hugo laid a heavy hand on his shoulder. 'I'll have you know, brother, that I can tool a carriage as well as you can…and better than my coachman, too. No one will give me a second look, especially if I wear a plain dark coat.'

Kit nodded. Hugo was right, of course. 'I shall wear the same,' he said. 'No point in offering a target for the Baron's pistol, if that is what he has in mind. You think he will try to shoot me, do you not, Hugo?'

'It's possible. We need to be prepared.' He paused. 'Unless you are willing to forget this appointment altogether? We could always go to the club, you know.'

'You know that is impossible, Hugo. We need to find out what is afoot. If I do not go on this occasion, they are bound to create another chance to attack me. Next time, I might not be forewarned. And I might not have my stalwart coachman to defend me!'

Hugo shook his head, laughing. 'Your coachman— with his pistol—will call to collect you in an hour. Go and find yourself a coat, brother. And make sure it is fit to be seen. If I am to bear your body home, I must have it elegantly clad.'

In the dusk, the shadows played tricks. Green Park seemed to be alive with movement, but it might have been nothing more than the wind among the leaves.

By the time Hugo had climbed down from the box, Kit had already found an urchin who would mind the horses for the promise of a shilling. At least one of them would return to pay the lad, surely?

'Couldn't see any movement,' Hugo said quietly, 'even from up there. If they're here, they must be well concealed. You have your pistol?'

Kit patted his pocket. 'And my cane. Katharina's note said that I must walk along the shrubbery path. She would come to meet me when she was sure I was alone.'

'Did she say which entrance you should take?'

'No. Why?'

'Because it gives us an advantage. You will start walking from this end. I will start from the other. They will not know which of us is Kit.'

'No, Hugo. This is my fight. I will not put you in the line of the Baron's bullet. I will go in alone. You may come to my aid if I need you. No doubt, you'll know soon enough.'

Hugo looked unconvinced.

'I mean it, Hugo,' Kit said grimly. 'I need to be able to give you back to Emma in one piece.'

Hugo frowned. 'At least, give me time to get to the far end. If I make my way into the shrubbery, I ought to be able to get to you the sooner.'

Kit recognised the sense in his brother's proposal, but still he hesitated. If anything happened to Hugo, there would be a widow and three fatherless children. Whereas he, Kit, had no one waiting for him. For Marina had rejected him.

'Kit? What do you say? You cannot object to that, surely?'

'Oh, very well. If you must. I will give you two minutes, and then I shall start along this path.' He held out his hand. 'God save you, Hugo.'

Hugo clasped Kit's hand firmly with one of his own and laid the other on Kit's shoulder. 'We have the advantage of surprise, Kit. Wellington would be proud of us. God bless you.'

He disappeared in the direction of the coach and the distant entrance to the shrubbery. Kit watched, counting the seconds. At the end of the agreed two minutes, he put his hand into his pocket, gripped his pistol and started along the gloomy path, swinging his cane.

Hugo had absolutely no intention of hiding in the shrubbery, waiting for Kit to be attacked, perhaps killed. Hat in hand, he raced along to the far end of the park, where the path met the roadway. There he paused to catch his breath, and to put on his hat once more, at exactly the kind of rakish angle Kit always used.

In the gathering gloom, no one would be able to tell them apart.

He pulled his pistol from his pocket and cocked it.

With his arm hanging loosely at his side, his pistol was hidden by his coat. He started forward at a measured pace.

It was just like the start of a duel.

He had covered no more than fifty yards when he heard a tiny rustle in the bushes to his left. He looked quickly down the path, straining to see in front of him. There was no sign of Kit. He must appear soon.

Hugo continued to walk steadily down the path.

'That's Stratton!' cried a man's voice from the bushes.

Hugo ducked automatically, but there was no bullet. Three hefty bruisers pushed their way out of the bushes. They were barring his way. And they had cudgels in their hands.

'So that is the way of it,' he said grimly. Unlike Kit, he had no cane.

From the corner of his eye, he caught a flash of colour among the trees. Good God, there was a woman in there!

'Behind you!' cried a female voice.

It came from the wrong direction.

Hugo whirled just in time to duck. The fourth man's club missed his head by a hair's breadth.

A woman screamed. And then another—a second voice.

Hugo ignored them. The force of his assailant's blow had bent the man almost double, exposing his neck. Hugo hit him with the pistol, but it spun out of his hand. He whipped round to face the other three—unarmed.

Kit had appeared as from nowhere. He was using his cane like a sword against two of the bruisers. Only one now faced Hugo.

Kit flashed Hugo a grin. 'I think the odds are fairer now, gentlemen,' he said calmly. 'Three against two.'

One of the pair risked a quick look behind him. A

mistake. Kit struck him hard on the wrist. With a howl of pain, the man dropped his cudgel and clutched his arm. 'Ye've broke it!' he screamed.

'Probably,' said Kit, squaring up to his last man. 'Let's see what you're made of, eh?' he snarled.

The man hesitated.

Kit stepped back a pace and looked towards Hugo. He was holding his own. Kit lunged forward. 'Now then!'

The man dodged.

Kit whirled, ready to parry the next blow.

A woman screamed again.

Kit looked towards the sound.

The man Hugo had felled was on his feet again. And he had an arm across a woman's throat.

It was Marina.

A murderous rage overcame Kit. In a split second, he had plunged his cane like a sword deep into his opponent's belly. The man dropped without a sound.

'Careful, Kit,' Hugo gasped, still struggling.

Hugo's voice stayed Kit's all-consuming fury. Instantly, he was icy calm. Waiting.

Two men were disabled. Hugo was about to overcome the third. But the fourth man had Marina.

'Let us go,' yelled the fourth man. 'Or I'll slit 'er throat. Swelp me, I will.'

Kit dropped his cane and took two paces forward, sliding his hand into his pocket. 'Let her go. Or I'll kill you.'

The man did not move. But his knife did. It glinted suddenly in the dim light. Kit heard a muffled groan.

'Let her go,' he said again, pulling the pistol from his pocket. 'Even at this distance, I can put a bullet in your head before you draw breath. Let her go.'

Hugo had his opponent in an armlock at last. 'Don't be a fool,' he yelled. 'He's a crack shot. He'll kill you.'

The man stood undecided.

The silence was rent by another scream.

Chapter Twenty-One

Marina struggled to turn towards the sound. Out of the corner of her eye, she caught a fleeting glimpse of a woman in the bushes, trying to fight free of a man. He seemed to have her by the hair.

'That's enough o' that, missy,' growled Marina's captor, pushing the knife higher up her throat. 'One more move an' I'll stick ye.'

Marina froze.

She was not afraid, even though she knew she might die here. All her senses seemed to have been heightened by the danger. She could smell her captor's unwashed body and fetid breath, overlaid with the sweet smell of the new leaves on the trees. She could hear his frightened breathing, and feel it on the back of her neck. His knife touched her throat with a cold promise of death.

And only yards away, she could see Kit's powerful shape, unmistakable in the gloom, preparing to shoot. He took another step forward.

'That's enough,' yelled Marina's captor. 'Any closer an' I'll kill her.'

Kit stopped. Slowly, he raised his pistol.

Marina felt her captor shrinking into her shadow.

There was no target for Kit but her own defenceless body. She held her breath. He would shoot only if he were sure. She loved him. So she must trust him.

She refused to close her eyes. If this was to be her last moment on earth, she wanted her gaze to rest on the man she loved.

'I think you might be wise to put up your pistol,' said a voice from the shrubbery.

Marina could not turn to see. It was a man's voice, though, and it had a foreign accent.

Kit did not take his eyes off Marina. Nor did his pistol waver by even a fraction. 'I think not, Baron,' he said grimly. 'You know my reputation. Tell your man that I can do exactly as I said. Tell him I will kill him if he does not let her go.'

'As I will kill you,' replied the Baron, moving out on to the path. Marina could see him now. His left hand was clamped around his wife's upper arm. When he pulled her out behind him, she moaned.

His right hand held a small silver pistol. And it was pointed at Kit.

No! Marina swallowed the scream that rose in her throat. She must not distract Kit. She must *do* something. But what? She had no weapons. She could not even kick out, for she did not have boots on her feet. She had run out, wearing the green silk evening slippers. They were now in shreds. Her feet were almost bare.

She could feel the man's panicked breathing slowing a little. He was beginning to think he was safe, protected by the Baron's gun. The hand holding the knife at her throat relaxed a fraction.

It had to be now.

She took a deep breath and rammed her elbow back

into the man's ribs with every ounce of strength she possessed.

He doubled up, groaning. The knife was no longer against her throat. She ducked away and threw herself towards Hugo, well out of Kit's firing line.

Kit had not moved. His pistol was still trained on Marina's attacker, now grovelling on the ground.

'Did he hurt you, Marina?' Kit's voice sounded hoarse.

'No. No.' Why was he concerned about her? He should be defending himself against the Baron. 'Take care, Kit,' she cried.

Kit smiled into the gloom. Without turning towards the Baron, he said calmly, 'If you were minded to kill me, sir, you really should have done it by now.'

The Baron hauled his wife a little closer. She whimpered.

'Do not imagine, sir, that I will lift a finger to protect your wife,' Kit said flatly. 'Our affair is long over. I suggest you would do better to address your complaints to her new protector.'

Marina closed her eyes in a moment of sheer terror. The Baron would never accept such insults. He was bound to shoot Kit now.

After a long pause, the Baron said slowly, 'Let these men go, Stratton. Your quarrel is with me.'

Kit glanced towards Hugo, who nodded and loosed his hold on his captive. The man hobbled over to where Kit's second victim lay on the ground and half-hauled, half-carried him off into the darkness. Marina's captor, and the man with the broken arm, simply took to their heels.

'Honour among thieves,' said Kit, turning slowly to face the Baron.

'And now it is stalemate, Stratton, I think.'

Marina started forward. If she could come between them—

Hugo caught her before she had gone a yard. He pulled her into the shelter of his arm and held her there. 'No, Marina,' he whispered into her hair. 'Do not interfere. Leave this to Kit.' When she still struggled to free herself, he laughed softly. 'Trust him, my dear. I promise he will come back to you.'

Marina was stunned into immobility. It sounded as if—

'Shall we play it out here? Or would you rather meet me on the field of honour, like a gentleman?' The Baron's tone made clear that he did not see Kit as a gentleman at all.

'As you choose, sir,' Kit said quickly. 'It will make no difference to the outcome.'

The Baron spluttered something in German. His wife groaned.

'Indeed,' said Kit. 'I am not your wife's lover now, sir. But I was. You have every right to try to kill me.'

'Are you saying, Stratton, that you have *no* such right?'

Kit said nothing.

Marina understood then. If they met on the duelling field, Kit would not fire on the Baron. He would just stand there, proud and defiant, allowing the wronged husband to have his revenge. It was Kit's concept of justice.

The Baron understood too, for he put up his pistol. 'I do not relish the idea of cold-blooded murder,' he said.

Kit nodded in the direction of the vanished bruisers. 'Do you not?' he said wryly.

'They would not have killed you,' replied the Baron

matter of factly. 'You would have become somewhat less attractive to the ladies. That is all.' He had not released his ferocious grip on his wife's arm. 'Katharina was happy to lure you here. She said she wanted to watch your beating. I fancied it might provide a salutary lesson—for both of you.' He looked down at her. There were streaks of tears on her ashen cheeks. 'So. So. It will do, I think.' He put his arm round her shoulder. It was not a loving embrace. 'We will go now,' he said. 'My compliments to you, Stratton, and to your brother. I had not expected anyone to overcome that nasty quartet.' He gave a stiff military bow, its precision marred by his hold on his wife. 'I am sure you understand that we shall not speak again.'

Kit returned the Baron's bow, but the man had already turned to leave. In a very few moments, they were out of sight.

Marina straightened and Hugo released her. She thought she felt a tiny, comforting squeeze before he let her go.

'That was a close-run thing, Kit,' Hugo said, shaking his head a little.

'Perhaps,' replied Kit.

Marina was almost sure he avoided his brother's eye.

'As for you, woman,' Kit said, advancing menacingly on her, 'what in heaven's name did you think you were doing?' He took her by the shoulders, as he had done once before. This time, he did not shake her. He just stood there, staring down at her, letting his gaze rove over her features. 'You are, without doubt, the most infuriating, idiotic, ungovernable—'

Hugo cleared his throat ostentatiously.

'Oh, go and see to the horses, can't you? You're a pretty poor apology for a coachman, I must say.'

Hugo burst out laughing. 'At once, sir,' he said with a mock bow. 'Just as you say, sir.'

'Marina.' Kit lingered over the word, all the while stroking her hair back from her face. 'Marina,' he repeated, 'you are quite maddening. How shall I ever be able to cope with you?'

She did not reply. She was sure she had not heard him aright. He must mean—

He drew her into his arms and began to kiss her face, beginning at her hairline, and moving to her forehead, her eyes... She groaned with the pleasure of his touch.

He stopped. 'Marina? Good grief, what am I doing? You are hurt. And cold. Here.' He shrugged out of his dark coat and wrapped it round her, imprisoning her arms. 'Your neck. Let me see.' With amazing gentleness, those strong, lean fingers lifted her chin so that he could see where the knife had been. 'Confound it! Can't see a thing in this light!' He tightened his grip on her. 'Come. There is a light on the coach.'

She stepped on something sharp and gave a little cry of pain.

'My God,' he exclaimed. 'Your feet!' He swept her into his arms, ignoring her attempted protest, and carried her out of the park to the waiting carriage. Hugo was on the box. A grinning urchin was at the horses' heads.

Hugo jumped down to open the carriage door. 'Spot of abduction tonight, is it, sir?' he quipped.

Kit flashed a smile in response. 'Drive back to Fitzwilliam House, my good man,' he said. 'Very slowly.'

Kit ignored Marina's protests that she had received nothing more than a scratch. He took her throat in his hands and gently, gently traced the red line the knife had made. There was one tiny drop of blood. He swore under his breath. He should have killed the villain when he had the chance!

'What is it?' Marina asked.

'You are bleeding,' he replied harshly. 'He cut you—'

'It was my own doing,' she said, putting her hand over his. 'I felt the prick of the knife when I pushed myself free. It is nothing.'

'You could have been killed, you beautiful idiot.'

Marina said nothing, but she smiled shyly. She seemed to be relishing his insults.

'And your poor feet…'

'That, too, was my own doing. I could have stopped to put on outdoor shoes…but then I might have been too late.'

'Too late for what, pray?' he asked, lifting her into the corner of the seat and raising her poor, bruised feet into his lap.

'To warn you that—' She stopped and looked inquiringly up at him. 'I suppose you will tell me that my warning was unnecessary. And that my arrival only served to put myself in danger.'

'Something of the sort,' he murmured, stroking the shreds of the green silk slipper from one foot.

A shiver ran through Marina.

Kit pretended not to notice. Slowly, he caressed the second slipper free.

She shivered again, more noticeably. 'What are you doing, sir?' she whispered hoarsely.

Kit began to stroke the bare skin of her foot where her stocking was torn and bloody. 'Trying to remedy the damage you have done, ma'am.'

He continued to run his fingers over her skin with a touch so light that, if she closed her eyes, she could not quite be sure that it was happening. She pushed herself back against the deeply cushioned seat, trying to escape from the feelings he was creating, yet at the same time longing for them to continue. In the end, she could not stifle a tiny groan.

'Mmm,' agreed Kit huskily. 'I fear these must be removed.'

Marina was floating. She barely heard his words. Her skin was alive, but her mind had been numbed by the magic of his touch.

He began to slide his fingers up to her ankle, and then to her calf. It was exquisite. She wanted to purr like a contented cat. When he raised her skirts to remove her ruined stockings, she could do nothing to resist him. He untied her garters, allowing himself a tiny caress of her inner thigh that had her moaning in her throat. Then he rolled the stockings down and gently peeled them from her bleeding skin.

She was still purring when he lifted her on to his lap and began to kiss her. She did not know where she was, only that she was in the arms of the man she loved, and that he was caressing her, kissing her, as if he loved her. A tiny, strident voice from her old self tried to scream that he was a rake, that he knew exactly how to seduce plain, innocent women like Marina, but she ignored it. The purring was too strong.

At first his kiss was light, hesitant, even unsure of her response, but as she began to kiss him back, everything seemed to explode. He pulled her close against his hard body, his hands stroking her spine and her hair. When it finally tumbled down her back, she heard a rumble of satisfied laughter, deep in his chest. Then the kiss was transformed. It was harder, more demanding, almost punishing, but she leaned in to him like a woman starving, craving for more. Innocent though she was, she responded to him with a lover's passion.

He groaned out her name.

If she never had another moment of passion in her life, she would remember the sound of her name in his throat.

His fingers had found their way to her bodice, had undone the tiny buttons and untied the ribbons of her chemise. Her breast was resting heavily in his hand. He groaned again, never lifting his lips from hers. And he began to roll her nipple between finger and thumb, gently at first, then more roughly. An arrow of heat shot through her, like the pull of a puppet's strings under his fingers, and she felt a sudden release of liquid fire in her belly. Her whole body was about to melt.

So this was passion—this unutterable longing for union, for fulfilment.

Kit broke the kiss, breathing hard.

Marina whimpered. She could not open her eyes. It had been so blissful.

'Forgive me,' he said huskily, pulling her head into the crook of his shoulder and applying his fingers to the buttons of her dress. 'I should not have done that.'

Slowly, she opened her eyes. They were huge and dark, and dazed with passion. He was not sure whether she was actually seeing him. He tried to concentrate on restoring her gown to a more decorous state, but it was almost impossible to do up those tiny buttons without touching the skin of her breasts. It was beautiful skin, like creamy silk overlaid with blush. And it was so very tempting…

'Kit,' she breathed through lips swollen from his kisses. 'Please—'

'No, my sweet,' he said, trying to hide the desire in

his voice, 'not here. Not in a dirty, smelly carriage, remember? In my bed. Willingly in my bed.'

She did not respond. He had lost her.

He knelt on the floor and, taking his handkerchief,
began to wipe away the grime and the blood from her
feet with featherlight strokes. He needed, desperately, to
prove to her how much she meant to him. He could think
of no other way.

'You must be bathed, Marina, to remove this dirt.
Emma will be able to give you some ointment, and ban-
dages—'

'Emma?' She sounded bemused.

'Emma. My sister. Hugo's wife. I am taking you to
her.'

'But you cannot!' she exclaimed. 'I am not your—
Oh, heavens! Look at me!' She put her hands to her hair,
desperately trying to put it into some kind of order. 'I
must go back to Lady Luce's house…where I belong. I
must… Oh, what will she think of me? How shall I ever
explain?'

Kit pushed the ruined stockings under the seat where
Marina could not see them. 'You will tell her the truth,'
he said, with emphasis. 'Or I shall. You ran out to save
a life.'

'But I—'

'And you succeeded. You are a very brave woman,
Marina Beaumont.'

Kit looked his fill at her. She was flushed with passion—and now with embarrassment, too. She was so
beautiful, he caught his breath.

A sharp rap on the roof brought him back to earth. It
took him a moment to realise that they were no longer
moving. He let down the glass and stuck his head out.
'Why have we stopped?'

'We are at Fitzwilliam House, y'r honour,' said Hugo respectfully.

'Are we, indeed? Well, turn this blasted carriage round and take the lady home.'

'Home, y'r honour?' Hugo queried.

'Yes. Back to the Dowager's house. The abduction has been postponed.'

Kit insisted on carrying Marina into the Dowager's house. His long dark coat was wrapped around her to protect her modesty from the servants' prying eyes, but there was no disguising the fact that her hair had come down and her feet were bare. He could almost feel her shame as he carried her up to the drawing room.

The Dowager had not yet returned.

'I could carry you up to your bedchamber,' he said.

'No!' It was almost a scream. 'It is bad enough that you have carried me here. I— Put me down, sir. And then, please leave.'

So that was to be the way of it. Well, it was time she learned otherwise. 'Marina, I will leave when you promise to stop behaving like an idiot.' He lowered her gently into a wing chair. 'What is the matter with you?'

'Lady Stratton said that your engagement to Miss Blaine was at an end. Is…is that true?' She was staring at her hands again.

'How could you think otherwise? After all, you were the one who secured my release, with those clever hands of yours. I don't believe I have thanked you for that.' He bowed formally. 'A woman like Tilly Blaine would drive a man to murder, you know. I need a woman who knows the value of silence—'

'Oh,' she sighed.

'And courage. My wife must—'

The door was thrown open. 'Good God!' exclaimed the Dowager. 'What are *you* doing here? I thought you were—' She turned and waved the butler away. Then she tottered across the room and almost fell into her chair.

Marina attempted to rise. 'Are you all right, ma'am? You—'

Kit pressed Marina back into her chair with a firm hand on her shoulder. 'Stay where you are. I will see to her.' He poured a generous measure of brandy and put it into the old lady's shaking hand. 'Drink this, ma'am. You will feel better for it.'

The Dowager, it seemed, needed no prompting from Kit. She tossed it off and immediately held out her empty glass to be refilled. With the second measure, however, she sipped in a more ladylike fashion, using her free hand to straighten her wig. 'That's better,' she announced.

Kit grinned across at Marina. His cynical mask had vanished, replaced by open delight…and love. Marina felt her insides melting at the intimacy of it. That icy husk around her heart—how vainly she had worked to nurture it!—had disappeared in the glowing warmth of his response. And he had talked of his wife… No, it was impossible.

'I suppose your being here would account for it,' said the old lady suddenly, setting down her glass.

'I'm afraid I do not quite… Account for what, precisely, ma'am?' Kit asked tersely.

Marina could see that Kit was determined to control his temper. He was finding it difficult.

'For your being here,' Lady Luce repeated. 'If you're here, you can't be there, can you? And that would account for it.'

The old lady was definitely rattled this time. She was talking in riddles. 'Did something happen, ma'am?' Marina asked gently. 'At your card party?'

The Dowager nodded a little shakily. 'Went to Méchante's after all. Some ruffians arrived. They were demanding money from Méchante. Apparently, for services she had arranged.' She cast a very scornful look in Kit's direction. 'I collect that they failed in their task. Naturally, she refused to pay, so they started to break up the house. Made a pretty good fist of it, too. It will cost her a small fortune to put all to rights.'

'Were you hurt, ma'am?' Kit asked quietly.

Marina realised that he was genuinely concerned. He knew, at first hand, that any one of those bruisers could have broken the Dowager's bones at a touch.

The Dowager shook her head. Then she gave a choke of laughter. 'Méchante was, though. They misliked the way she tried to order them out. She will be more than a little bruised tomorrow. Black eye, too, I dare say.'

Marina caught her breath, and then sighed. Perhaps Lady Marchant had received no more than she deserved.

'And you think *I* am well served, too, eh? Don't you?' added the Dowager tartly.

Kit said nothing. He was looking at Marina.

The Dowager appeared not to have noticed. 'Well, perhaps you are right. I had rather hoped those devils would change your looks, but…having seen them in action, I admit I was wrong to…' She pushed herself up from her chair. 'I want to go to bed. You, sir, should not be here. You must leave. Pull the bell.'

Kit did so and then politely offered her his arm. 'I had understood, ma'am,' he said quietly, 'that, even under your stern rules, a betrothed couple were permitted to be alone together.'

Lady Luce's gasp was so loud that it drowned out Marina's. For probably the only time in her life, the Dowager was totally at a loss for words. And as for Marina...

He led the Dowager towards the door. 'You should know that Miss Beaumont has done me the honour of agreeing to be my wife, ma'am. But I know you have had a distressing evening. Tomorrow will suffice for your congratulations. Marina will be removing to Fitz-william House in the morning. You will be very welcome to call on her there.'

'Kit! You—!'

'Later, Marina, my love. Later. Do not embarrass Lady Luce with such shameless protestations of affection. She needs her rest.' He smiled over his shoulder at her, but his expression was quite serious again by the time he had turned back to Lady Luce and her hovering abigail. 'Goodnight, ma'am,' he said, bowing. 'Sleep well.'

He closed the door firmly on them and returned to Marina. She was bristling. Again. She probably had cause.

'If I had been able, Kit Stratton, I should have run across the room and slapped that stupid smile from your arrogant face. How could you say such things?'

He tried to look sheepish. She was not deceived. She laughed. It was the glorious, joyous sound he had longed to hear. 'You are a rogue, sir, as well as a rake. And I have *not* agreed to marry you. You—'

He reached for her and drew her into his arms. Then he kissed her, thoroughly, until she had stopped resist-ing. 'Now, Marina, I am going to send for hot water and towels to bathe your feet and you, my sweet, are not going to protest. Indeed, you may sing to me while I see to your hurts. After that, I shall carry you up to your room—'

'No!'

'Accompanied, for propriety's sake, by one of the maids. Tomorrow, you will remove to Fitzwilliam House while I make arrangements to convey you home to Yorkshire and—'

'Stop, stop! You are impossible, Kit Stratton. I will not permit you to order my life like a…a…' She could not think of a suitably insulting description of his high-handed behaviour. And she did not really wish to try very hard. Not now, when there were more important things to be said. 'Besides, I have not said that I love you. Or that I will marry you—'

'But you do, don't you?' he said, planting tiny kisses on the side of her neck until she melted into his arms once more. 'And you will.'

'Only if you love me,' she whispered.

'To distraction,' he said and found her lips.

*   *   *   *   *

HEAD FOR THE ROCKIES WITH

Harlequin Historicals®
Historical Romantic Adventure!

AND SEE HOW IT ALL BEGAN!

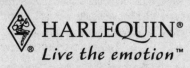